HAUNTED

HAUNTED

SUSAN COOPER

JOSEPH DELANEY

BERLIE DOHERTY

JAMILA GAVIN

MATT HAIG

ROBIN JARVIS

DEREK LANDY

SAM LLEWELLYN

MAL PEET

PHILIP REEVE

ELEANOR UPDALE

ANDERSEN PRESS • LONDON

First published in 2011 by
Andersen Press Limited
20 Vauxhall Bridge Road
London SW1V 2SA
www.andersenpress.co.uk

6   8   10   9   7   5

The rights of Joseph Delaney, Susan Cooper, Mal Peet, Jamila Gavin, Eleanor Updale,
Derek Landy, Robin Jarvis, Sam Llewellyn, Matt Haig, Philip Reeve and Berlie
Doherty to be identified as the authors of this work have been asserted by them
in accordance with the Copyright, Designs and Patents Act, 1988.

British Library Cataloguing in Publication Data available.

ISBN 978 1 84939 321 8

CONTENTS

THE CASTLE GHOSTS

Joseph Delaney

THE CASTLE GHOSTS

I looked up at the castle and tried to be brave. After all, I wasn't going to be imprisoned there. I was going to guard the prisoners: murderers, common criminals and convicted witches. That was my job. Or at least it would be once I'd finished my training.

There was a new moon, slender and horned, about to be overwhelmed by the dark clouds blustering in from the west. I shivered but not just with cold. I'd heard stories about the castle after dark, about things long dead that walked its damp corridors.

The building was large and forbidding, set on a high hill about three miles from the nearest town and surrounded by a dense wood of sycamore and ash trees. It was constructed from dark, dank stone with turrets, battlements and a foul-smelling moat that was rumoured to contain the skeletons of those who had attempted to escape.

I'd never wanted to be on the night shift. But my feelings counted for nothing. Orders were orders and, after just two weeks preliminary training, I'd been told to report one hour after sunset. But, being unused to going to bed in the afternoon, I'd overslept. I was already over half an hour late and castle guards were supposed to be punctual.

There was a clanking grinding sound and then the portcullis began to rise. They knew I was there. Nobody approached the castle without being noticed. Behind the portcullis there was a huge wooden door studded with iron. It was another five minutes before that opened and I waited patiently as a light drizzle began to drift into my face.

At last the door started to grind back on its hinges to reveal a burly guard. He scowled at me. 'Name?' he demanded.

'Billy Calder,' I answered.

He knew my name and knew exactly who I was; he'd been letting me in every day for my training. But he was following the rules. Anyone entering had to identify himself.

'You'll be working under Adam Colne. There he is,' he said, pointing to a man in the distance who held a huge bunch of keys. 'He's waited over half an hour for you and he's not best pleased to say the least. I wouldn't like to be in your shoes, boy.'

I approached Adam Colne warily. He was big and scary with a reputation for being tough and ruthless. He'd once thrown a trainee guard from the battlements into the moat. The boy had been lucky to survive. Colne stared at me hard, without blinking, making me feel very nervous. It was the first time we'd met and I knew I hadn't made a good impression.

'You're late!' Colne growled. 'There are only six guards on the night shift and it's important that we are all present. So it won't happen again, will it, boy? Those who work for me never make the same mistake twice. Not if they want to carry on breathing. You have to know your place in the scheme of things. Do I make myself clear?'

'Yes, sir,' I answered.

'Good, as long as we've got that straight I'll forget your lateness and we'll make a fresh start from now. You'll be happy here, boy. We're just like a close-knit family on the night shift.'

I didn't know much about families because my parents had died when I was very young. I'd been brought up in an orphanage. This was my first job since I'd turned fifteen and had been thrown out to make my own way in the world. I was a stranger to the district and hadn't made any friends yet.

'So first things first,' Colne continued. 'Do you know why you've been transferred to the night shift?'

'No, sir.'

'Somebody asked for you. Somebody politely requested your presence. Someone we have to keep sweet. "Let the young Calder boy guard at night," she begged. Wouldn't you like to know who she is?'

I nodded. I hadn't got a clue.

'Then why don't you take a guess?'

Who could it be? There were some female as well as male prisoners but certainly no female jailers. The castle was run by men. But as far as I was aware, I knew no one imprisoned in this castle – or any castle for that matter.

'Is it one of the prisoners, sir?'

'Her name is Netty and she *was* one of the prisoners, boy. But she's a prisoner no longer.'

That didn't make any sense. If she'd been released why had she requested my presence on the night shift?

'Where is she now?' I asked.

'Mostly she's to be found in Execution Square. One of her favourite places it is, because that's where they hanged her.' My face must have shown my shock. 'Netty is a ghost, and we need to keep her sweet or it's bad news for everybody. Some call her "Long-Neck Netty" on account of how stretched her neck was by the rope. But don't let her overhear you using that name. She doesn't like it. Even when she's in a good mood she raps and bangs and wakes up the prisoners. Sometimes she turns the milk sour or gives us nightmares. No, it don't do to cross Netty. So follow me, boy! If it's you she wants on the night shift, it's you she'll get.'

He walked off swinging his big bunch of keys, and I followed him through a tunnel and into the castle yard.

'But how does she know who I am, sir?' I asked.

'Must have seen you during your training and taken a shine to you.'

'Are we going to see her now?' I asked, my knees beginning to tremble. The thought of facing a ghost had suddenly turned me right off the job. *Why on earth had I wanted to be a prison guard?*

'Nobody *goes to see* Netty, boy. She comes to see you. No doubt she'll turn up when she's ready. Of course there's more than one ghost haunts this prison.' He pointed at two cell windows high on the wall. It wasn't time for lights out yet and they were the only two cells in darkness.

'We never put prisoners in those two cells, boy. Not now, anyway. Know why?'

'Are they haunted, sir?'

'They're haunted all right, but by exactly what we're not sure. About ten years ago the castle was filled to bursting with prisoners so we had to use those two cells. We knew they were supposed to be haunted by something unpleasant but there were no precise records, so we took a chance and locked up two drunken farm hands for the night. Got into a fight they had, and then battered the parish constable who'd tried to separate them.

'The morning after, they were trembling like leaves in an autumn storm. And both told the same tale. In the middle of the night something invisible but very strong had grabbed them by their throats and tried to drag them into the wall. But that weren't all...'

Colne stood there for a while staring into the darkness, shaking his head and muttering to himself as if he were reliving the experience. He seemed to have forgotten all about me.

'What happened? I asked.

'Well, as I said, the castle cells were all occupied so we had to put them back in the same quarters again the following night. Come dawn we regretted it. We should have sent them off elsewhere to be locked up, but we hadn't the man power to transport 'em. In the morning one of them was dead. He'd been strangled and there were fingermarks embedded in his throat. His eyes were bulging too – it wasn't a pretty sight. But the other had disappeared; or at least most of him had. There was a large pool of blood on the cell floor, and in it were his teeth.'

'His teeth? Was that all that was left of him?'

'His dentures, boy, to be precise, which were made out of wood. And whatever had taken him couldn't get them through the stone wall as well. Flesh and bone, yes, but not Rowan wood. It's a wood that has certain properties. Witches aren't supposed to be able to touch it and some say it wards off dark apparitions. Anyway let's get inside, out of this drizzle. I need something to warm my belly.'

We passed along two corridors and at the end of each was a sturdy door to be unlocked. Moving even a short distance across the prison took some time because of all those locks; no wonder each jailer carried a big heavy bunch of keys.

At last we emerged into a large room with a small fire in the grate, three big wooden tables and lots of chairs.

'This is the quarters for the night shift,' Colne said.

I'd never visited the room because it was always locked during the day. But there was little evidence now to suggest that it was ever occupied. There were no cups, cutlery or plates on the table tops. The room was tidy – too tidy. Something about that made me feel very uneasy.

'Of course,' Colne said, 'we don't use it much. Not a nice place this.'

'Is it haunted as well?' I asked.

'By night the whole castle is haunted, boy, but a lot depends on what's doing the haunting. There are some really nasty things that rap and bang in here so most guards prefer to take their rest in other places.'

I didn't speak. I just waited in silence. I knew he had more to say.

'About twenty years ago, when I first started on the job, I was braver, much braver, and I sat in here one night eating bread and ham that my wife Martha had packed for me. She's dead now, poor soul. It's funny, isn't it? All these castle ghosts but never once did the spirit I most wished to see come back to say farewell.' He shook his head sadly. 'Anyway I was sitting in that chair over there chewing my food...'

He pointed to a wooden chair. It looked just like all the others but it was the one nearest the door.

'At last my stomach was full and I started to doze. Then something woke me. A strange noise from behind that raised the hairs on the back of my neck and sent chills running down my spine. It sounded like something was gnashing its teeth together hard, at the same time as growling deep in its throat. Whatever it was shot past my chair. It was small and dark and it scuttled across the flags quicker than I could blink.

'It scared me, boy. I tried to tell myself that it was just a rat but it had passed straight through a closed door so I knew that it was something else. And there was a smell too – a stench of fire and brimstone. So it was something evil. Something it's better not to think about. Something straight from hell. I rarely eat in here now – at least not when I'm by myself. One funny thing about ghosts is that they're most likely to put in an appearance when you're alone.'

He sighed then shook his head. 'But there are worse

places in this castle, and the worst place of all is the one that I have to visit every night. And I have to visit it alone. It's a place we call the "Witch Well". There's a prisoner down there that it's best to keep away from. He's tethered to a ring in the dungeon floor by a long chain. He sleeps all day but is wide-awake after dark and has to be fed at midnight, or things could get really awkward for everybody who works here. Someone has to do that dangerous job and as the most experienced guard on the night shift it falls to me. As well as the special prisoner, the well has something else to make it a fearsome place. It's haunted by foul things – the ghosts of those confined there long ago. I only wish I didn't have to go there, but duty is duty. I'll show you where the well is later, but first I'll make us both that hot drink to ward off the chills of the night.'

Ten minutes later we set off again and Colne led me through another series of corridors with occupied cells on either side. By now it was after lights out and you could hear prisoners moaning in their sleep or sometimes crying out as if in the grip of a terrifying nightmare. Colne opened then locked each door behind us after slamming it with a clang.

'Never leave your keys in the lock, even for a moment, boy,' he warned. 'Always fasten them back onto your belt. It's the safest way, so nobody else can ever get their hands on them.'

At last we ended up in the open again, the drizzle falling straight down on our heads, the castle walls rising sheer on all four sides. It was a small claustrophobic area, about twenty paces by twenty paces, and most of it was filled by a large wooden structure that I recognised as a gallows. This was another place I hadn't seen during my training. It was Execution Square – the place haunted by Netty!

'Yes, boy, this is where the condemned get their necks stretched! But over there is what we've come to see.' Colne pointed to the furthest corner of the square. We passed the gallows and halted about four paces away from an iron door with a massive lock. I could hear water trickling in the near distance.

'This is the entrance to the Witch Well, and behind that door you'd face your worst nightmare. So just be glad you're not in my shoes!'

After a week or so I began to feel a lot better about being on the night watch. The duties were much easier because it wasn't necessary to feed the prisoners. Only the prisoner in the Witch Well got fed at night and that was Adam Colne's job. The other inmates were mostly sleeping or groaning or crying. I just had to patrol the corridors.

I never saw the ghost of Netty but I suspect that she came close at times. Once I was sure someone touched the back of my neck. It felt like the tip of an ice-cold finger. But when I turned to look there was nobody there – or at least nothing that needed to draw breath. There were whispers too but very faint, and I never could quite make out the words. I would have been all right and probably still doing that job but then the 'Purple Pestilence' came along and changed everything for a while.

The disease swept straight through the nearby villages and towns. Some people got sore throats so severe that they couldn't breathe. Then, just before they died, they turned a deep purple colour. It was mostly the very young and the very old who died but the survivors had a very hard time of it too, and were confined to their sick beds for weeks.

One night I went to the castle and Adam Colne wasn't there. Three other guards were also sick. That left just me and the gate guard.

'You'll have to do it, boy!' he told me. 'The prisoner in the Witch Well has to be fed at midnight and there's only you available to do it tonight. I can't afford to leave the gate.'

I knew that anyone could guard the gate but, although he was older and more experienced than I was, he was scared to feed the prisoner and was using the gate as an excuse.

'Where's the food?' I asked, my knees knocking just at the very thought of entering the Witch Well.

'There are two buckets waiting for you in Execution Square – directly underneath the gallows. Give the prisoner the first at midnight then the second course about ten minutes later. Just tip each bucket down the steps. Don't linger. Get out of there just as quickly as you can. So off you go on your rounds but when you hear the church bell sound at quarter to the hour make your way to the Witch Well.'

So, carrying my big bunch of keys, I set off on my patrol of the corridors. I was really scared but just wanted to get it over with and I was glad when I heard the church bell in the distance telling me that it was time to go and feed the prisoner.

Between the main gate and Execution Square there were seven corridors to walk and eight stout doors to unlock and lock. At last I reached the square. It was raining even harder than usual. I picked my way between the puddles towards the gallows where the two large wooden buckets of food were waiting.

Each was covered with a piece of wood to stop the rain getting in, and there was a stone on top to keep it in place. Why the stone was necessary I hadn't a clue. The four sheer walls that enclosed the gallows meant there could be no wind.

In the distance the church bell began to ring again. At the twelfth peal I picked up the nearest bucket and carried it towards the gate of the Witch Well. It was heavy. What on earth could be inside? I lowered it to one side of the gate and fumbled for the right key. The lock seemed stiff but at last it yielded, and very nervously I pulled open the door.

There was a torch flickering on the wall just to the side of the door. It lit the entrance adequately but the steps descended into absolute darkness. With one hand on the door jamb, I listened. For a moment I could hear nothing at all but then from far below came the faint sound of breathing.

I lifted the stone from the wooden cover of the bucket and placed it on the floor. Next I removed the cover. I was instantly assailed by a strong metallic coppery smell. The bucket was full of blood! Surely this wasn't food intended for a human being? What kind of creature could be imprisoned below?

I didn't intend to linger long enough to find out so I did as the gatekeeper had instructed. I lifted the heavy bucket and I tipped it, allowing the contents to cascade down the stone steps. The blood flowed like a waterfall carrying big chunks of raw meat along with it.

Wasting no time, I carried the empty bucket outside, closed the door behind me and locked it. As instructed I waited ten minutes before getting ready to feed the creature what the gatekeeper had called its 'second course'. At one point I thought I could hear faint noises from behind the door so I leaned against it and put my ear to the wood. I could definitely hear chewing, snuffling noises, but after a while it became quiet and I judged it time to unlock the door and feed the prisoner again. I was more nervous than ever. What if he was lying in wait for me behind the door? I eased it open.

To my relief it was exactly as before, the steps leading down into absolute darkness. The only difference was that the stones were now red with blood. Then a thought struck me. They had been clean before I'd tipped the first bucket. Who had done it? Was that part of Adam Colne's job too?

This second bucket was also filled almost to the brim with blood so, wasting no time at all, I tipped it down the steps. It proved to be different from the first course; this had bones in it rather than pieces of raw meat. I turned, intending to get out of there fast. It was then that disaster struck. I heard the door creak on its hinges, and then it started to close!

I took two quick steps towards it, but the door slammed shut before I could reach it. Then I remembered with a sickening jolt that I'd left my key in the lock! In my nervousness to tip the second bucket down the steps and get the job over with, I'd broken an important rule.

And there had been no wind, so why had it closed? It was almost as if someone had shut it from the outside. When I tried to push the door open it didn't yield and I began to panic. But there was worse to come.

To my horror and dismay, I heard the sound of the key being turned in the lock. I tried to push the door open again but it wouldn't budge. Someone had locked it. But who could have done it and why?

And now I was trapped in the Witch Well with the prisoner. I could hear him somewhere below starting to eat his second course.

First there came the lapping and slurping of a big tongue drinking the blood that I'd poured down the stone steps.

How big was the tongue? No human tongue could make so much noise!

Next there came the crunching and grinding of large teeth chewing the bones that had been carried down to him by the red tide.

How big and sharp were the teeth? No human teeth could chew through bones like that!

I tried the door for the third time, again without success. Then I sat down resting my back against it, thinking desperately about what I could do. It was no good shouting for help because the gatekeeper was too far away. And if I did call out, the prisoner would certainly hear me, and might come up the steps to investigate.

The gatekeeper wouldn't expect me back until the end of my shift. It was only then, when the day shift arrived, that someone might discover my disappearance and come to release me from the Witch Well. But that was still many hours away.

Maybe if I stayed at the top of the steps, quiet as a little mouse, the prisoner would stay down there.

No sooner had that thought entered my head than the chewing below ceased. The prisoner must have eaten all the bones. Perhaps he would now be full to bursting and fall asleep?

That hope was quickly shattered. There was a new sound, like a broad-toothed file rasping on wood. What could it be?

The sound went on for a long time and seemed to be getting gradually nearer and nearer. There was also the occasional clank of a chain. Something deep inside my brain must have figured out what the noises meant because the answer popped into my head very suddenly and I started to tremble.

The creature was slowly climbing the steps and dragging its chain behind it. The rasping sound was being made by its large tongue. Nobody needed to clean the steps of blood because the prisoner did it himself. He was climbing upwards, licking each step in turn, not wanting to waste even a drop of blood.

I had one hope left. A lot depended on the length of the chain that tethered him to the ring in the dungeon below. It seemed sensible to me for the prison authorities to have made it long enough so he could reach the top step with his tongue – that would save on the need to send someone in to do the cleaning – but not long enough to allow him to reach the door. That way anyone feeding him would be safe as long as he stood very close to it.

But if that was the case why had the gatekeeper told me to get out as quickly as possible? Was there some other danger that I hadn't foreseen?

The sound of that tongue licking the step was getting nearer and nearer, I stood and pressed my back against the door to get as far as possible from the top step. Next I braced myself ready for my first view of the creature. I didn't have long to wait. The first thing to emerge into the light, cast by the flickering torch, was the tongue itself. It was huge and swollen and purple, like the faces of those who died from the pestilence.

Next came the huge head and I shuddered at the sight of it. Rather than hair it was covered in green scales, and its ears were long and pointy with a sharp piece of bone protruding from the tip of each. What was it?

As more of the prisoner came into view, I gradually became aware of its size. It was far bigger than a man, perhaps nine feet tall, with strong muscular shoulders and a naked hairy back. Instead of fingernails it had long, sharp talons, each one more lethal than a dagger.

Its tongue was licking the top step now and so absorbed was the creature in slurping up every last drop of blood that, so far, it hadn't noticed me. My heart was in my mouth and I pressed myself even harder back against the door.

But the moment it finished it looked up, and its big, green, cruel eyes looked directly into mine. For the first time, I saw its teeth. It had two long yellow fangs that curled down over its bottom lip. With a snarl it leaped towards me. The chain brought it up with a jerk, and it thrashed against it, straining to reach me, its claws just inches from my shoes, saliva dribbling from its open mouth in anticipation of eating my flesh.

Would the chain hold it? For a moment I waited, trembling in dread, expecting one of the big links to break. But they remained intact and the creature's attempts to reach me slowly became less frantic. I tried to remain calm. The only risk to my life was if I grew tired and fell forward away from the door. But I was hardly likely to fall asleep with the hungry, open, fanged mouth of that monstrosity a few feet away and its claws mere inches from my shoes.

Slowly my fear began to ebb. I told myself that I could survive here until daybreak. But then, just as I was becoming calmer and more hopeful, there was a sudden draught and the torch began to flicker. The draught became a gust, the gust became a howling wind, and the torch went out. I was plunged into darkness.

For a moment I could see nothing and then there was a faint glow from the side of the steps. The glow became a tall column of light that lit the walls and steps better than a candle, and a human form started to materialise.

My heart began to beat faster. This was one of the castle ghosts, and it only took a few moments for me to realise which one. At first glance the body looked solid and the red lips, brown eyes and green dress could have fooled you into thinking that this was a living flesh-and-blood woman. But she was standing in front of the creature from the dungeon and you could see through her to his glaring eyes and twitching talons.

She was a tall woman who once had been beautiful but the high cheek bones and glossy black hair were ruined by two things: her bulging eyes and her stretched and twisted neck with its knotted veins. I shuddered with fear. It was the ghost of Long-Neck Netty, the woman who'd been hanged in the castle's Execution Square.

Netty smiled without warmth and then she spoke; her voice was as cold as the north wind. 'What do you think of my son?' she asked.

I didn't answer, and she turned and gestured towards the taloned creature on the steps which was still straining against the chain, making fresh efforts to reach me. 'He's a good lad and deserves the best,' she said. 'He didn't ask to be born in that shape and he's always hungry. It was my fault, you see. I met a young man, the most handsome that any woman had ever seen. He had blue eyes, curly blonde hair and a dazzling smile that melted my heart. I'd have done anything for him.

'But I was young and foolish and never questioned the fact that he only ever wanted to meet me after dark and alone. I was a witch but I was self-taught and belonged to no coven, so I had nobody to advise me and point out the great danger that I was in. I bore a child to that handsome young man and it was only afterwards that I learned the truth. He was the devil! And some offspring of a witch and the devil are born as abhumans. My poor child, he never asked to be brought into this world so ugly and misshapen so I try to make it up to him whenever I can. I feed him a choice morsel: some tender flesh and sweet young blood. That's why you are here, boy. That's why I asked for you to be transferred to the night shift! You aren't the first young lad that Adam Colne has put my way. He daren't refuse me or *he'd* be given to my son instead!'

From the moment that she had demanded I be moved to the night shift, her intention had been to feed me to her son.

'Why don't you make it easy for yourself?' Netty cried. 'Just walk down the steps and get it over with. The pain won't last long!'

I was too terrified to reply. But I still had hope. She was just a ghost and although she could scare me, Netty couldn't actually make me do anything. I could still wait at the top of the steps until someone from the day shift came to unlock the door and set me free.

'Do we have to do it the hard way? Do I have to drag you down the steps?'

'You're just a ghost!' I shouted, my knees trembling. 'You have no substance. You can't drag me anywhere!'

'Oh! Can't I, boy? You don't know very much about ghosts, do you? Who do you think turned the key and locked you in here?'

Netty moved closer and stretched out her left hand towards me until her ghostly fingers were touching my neck. I could actually feel her cold fingertips! Then there was a sudden tug at the collar of my shirt and for a moment I lost my balance. I tottered at the top of the steps and almost pitched forward into the waiting talons of the abhuman. It was straining against the chain again, slavering in anticipation of eating my flesh and drinking my blood.

But somehow I managed to remain upright and, once more, pressed myself back against the door.

'You're stronger than you look, boy!' Netty said. 'Not to worry. It's easy enough to summon up a little help. There are plenty here that owe me big favours. Either that or they're scared of displeasing me. Even a fellow ghost can be hurt by someone like me! The ghost of a witch is very rare but also very powerful!'

Long-Neck Netty began to mutter under her breath and the air instantly became very cold. Suddenly there were other presences moving up out of the darkness of the Witch Well, each surrounded by a nimbus of baleful yellow light.

Some crawled up the steps towards me with heavy ponderous intent; others soared up into the air above the abhuman and circled at great speed making me dizzy just to look at them. They were hideous and misshapen, with teeth like needles and long matted hair trailing behind as they flew. Round and round they whirled, shrieking loud enough to burst my eardrums. Then they began to tug at my clothes and pinch my skin with their sharp fingernails.

I fought to keep my balance but the castle ghosts were relentless, and their attempts to tug me down the stone steps went on and on whilst Netty grinned at me and her son drooled in anticipation of the feast to come.

But I was determined to survive. I just had to hang on for a few hours. Help would eventually arrive. I could do it!

Never give up! I told myself. *Never give up!*

All that happened a long time ago and my memories of that terrible experience have now faded somewhat. I've walked the corridors of the castle for many years and I've got used to the ghosts, so most of them don't scare me that much any more. But I always stay away from the Witch Well; it still doesn't do to get too close to Long-Neck Netty and her abhuman son.

Guards come and go. Adam Colne has now retired and his son has taken his place. It seems to be a family tradition. Four generations of Colnes have guarded the Witch Well. No doubt I'll still be around when Adam's grandson takes over. I'll be here as long as the walls of the castle still stand. I know my place in the scheme of things.

Because now I'm one of the castle ghosts.

THE
CARETAKERS

Susan Cooper

THE CARETAKERS

Last summer was Normandy, and for two years before that it had been Spain, but this summer my Dad said he wanted to hear his own language spoken, so it was Devon. And not even a place you've ever heard of, but a bed and breakfast a long way from anywhere, on the edge of Exmoor. I did a lot of whining but it had no effect at all. James didn't object, but then he never has an opinion on anything except his own weird interests.

We drove there. That meant endless hours in the back seat with my big brother, but though James is tall for fourteen he's very thin, so we could each pretend the other one wasn't there. I texted Melissa and Becky on and off all the way, and James played one of his elaborate games. Or maybe he was texting his own friends, not that he's ever talked about having any.

Mum had packed one of her 'Great British Picnics', as James calls them: bread-and-butter sandwiches, boiled eggs and sausage rolls, carrot sticks, apples and slices of date-nut bread, with a thermos of tea for her and Dad, and Coke for us. The Coke was her token recognition of the twenty-first century. We ate it all in a field, sitting on a blanket. There were six cows in the field, but my dad said confidently that they wouldn't come near us unless a bull was around. He's a pharmacist, with no experience whatsoever of animals, but he's a very confident man.

I don't think James was happy about the cows. He was doing one of his twitchy routines, touching everything three times if he'd touched it once. But he didn't get angry, not till we got to the house.

Bucklewood Farm, it was called, though it wasn't a farm at all. It looked more like a stately home, impressive but gloomy. For a moment I wondered if we were in the right place. The house was big and grey, with stone steps up to its front door and two round stone columns on either side. There were massive old trees in the garden, and beyond that a meadow of tall grass stretched down to a lake.

The moment Dad stopped the car at the front, the door opened and two people came down the steps. A man and a woman; they must have been watching out for us.

'Welcome!' said the man heartily. He was quite old but very upright, with a little grey moustache twisted into points.

The woman was grey-haired too. She had beady dark eyes that didn't smile, though the rest of her face was smiling at us.

'Welcome to Bucklewood Farm!' she said.

Mum knew they must be Captain and Mrs Miller, the owners, so she introduced us and there was a lot of hand-shaking. I stood close to James to be a good example, so he wouldn't dodge it; he doesn't like touching people. So he did put out a limp hand, a little way, and Mrs Miller tried to shake it. The captain just gave us both a manly nod.

They helped us unload our suitcases and carry them inside. There were a lot of cases; four from the boot and two from the roof of the car, because Mum always packs as if we're leaving for a year instead of two weeks. Inside, the house was still impressive, with dark, solid furniture and a loud grandfather clock. The Millers led us up a broad curving flight of stairs, and showed us that we had a whole wide corridor to ourselves, with three bedrooms and a big bathroom.

There was a double room that would obviously be for Mum and Dad. At the end of the corridor was a small room that looked somehow older than the rest; it was a bit dark and spooky but its one window had a fabulous view. You could see the lake, and a tree-covered island in the middle of it.

'This one's mine!' I said, and took my suitcase inside.

Captain Miller said that at six o'clock there would be dinner for us, this being our first night, and that they'd leave us to settle in. We weren't supposed to get any meal except breakfast, so this was nice of them. They both went away, their shoes clopping against the gleaming wooden floor.

James came into my bedroom and crossed to the window. He looked out at the lake for a long moment and then he gave his head a sudden fierce nod, as if he were answering a question nobody had asked.

'Me!' he said loudly. 'This room is for me!' He was standing rigid as a lamppost, with his arms straight down and his fists clenched, and he had started to shake.

Mum sighed, and looked at me. I was cross, and I thought about insisting on having the room I wanted; everyone gives in to James, just to avoid him having one of his scenes. But she sounded exhausted, so I sighed too, like an echo, and she squeezed my shoulder.

'You want this one?' I said to James. 'It's really small. But go ahead, it's yours.'

He didn't even say thank you. He went off to get his luggage, and it was Dad who picked up my case and took me to the other single room.

'Good girl, Anna,' he said.

'That's OK. I'm fine in here.' And I was; it was a brighter room with an interesting shape. The ceiling slanted down on one side, following the line of the roof, and there was a rocking chair and a little desk. It all looked rather like a picture from an old-fashioned children's book.

I suppose you're wondering why I gave in to James. There's no label for what's different about my brother. There are long medical Latin names for it, but all we really think about are the rules we've grown up with, that make it possible for him to live at home in the family. He can't do anything on his own, it isn't safe. His problem isn't autism, or Asperger's, but like those people he isn't able to understand anyone else's feelings. Or his own. He walks on an edge, and we have to keep him from falling over it. If we handle him right, he will have his furious moods but he'll come out of them. I've known about all this ever since I was little, it's just the way things are.

Dinner was ham and salad, with rolls and butter, and four pieces of apple tart; it was all on the table waiting for us, and we saw nobody else except Captain Miller, who came in with a tray of coffee afterwards and said, 'Goodnight. Sweet dreams,' with a stiff little smile, and left.

'Goodnight!' Dad called to the closing door, and I saw him raise his eyebrows at Mum and roll his eyes.

'No help?' he said.

'Must have come down in the world,' whispered Mum.

I said, 'What d'you mean?'

'*Ssh,*' Mum said.

But nobody was listening to us.

It was an amazingly quiet house. I opened my window before I went to bed, just in case there was anything to hear. Somewhere out in the still twilight there was a long chirring, rattling sound, and a few squawks, and a noise like something falling out of a tree. But it was just a bird flapping away.

Maybe that's why I woke out of a falling-down dream in the middle of that night. You know the kind: suddenly you're falling, falling, and you wake up *snap*, first in a fright and then grateful that it's only a dream, even though your heart's still pounding. I lay there, breathing fast, with no idea what had been happening in the dream I'd been falling out of.

Then I opened my eyes, and in the summer almost-dark I could see the rocking chair in the middle of the room. It was rocking, even though nobody was there. To and fro it went, to and fro. For a moment I was really spooked. I told myself it must be the wind. I thought about closing the window, but I didn't have the courage to get out of bed. It was a while before I fell asleep again.

Breakfast was waiting for us the next morning in the dining room, just as dinner had been. It was a good breakfast; Dad was finishing a thick slice of toast and marmalade, and James scoffing a plateful of scrambled eggs and bacon. There were promising covered dishes on the sideboard.

'Get a move on,' James said to me. 'We have to go down to the lake.'

Dad gave me a big encouraging smile through the toast. We both knew that if my brother said something positive, it was wise to act on it right then before he changed his mind. So I ate fast, while Mum came drifting into the room, looking nine hundred per cent better after a good sleep, and poured herself some tea.

James strode off through the meadow, towards the glimmering water that was just visible beyond, and I followed him. There were some pretty wildflowers I didn't recognise in among the tall grasses, and even butterflies, but I knew I couldn't stop to look.

At the bottom of the field the grasses changed to reeds and bulrushes, and you could see that the lake was really big, with an island in the middle of it covered in trees. Two ducks skittered along the water and into the air as we got closer. The ground began to feel squishy.

'There's the boat!' James said. 'He told me there'd be a boat.'

'Who did?' I said. 'Captain Miller?'

James didn't answer. He scrambled down to a

wooden jetty sticking out into the water from the reeds. It was old and rickety, with some boards missing, but the square posts at its edges looked sturdy enough. A little dinghy was tied to one of them by a rope.

James went out on the jetty, and the boards creaked. 'Be careful!' I said.

'It's perfectly safe.' He took hold of the post and stepped down into the boat. It swayed wildly.

'There's oars,' James said. 'Come on.'

I've seen him row before, and we both know how to swim, so I went and untied the rope. The boat sank deeper into the water when I stepped in, wobbling so much that I had to grab James's head. He flinched. I let go as soon as I could, and sat in the stern. He started to row, rather splashily.

Everything was fine till we were right out on the water, halfway to the island. Then suddenly I was terrified. Nothing happened, but it was as if a huge noise swallowed me up, awful, a great hostile wave. I'd never felt anything like it, ever. I was so frightened that I heard myself scream, and I was clutching the sides of the boat so hard that my fingers hurt.

'No! James! Go back! Go back!'

He shook his head calmly and went on rowing. 'Come on, Anna, there's nothing wrong. Don't be silly.'

'Stop stop stop! Turn round! Go back!' I can't describe how scared I was; I was still screaming, it was like hearing someone else's voice. It went on and on.

James stopped rowing. He scowled. But because I was still shrieking, he pulled on one oar so that the boat turned, and he rowed us back to shore. We'd gone only a few yards when the awful fear vanished as suddenly as it had come, and I stopped yelling and sat there gasping as if I'd just run a race.

I couldn't understand it.

James said crossly, 'You spoiled everything – now he's gone!'

'Who's gone?' I said.

He just made a terrible face at me and went on rowing. He wouldn't say another word.

When we reached the jetty, I clambered on to it and held the boat so that James could get out and tie it up. Then we both went back through the meadow in silence; James first, me following. I could tell how angry he was by the stiff fast way he walked.

He marched into the house and slammed the door of his bedroom, and I explained it all to Mum and Dad. Only I left out the feeling that had hit me. The terror. I couldn't have described that without sounding crazy. I just said James and I had had a fight.

'Oh, Anna,' Mum said wearily. 'You know what happens.'

James stayed in his room for hours. Dad and I went for a walk on the moor and saw a deer. Mum stayed behind and read a book. She said she heard James talking angrily behind his door once or twice, but that was all. We drove to the next village for dinner, and James was OK, though he was a bit manic, going on about the lake and the island to Mum and Dad. Not to me; he was still cross with me.

That night I didn't dream, but twice I was woken up by a sudden loud noise, like something heavy falling down. The third time that's just what it was: my suitcase fell off the top of the wardrobe. Dad came into my room in his pyjamas; it had woken him too. He looked down at the suitcase.

'It just fell,' I said.

'Had you moved it?'

'No. You put it up there.'

'I did. Very carefully, like this.' He picked it up and put it back, squarely on the top, and he looked at me a bit oddly.

'This time it'll take a major earthquake,' he said. 'Goodnight, chicken.'

'Leave the door open,' I said.

Dad looked at me with his eyebrows raised, and I gave him a feeble grin. He did leave the door open though.

As he left I heard a whispery noise that sounded incredibly like a sneering little laugh. Then again from further away, as if the laughing person were leaving. It absolutely wasn't Dad's voice. But it could have been the scuff of his slippers against the floor, and the noises had made me jumpy. I told myself it was nothing, and there was quiet after that.

Captain Miller was setting up the coffee percolator in the dining room when we came down to breakfast. He gave us his stiff little smile. 'Everything tickety-boo?' he asked.

'Except for the bumps in the night,' Dad said cheerfully.

Captain Miller's hands stopped moving. *'Bumps?'* he said.

Dad blinked. 'Surely you heard them?'

'Things falling,' Mum said. 'My husband thought it might have been an earth tremor. Is there anything in the paper?'

'We heard nothing,' Captain Miller said. He got very busy with the coffee tray again. 'I'm sorry if you were disturbed.' And he went away fast, almost as if he were escaping.

James was intent on going out in the boat on the lake again. He wanted to get to the island. 'You don't have to come too,' he said to me. 'No girls required.'

I know better than to answer when he says things like that. Besides, nothing on earth would have induced me to go back on that lake. We all went down to watch, to let him row to the island. On the way, we weren't pushing through the tall grasses this time because someone had mowed a wide path for us, right down the centre of the meadow. By the lake I saw the someone, still mowing. Mum and Dad hadn't noticed him, they'd gone ahead, following James, but I went over to watch.

He was a little old man in a long-sleeved shirt and a leather waistcoat, with a very wrinkled brown face and a lot of white hair, and he was mowing with an old-fashioned scythe. I'd never seen one before, except in pictures of Old Father Time. It had a fearsome long blade at right angles to its long handle, and he held the handle upright in both hands and swung the blade over the ground before him in a great sweeping curve that took down everything in its path.

I was fascinated, and I asked if I could try it, but the old man shook his head, smiling.

'Dangerous thing if you're not used to it,' he said.

He had a lovely Devon accent, unlike the Millers. His name was Harry Ridd, and he said he'd always looked after the Bucklewood garden. 'The place,' he called it. Everything about him was old-fashioned: his clothes, his manners, the way he talked. He was like someone out of a history book.

He paused in his mowing and watched James getting himself into the dinghy and fitting the oars in the rowlocks.

'He wants to take care on the lake,' he said to me.

'Don't worry,' I said. 'He's a good rower. He's dying to get over to that island.'

Harry Ridd paused for a moment, leaning on the handle of his scythe; he cocked his head, almost as if he were listening for something. Then he said, 'Well, he's calm today. There'll be no trouble, not if your brother

38

leaves before dark.'

It seemed an odd thing to say, but before I could ask him what he meant, he smiled again and gave me a very polite nod that was almost a bow. He was so gentlemanly that he didn't seem at all like a gardener. *A cut above,* as my dad would have said.

'Good day to you, young lady,' Harry said, and he started his mowing again, moving gradually away to make a path along the bank of the lake.

I could see James out on the water, rowing. I ran to catch up with Mum and Dad, who were standing watching him from the little jetty.

Mum said brightly, 'Let's walk around the lake!' She's always worried about James, and always trying to pretend that she isn't. So off we went, in the other direction from Harry Ridd and his mowing, through trees, along grassy banks, sometimes through twiggy little bushes. Mum kept looking out across the lake at the island as we moved round, to see if she could spot James and the boat.

It was quite a wide lake, and it took us almost an hour to get all around it. We saw James just once; he'd reached the island, and he was pulling the dinghy up onto the bank. Mum called to him, but he didn't hear; he'd turned to go into the trees.

And it was the weirdest thing: I thought I saw another boy there in between the trees, waiting for him. I could even dimly see his face; he was laughing.

But nobody else seemed to have noticed, and in the next moment there was nothing there. It must have been just a moving shadow – the sun was in and out of clouds all day.

'I don't like him being so far away,' Mum said.

'Come on, Mary,' Dad said. 'You can't watch him every minute. Let him have fun playing explorer for a while.'

'It's not a very big island,' I said, trying to be comforting.

So eventually Mum let Dad talk her into spending a peaceful afternoon in a garden chair reading a book, and off they went back to the house. I roamed about the edge of the lake for a bit, and saw the old man, Harry Ridd, still mowing, with long slow strokes of his scythe.

He paused and waved to me. 'I'll be watching out for him, never fear,' he called. It was if he was reading my mind – or Mum's.

'Thank you,' I said.

'All's calm today,' said Harry Ridd, and he went on sweeping his scythe through the grass.

James did come back, but not for hours. By about six o'clock Mum was getting really worried and Dad was demanding that the Millers find them another boat. Mrs Miller was unhappy and silent, and Captain Miller kept saying to Dad, 'The lad can look after himself, I'm sure.'

Then James came up through the meadow, along Harry Ridd's newly mown path.

His shirt and his shorts were full of rips and tears and there were little patches of dried blood on his arms and legs from cuts and scratches, but he was smiling. James doesn't smile easily.

Mum was in tears suddenly. 'Where have you *been*?'

James stood tolerantly still as she flung her arms round him. 'On the island,' he said. 'Where else would I have been?'

Dad erupted then, and there was an awful row, full of shouting and reproaches, the kind they don't often throw at James because they always say he can't help it, whatever 'it' happens to be at the time. James did a lot of shouting back, not making much sense.

When he'd sullenly gone to clean himself up, the Millers brought us dinner, because they said it was too late to expect us to go out and eat. I got an odd impression that they were feeling somehow guilty.

I never did find out what James had been doing all that time, on the little island. I don't think Mum and Dad did either, but for once they were completely fed up with James's complete refusal to care about anyone else's feelings or concerns. They announced that for the rest of our time here we were going to do what most families did on holiday: go to the seaside.

So every day we drove to the coast; to Lynmouth or even Combe Martin, and we sat on the beach and took long walks and had swimming races in the cold water. Mum always won; she'd been a swimming champion when she was young. Every day we ate picnic lunches and seafood dinners until we were sunburned and exhausted, and drove back to Bucklewood Farm and fell into bed. The sun shone and the winds were gentle; it was perfect summer weather and we had a wonderful time.

All of us except James, who sulked and glowered even while the sun and the seawater helped his cuts and scratches to heal. He was angry all the time.

He kept saying, 'We're staying at this place, and there's the lake – I don't see why we can't just be here. It's a perfectly good house and it's peaceful.'

Except that it wasn't peaceful. Not now.

The noises had started again, at night. Out in the corridor there'd be a crash that was loud enough to wake everybody, but when you opened the door to look, nothing was there, nothing had moved. You'd go back to sleep, and before long you'd be woken again by a crash *inside* your room. But Mum and Dad never found anything that had moved, and my suitcase never fell off the top of the wardrobe again. It was really weird.

James slept soundly in his room and said he never heard any noises at all. The Millers said they didn't either, though I thought they had that funny guilty look when they said it.

Every night the noises went on, getting louder and louder.

'I don't understand it,' Mum said. 'D'you think the Millers drink? Maybe they have terrible rows at night and throw things at each other.'

'They're certainly a mystery,' Dad said. 'Great big house, no one to help, and no other guests. Where did you say you found this place?'

'There was an ad in *Country Life*,' Mum said, sounding as if she was talking about the Bible. 'I saw it at the hairdressers.'

'Maybe the house is haunted,' I said.

'Oh, for goodness' sake, Anna,' Dad said irritably. 'I don't want to hear any foolish talk like that. Keep it for your vampire books.'

He's a total realist, my father: he knows everything can be explained, just the way everyone can be cured of their problems with a pill. Except James, of course.

But he didn't have a good explanation for the noises.

There was a fine rain falling and the clouds were solidly dark, so we stayed at the house that day. Mum drove off to get some things for lunch, Dad was reading a book, James was shut in his room with his laptop. There was no sign of the Millers – but then there never was, once breakfast was cleared away. When the rain slacked off I put on my anorak and went for a walk under the grey sky.

As I went down the front steps, out of the corner of my eye I thought I saw someone swinging on the swing that hung from the old oak tree next to the house, but when I looked straight at it, there was nobody there. The swing was just moving to and fro on its own in the breeze. I looked at it nervously all the same. I didn't feel easy in this house.

In the lane outside the house I heard a chopping sound, and I came across old Harry Ridd swinging a long axe. He was cutting up a big branch that had fallen off a tree. It was a hefty branch, and the axe looked really heavy for a small man. Besides, he was old.

'They should get you a helper,' I said to him.

'My favourite occupation,' said Harry Ridd. 'I was always a gardener at heart.' He smiled at me, and all the lines on his face curved upwards; he looked like a happy, wrinkled apple. Then he looked at me more closely, and his face changed. He let the head of the axe drop to the ground, and stood there leaning on the end of its handle.

'Anna,' he said. 'It is Anna, isn't it?'

'Yes,' I said.

'What's wrong, Anna?' said Harry Ridd.

And his voice was so gentle and he looked so kind that I found myself telling him all about the noises in the house and the suitcase dropping off the wardrobe. I told him about how terrified I'd felt out on the lake. I even told him a bit about James.

'Oh dear,' he said, and he gave a long sigh.

I said all in a rush, 'I know it sounds silly and I know there's no such thing as ghosts but ... is there anything wrong with this house?'

'In a manner of speaking, there is,' said Harry Ridd.

He let his axe drop and he sat down on the thick end of the branch. I sat on a log. It looked a bit damp but I was damp anyway.

'There was a boy,' he said. 'Two hundred years ago, they say. His name was Charles. Charlie. Some people still call that little island in the lake "Charlie's Island".'

'Was it his special place?' I asked. There's an old tree in our garden at home that Mum once called 'Jamie's tree', because James used to sit in it for hours.

'So they say,' said Harry Ridd. 'Charles was the grandson of the man who built this house, and he was a wild boy, often angry. It was just the way he was made, I suppose. He had a terrible row with his grandfather one day and went out on that lake in a storm, and he drowned.'

I tried to imagine the lake in a storm. 'His boat tipped over?'

'I suppose so,' Harry Ridd said. 'And the grandfather went in to try and save him, but he drowned too.'

I said, 'That's a terrible story.'

'Very sad,' he said. 'And they say the boy's still here.'

I felt cold suddenly. 'You mean Charlie's ghost?'

'Charlie and his anger,' he said. 'It's always been here. So they do say. And it loves to find another angry boy – to fuel the fire, so to speak.'

I thought: *Of course*. I said, 'Like James.'

'I'm afraid so, my dear. Yes.'

45

I said, 'Do Captain and Mrs Miller know about Charlie?' And as I said it, I knew that they did, but that they were trying not to believe it.

'They are new people,' Harry Ridd said. 'They were not fated to be always taking care.'

It was an odd thing to say, perhaps, but I didn't notice that at the time.

'It's a handsome house,' he said wearily, 'but none of them ever stays long.'

He got to his feet and picked up his axe, and for a moment he was looking at me hard, like a warning.

'Look out for your brother,' he said. 'If ever he heads for the lake in anger, go after him. Charlie likes company.'

A car came down the lane; it was Mum. She stopped beside me and lowered the window. She looked pleased with herself. 'Hop in, Anna!' she called. 'I've got ice cream, and it's going to melt.'

'Thank you,' I said to Harry Ridd, but he had gone.

I got into the car, shaken, trying not to think about what he'd said.

Mum hadn't even noticed him. 'Chocolate and strawberry,' she said. 'Everyone's favourites. Let's hope Mrs M will give me space in her freezer.'

'Brilliant,' I said.

All that day the weather got worse and worse. The wind picked up, and the sky got so dark that we had to turn on the lights in the dining room. Rain lashed against the windows, and once in a while you could hear a rumble of thunder. It affected everyone's mood, but particularly James's.

He was in one of his manic phases. Even though we obviously weren't going anywhere in the rain, he kept complaining again, over and over, about our drives to the seaside. It wasn't fair, he said; it wasn't fair that he had to do things he didn't want to do. He went on and on, and even though Mum and Dad didn't argue with him but tried to stay calm, he worked himself up into such a rage that finally Dad snapped and shouted at him to go and sit in his room till he could behave like a civilised person. James jumped up, angrier than ever, and rushed up the stairs.

Mum pushed back her chair to get up, and Dad glared at her. 'No!' he said. 'Don't go after him and be soothing – it never works! He has to learn there's more than one person in this world.'

But there was a huge crash upstairs, the sound of breaking china, and after a sort of frozen moment they both jumped out of their seats and ran upstairs, with me tailing after them.

James was standing in the corridor, and a big china lamp that had stood on a table outside my room was lying on the floor in pieces.

'For God's sake, James!' Dad said furiously. 'Are you mad? This isn't our house!'

'It wasn't my fault!' James yelled. 'It wasn't!' His

voice cracked, as if he was about to cry, and he flung himself round and ran back towards the stairs, past us. For an instant I saw his face and it wasn't a way I had ever seen him before, it was an awful mixture of rage and fear, and hardly looked like him at all.

He rushed down the stairs. Mum turned to follow.

'No!' Dad said, tight and low.

From outside there was a flash of white light suddenly, right on cue as if we were in a horror film, and a huge crack of thunder straight after it. It was ridiculous to think James might have gone running outdoors in a storm, but all at once my head was full of old Harry Ridd's voice: *If he heads for the lake in anger, go after him . . . if he heads for the lake . . .*

It seemed to get louder . . . *Go after him . . .*

I ran down the stairs. I didn't stop to grab a coat. I went out of the house into the rainstorm, and ran and ran. Across the lawn, into the meadow, rain whipping against my face so I couldn't see. I was soaked in five seconds. Another flash of lightning lit up the meadow, the tall grass all bending under the rain, and the dark water of the lake ahead. Behind me through the noise of the wind I could hear Mum's voice faintly calling. But ahead of me, sure enough, I could just see James's running figure.

When I reached the lake, there he was, out on the water in the little dinghy, tossing on the waves whipped up by the wind, struggling to get the oars into the rowlocks. It was a crazy thing to be doing, totally crazy, but he never does think properly when he's really upset. My mind kept saying to me: *If he heads for the lake... Charlie likes company...*

Water was splashing up at me from the waves breaking on the bank. I could see James rowing, fast, clumsily, and the boat tossing.

And in the boat with him I could see another boy. He was laughing.

I didn't think, I just moved. I kicked off my trainers and splashed into the water and started to swim. Looking back, I just remember how cold it was. And I was just as crazy as James, because I'm not a very strong swimmer. But I wasn't going to let Charlie get my brother.

Lightning flashed white on the water, and through the waves I could just see the dinghy ahead of me. I swam and spluttered and swam, and it didn't seem to get any closer. Then suddenly it was as if the dinghy hit something; it reared up in the air, throwing James out, his oars spinning up around him. I heard a muffled shout and a lot of splashing. Another flash of lightning made me blink, and as the thunder came after it I found someone swimming up to join me, a sleek dark-haired head, arms flashing to and fro. It was Mum, of course. I should have known she'd do the same thing. I've never been so glad to see anyone in my life.

The rain was whipping the water; the boat was upside down ahead of us.

'Can you see him?' Mum yelled.

'Over here!'

I could just see James through the waves and the rain; he was beginning to sink, he must have banged his head. I grabbed his arm, Mum got his shoulders, and between us we turned him so she could swim backwards to shore, pulling him by his shoulders the way they teach you to do in life-saving. But I'd only had one life-saving lesson, last term, so if I'd been there alone Charlie would have got James and maybe me too.

We got to the shore quite soon, I suppose, but it seemed like for ever. Swimming with all your clothes on is like walking through treacle, and even worse when you're terrified.

Dad came running up in his anorak; he must have come out all calm and rational, following us, and then found himself in a nightmare. He waded into the water to help, and we all pulled James up through the mud on his back. He was white and unconscious and incredibly heavy. The rain was still pelting down. Nobody said anything; we were all working too hard. Mum bent over, retching, spitting out water. Dad turned James's head sideways.

'Anna!' he said urgently. 'In my pocket, right pocket – get my mobile! Call nine-nine-nine!'

It's a long blur, everything after that: Dad starting CPR on James while I burrowed for the phone; the lovely calm Devon voice talking to me; Mum saying a prayer; James's white face and the water coming out of his mouth; Dad giving him breaths, like kissing him, between those long pumps to his chest... and then the joy of seeing James give a spluttering breath of his own...

By the time the ambulance came bumping through the meadow, obliterating Harry Ridd's carefully mowed path, James was breathing normally. He was conscious, though I don't think he really knew what was going on. The Millers came running after the ambulance. The storm was almost over, the sky clearing as the wind blew the darkest clouds away. The rain had stopped. There were two ambulance men, very gentle but quick, they put James on a stretcher and into the ambulance, and Dad went with them.

One of the men spoke firmly to Mum and me; he told us to go and get warm and dry right away, and said we could drive to the hospital only after we'd done that. Mum was exhausted and shivering, but paid attention now that she knew James was going to be OK.

So we found the shoes that we'd both kicked off when we went into the lake, and as the ambulance drove away, we went back to the house with the Millers escorting us like quiet sheepdogs. Mrs Miller ran two hot baths while we got out of our wet things, and

Captain Miller brought two glasses with an inch of brandy in each of them, and told his wife to make sure we drank it at once. The brandy made me cough, but it did warm me up from the inside.

The Millers were hovering anxiously in the corridor when I came out of my room. They said they'd like to drive us to the hospital, when Mum was ready. Mrs Miller was upset, and it made her want to talk; I saw now that she was a thin, worn-looking woman. She was holding Mum's empty glass, and she kept turning it round and round in her hands.

'Oh dear,' she said unhappily. 'We've never had anything like this happen before. People love the lake and the little boat.'

'Nothing wrong with the boat,' said Captain Miller. 'Perfectly safe, if you handle it right.'

Mrs Miller seemed to be fumbling for words, more as if she were trying to avoid saying something than saying it. 'I did wonder,' she said to me, 'about your brother and what he . . . I mean, we haven't had children here before. Perhaps we should have thought. I mean, he's a disturbed boy, isn't he?'

Captain Miller said, 'His parents are in charge, my dear.'

'He's . . . unusual,' I said. 'He's going to be fine, Mrs Miller, don't worry.'

'Oh dear,' she said again.

I suddenly felt very sorry for her.

'Look,' I said, 'it's all right, because I know all about angry Charlie. I think Charlie must have sort of . . . woken up when he found James was here. Maybe he'll go to sleep again when James has gone away.'

'I have no idea what you're talking about,' Captain Miller said. But he didn't sound very convincing.

And Mrs Miller knew; I could see it in her face.

'It was Harry Ridd who saved James's life,' I said. 'He was the one who told me about Charlie and his grandfather drowning, and about Charlie being still here, still angry.'

'Harry Ridd?' Mrs Miller said. All at once she looked not just upset, but frightened.

'That's his name, isn't it? Your old gardener. He told me the story, he warned me about the lake. That was why we went chasing after James. Otherwise he would have drowned too.'

'We haven't got a gardener,' said Captain Miller.

'He was mowing a path through the meadow with a big old-fashioned scythe.'

Mrs Miller said, 'We have no help at present. Nobody looks after the garden but my husband.'

I said helplessly, 'He told me he'd always taken care of the place. He told me he was always here.'

'Harry Ridd was the name of the man who built this house,' Captain Miller said. 'In eighteen thirty-one.'

We all three looked at each other for a very long moment, and nobody said a word.

Then Mum came out of her room, and Captain Miller sprang to attention. 'All ready?' he said. 'Let's drive to the hospital!'

James was fine; in fact he was asleep when we arrived. The doctor said they wanted to keep him there overnight, just to be sure. So the Millers drove us back again with Dad, and Mum started packing. None of them talked about anything much except the weather. It was their way of coping, I suppose.

Next day we drove home, picking James up on the way. That meant that he never saw Bucklewood Farm again, but he didn't seem to mind. He never mentioned Charlie, not then nor ever since. In the car, all he wanted was his favourite game, so I played it with him nearly all the way home. He hasn't had one of his angry attacks for weeks. But he will, of course.

The day we left, I got up very early and went outdoors. The sky was clear, the birds were singing, there was still a white morning mist round the hedges and trees. It was beautiful. I sat on the swing that hung from the big oak tree, and I said a silent goodbye to my friend Harry Ridd, and thanked him. He would go on, and I would go on. It's just the way things are.

GOOD BOY

Mal Peet

GOOD BOY

You are walking down the garden path. You are wearing strange and heavy clothes. Your hands explore them but do not recognise them. It's very dark, but your feet know the way. The gate opens without you touching it. You walk through it but then you are not where you ought to be – on the street where the parked cars wait calmly for the morning. No, you are in a wild and limitless space. The wind's moan swells, fades, swells again. You walk on, but then your clever feet refuse to move because you are at the edge of a precipice. You don't want to look down, but you can't help yourself. So you do look down, and at the bottom of the black and measureless drop there are bright wriggling worms, yellow and white and red. Because

57

they make you feel dizzy and sick, you lift your eyes away from them. You turn back the way you've come, but the garden and the house have gone. All you can see is the ragged horizon where the pitch-dark of the land meets the dark grey of the sky.

You understand that you're waiting for something.

And here it comes. Walking along the horizon.

At first it's just a ripple, like something behind a curtain. Then the moon opens its eye and you can see that the thing walks on all fours with its head lowered. It's a dog, a very large dog and, although you have never been afraid of dogs, this one fills you with terror. It's as though you are drowning in fear, it's as though fear has filled you up right to the top of your throat and you have only one last breath to scream with.

So you scream.

The dog hears you and turns its head, its ears twitching. Then it disappears, its black shape lost in the surrounding blackness. But you know it's flying towards you and there's nothing you can do except stand there with your back to the abyss and wait while your last scream echoes and echoes and echoes.

Then there is light and warm arms and a voice.

'Hey. Hey, Katie. Katie? It's all right. Ssh. It's all right. It's all right, sweetie. God, you frightened the life out of me with all that screaming.'

The biscuity smell of her mother's bed-warmth.

But still the dog coming at her out of the night.

Then the bedside light making everything shock-ingly familiar.

Gone.

'You were having a bad dream, babe. That's all. It's OK.'

The child's heart beats against her ribs as if it were trying to escape its cage.

'Can I sleep with you, Mum?'

'Sure. Come on.'

In the big bed she snugs herself against her mother's body.

'Wanna tell me about the dream, Katie?'

'It was about a big bad dog.'

'We all have those, sweetie,' her mother murmurs. 'It's normal. Don't worry about it. It's OK.'

But it isn't OK, and it isn't normal. The dog continues to haunt Katie Callan's sleep. Often it is just a dark flicker that passes through her dreams like a shadow along a wall. A glimpse of a black muscular shape patrolling the edge of a gloomy sky or turning to look at her. Then gone. At such times Katie's breathing will stumble, or she will groan, then sleep on, more or less peacefully. At other times, it's the full nightmare: the terrible drop at her feet, the dog getting invisibly closer, then its eyes, blank mirrors of moonlight, emerging from the darkness, closer – much closer! – than she'd expected.

MAL PEET

Its harsh and eager breathing. Then the screaming starts and Katie wakes into a room full of screams.

Sometimes months pass before the great black dog comes in the night. But Katie always knows it will return. She grows to fear sleep. She fights sleep off. But sleep is a crafty enemy, and starts to sneak up on her during the daytime.

When Katie is ten years old, her head teacher invites her mother to come to the school to discuss 'the problem'. A visit to a child psychiatrist is arranged.

The psychiatrist is a softly spoken woman who wears spectacular earrings, which Katie envies. Her name is Aziza.

Gently, while talking about other things, she teases the details of Katie's nightmare out of her. After their third session she asks to speak to Katie's mother alone.

'The truth is,' Aziza says, 'that we have very little idea about what causes recurring nightmares unless they are about something that has actually happened to the person having them. Katie tells me that she has never been attacked by a dog, or anything else. Is that true?'

'Yes. As far as I know.'

Aziza thinks about that answer.

Then she says, 'I'm sorry, Mrs Callan, but I need to ask you this: you are a single parent, is that correct? And you have a part-time job in the Post Office?'

'Yes. So what?'

'So, well, I'm sorry, as I say, but...'

Jenny Callan says, stiffly, 'Katie is never left alone. I don't neglect her. And if anything bad had happened to her I'd know about it. We don't have secrets from each other. Is that what you were getting at?'

A tense moment like an intruder in the room.

Then Aziza says, 'OK. Thank you. So, another possible explanation for recurring nightmares – the same nightmare – is that it's a sort of habit. That even though it's weird and frightening, it becomes... familiar. That the dreamer starts to expect it. Unconsciously, might even *want* it. Does that make any sense to you?'

'Yes. I suppose so.'

'So the trick is to break the habit somehow. Look, this might seem a rather odd suggestion, but have you ever thought about getting a dog? A puppy that Katie could care for? In Katie's mind, *dog* is connected to *fear* and *violence*. I'm thinking that if we could break that connection, if she could see a dog in terms of *friendship*, *protection*...'

Jenny frowns. 'What, like a sort of antidote?'

Aziza the psychiatrist leans back in her chair and says, 'Yes, exactly. An antidote. Is it worth a try, do you think? Could you fit a dog into your life?'

The puppy is a mongrel, his coat random splashes of brown and white and black. He looks as though he'd got in the way of a team of sloppy decorators. His feet belong to a much bigger dog, and he falls over them when Katie plays with him on the wee-scented rug.

'His mum's a spaniel,' the woman who'd put the advert in the local paper tells them. 'I can't honestly say what the father is. Some sort of terrier, at a guess. There's one up the road that might've done the dirty deed.'

They take him home.

Katie wants to call him Rabbit on account of his long dangling ears, but her mother thinks it would sound daft if they went on walks and shouted, 'Here, Rabbit!' at a dog. So they settle on Rabbie. He turns out to be intelligent. When he's spoken to he has an attentive way of tilting his head and sharply focussing his eyes, those bright black buttons set in his patchwork head.

Rabbie sleeps in a quilted cloth basket under Katie's bed. Soon, and somehow, he comes to understand why. When the terrible black dog descends from the skyline of Katie's dreams, when she twists and groans, Rabbie emerges from under the bed with a warning resounding in his throat that swells into a bark. Two of those do the trick: Katie slips free of the nightmare and reaches down to Rabbie, sleepily fondles the little folds of skin between his ears.

'Good boy. Good boy. It's all right. It's all right now. Go back to sleep.'

Gradually the gaps between the dream-dog's visits grow longer. And when it does come it keeps its distance, only watching her with glittering eyes while stalking by.

Then she'll hear Rabbie's warning rumble.

'Good boy.'

Her hand on his warm head, then moving down to the soft place between his narrow shoulders.

'Good boy.'

And, eventually, the beast vanishes from her nights.

When Katie Callan is eighteen she goes away to university. She drops the 'i' from her name; 'Kate', she thinks, is more grown-up. Sophisticated. She is happy, most of the time, for the next three years. Her world gets bigger. Rabbie misses her more than she misses him. When she comes home between university terms he greets her with a delighted dance, up on his back legs with his front paws dabbing at her. She takes him for walks, but talks to her mobile more than she talks to him.

Kate leaves university and spends a year doing any old job for money. She doesn't come home very often. Then she decides, or discovers, what it is that she really wants to do. She fills in, very thoughtfully, an application form. It takes her two days. She goes for an interview, then another one.

She rings her mother.

'Mum? Mum, I did it! I passed the interview!'

'That's fantastic, sweetheart. I knew you would. Well done.'

There's something wrong with her mother's voice.

'Mum? Aren't you pleased?'

'Yes. Yes, of course I am. I'm very proud of you, love.'

It still isn't right, though.

'Mum? What's the matter?'

'It's just . . . It's terrible to have to tell you this, today of all days, but . . . well, Rabbie died this morning.'

'Oh no,' Katie says. 'Oh my God. What happened? Was he ill? You never said anything.'

'No. He was getting a bit blind, as you know. And he must've wandered into the road and got hit by a car, or something. A neighbour found him. I know it's stupid, but I've been crying all day.'

'Oh, Mum. I'm so sorry.'

'It's all right. I really didn't want to spoil your day. It's ridiculous to get so upset over a dog.'

Later Kate makes other calls, and goes to a pub to celebrate her new job with her friends. At one point she gets tearful about her dog dying. Her mates tease her, and eventually she laughs at herself. Then she goes back to her flat and stumbles into bed.

You are walking down the garden path. You are wearing . . .

No.

You are not where you ought to be – on the street where the parked cars wait . . .

No. Please, no.

It appears on the horizon. It's just a shape at first, like a ripple behind a curtain . . .

Sweating. A scream climbing up through her chest.

Your heels at the edge of the drop. The bright worms way, way down there.

She reaches for Rabbie. Her hand knocks over a glass of water.

And now it's nearer than ever before and you see the moon madness in its eyes and its lips drawn back from its teeth and the rippled roof of its mouth and its slobber and it launches itself at you, its body all muscle and hot stink . . .

Screaming.

'Good boy! Good boy!'

She gropes, fingers finding only wet carpet. She sits up. Her hand clatters the bedside table, finds the lamp.

The terror fades into the light but it's like it's never been gone.

Nor does it leave her now. It haunts her days as well as her nights. Shadows of its shape slip across walls, along corridors, down alleyways. She glimpses its reflection in shop windows. It emerges from innocent hedges and sits, tensed, waiting for her to come closer before it disappears.

As when she was a child, she starts avoiding sleep. It affects her work. She is tired, she forgets things. After a few months her boss suggests the she should talk to a therapist.

This one is not at all like Aziza. He is bald but has a small beard. It's like his hair has slid down his head and gathered at his chin ready to fall into his lap. His name is Mark.

She tells him about the dog that haunts her life.

'What do you do for a living, Kate? Is it OK if I call you Kate?'

'Sure,' she says. 'I'm a police officer.'

'Really. Like a detective?'

'No. An ordinary copper.'

'Hmm. That can be a high-risk job, can't it? Especially in this city. So would you describe yourself as a brave person? A confident person?'

'I used to be,' Kate says.

Mark nods and picks up a pen. 'So tell me what frightens you. Apart from the nightmare dog, of course.'

'The usual things,' she says. 'Spiders, nutters with axes in their hands, cancer, heights...'

He interrupts. 'Not everyone is scared of heights, actually. Mountaineers, for instance. Scaffolders.'

She shrugs. 'I guess.'

After a pause Mark says, 'The black dog is sometimes a metaphor for depression. Do you think you're depressed, Kate?'

'No.'

All the same Mark describes the symptoms of depression. Kate has to agree that some of them match her own. Mark writes her a prescription for anti-depressant tablets and arranges another appointment in a month's time.

Kate doesn't take the anti-depressants. She doesn't think the nightmare dog is something you can get rid of with pills. After a fortnight she flushes them down the toilet. She skips the next appointment with Mark. And the one after that.

The dog continues to haunt her.

On a November night, with the sky a dark blank above the sullen yellow street lights, Kate Callan is in a patrol car with her regular partner and driver, PC Simon 'Wheelie' Binns. They're thinking about picking up a couple of coffees when Control comes on the radio.

'Oscar Papa three-zero,' Katie says into the mike. 'Go ahead.'

'Reported violent incident at Dover House on the Eden estate.'

'Well, fancy that,' Wheelie murmurs, swinging the car left to make a U-turn.

'Probably a domestic,' Control says, 'but watch yourself. Whisky Bravo also alerted.'

'Wilco,' Katie says.

Wheelie turns on the flashers and the siren. Accelerates. The street lights race backwards like a madman's blinking.

Like the other three buildings on the Eden estate, Dover House is a huge slab of a place jutting rudely up into the sky. Walkways run along each of its ten levels. *It's the kind of place*, Kate thinks, *you'd only live in if life had had dealt you a very bad hand*. When they get out of the car, there are people waiting for them; they back off and stand watching like humans witnessing the arrival of an alien spacecraft. But there is screaming and shouting from up the face of the building. Silhouettes against the broken and flickering light along the walkways, pointing in various directions.

Kate and Wheelie stand, staring up, uncertain. Then a man in dreadlocks, an older man, says from behind them, 'It's kickin' off on level six, man. But I wouldn' go up there if I was you.'

Wheelie says, 'What d'you think?'

'Call backup,' Kate says.

Wheelie reaches into the car and talks into the radio.

Then there's two pops like cheap fireworks and a chorus of screams.

'C'mon!' Kate shouts, already running towards the entry.

'No!' Wheelie yells, but she's gone.

At ground level there's nobody, just a long line of bin bags sitting like black toads, some of them spilling their guts. At the end of the corridor there are two lift doors covered in graffiti. Kate whacks her palms against both sets of buttons but, as she expected, nothing happens.

She starts to climb the stairs. By the time she gets to level six, her lungs feel like they're full of broken glass. She leans against the wall of the stairwell, dragging in air, then risks a peek round the corner of the walkway.

There's a young guy, a boy, sitting on the concrete ten metres away with his back against the wall. His mouth is open but he's making no sound. A girl is kneeling in front of him, rocking her body back and forth, holding her hands out as if she's begging, or praying.

'Ash. Ash, man,' she's saying, over and over.

There's no-one else. All the doors along the walkway are shut.

When Kate approaches, the girl looks at her and lifts her hands. They are bloody.

Wheelie is yelling in Kate's earpiece. She ignores him and switches her collar-mike to 'send' and jabbers the codes for Ambulance and Armed Response Units.

She gets to the girl and puts her hands on the girl's shoulders and says, 'It's OK. It's all right.'

Which it isn't, obviously. The girl is shaking like there's electricity running through her. The boy's hands are clutched at his stomach, but they're not stopping the blood leaking onto his lap. Shock has locked his face into a vacant smile.

Kate kneels.

'Ash? Is that your name? Ash, can you look at me, please?'

The kid's eyes roll slowly towards her.

'Ash, I need to see what's happened to you. You've got to take your hands away so I can see. Can you do that?'

The boy shakes his head.

The girl says, 'Denny shot him. It was Denny. I told Ash...'

There's a sound from the stairs end of the walkway and Kate stands up. Her hand reaches for her taser, but it's Wheelie. She's surprised he got up here so fast; he's not the slimmest or fittest man at the station. He's bent over, his hands on his knees.

'Callan,' he gasps. 'Callan, you—'

Then he takes in the scene.

'Dear God.'

Kate pushes past him.

'Do what you can for them,' she says. 'The shooter went up, or we'd have met him on the stairs.'

'Kate, no.'

But she's gone.

Climbing the last four flights, fear and exhaustion thud her heart. At the tenth floor, as before, she peers round the corner. No one. Behind and to the right of her there's an unmarked door. She risks pushing it. It opens. Nothing terrible happens. Behind the door there's a space not much bigger than a cupboard. Two of the walls have thick power cables running down them. On the third there's a metal ladder. She climbs it and

GOOD BOY

feels the cold breath of night on her face. Then, as she'd feared, she finds herself on the roof.

It's a flat area more or less the size of a football pitch. Towards one end there's a metal thicket of telecom aerials. Running down its centre there are four low structures a bit like sheds with slatted walls. The surface is puddled and gritty underfoot. Kate walks cautiously to the far side of the roof to the fire escapes and looks down. As far as she can see, there's nobody on them. Far below, the lights of traffic are twisting worms of red and white and yellow. And blue, flickering. The moan of approaching patrol cars swells, fades, swells again.

The roof of the next block, Folkestone House, is level with her, and close. You could almost jump the gap. But not quite. The thought sickens her.

She retreats from the edge of the precipice. She should not be up here. The voices in her earpiece are telling her that. She is, suddenly, both sensible and afraid.

She heads back towards the roof access, but before she can reach it a hooded human shape steps out from behind one of the shed-like things. He's holding a gun in both hands. Light from somewhere makes a blue line down its barrel.

He giggles.

It's the giggle that chills Kate to the core. She knows that a man who giggles when he's aiming a gun at you is not the kind of man you can reason with.

All the same, she tries. She spreads her arms away from her body.

'I'm unarmed. Put the gun down. Please don't be stupid. You've got nowhere to go.'

Wrong thing to say.

He takes a step towards her. All she can see of his face is the tip of his nose and then a flicker of tongue as he licks his lips.

'Yeah,' he says. 'I got nowhere to go.'

He laughs like he's choking.

'I'm goin' nowhere. Tell you what, though. I don' fancy goin' alone. I fink I might take you wiv me.'

Kate turns her head and measures the distance to the fire escapes.

It's worth a try, she thinks, then her heart seems to stop its mad beating. She stops breathing because the black dog is stalking along the parapet of Folkestone House like a ripple in the dull sky. Its ears are alert triangles. Its eyes are two orange flames, watching her. She can see the flesh bunching in its shoulders and haunches. It lifts its upper lip in something like a smile. Kate hears the long low growl deep in its throat; a sound like bubbling blood.

She understands.

She understands why this dark and terrible animal has been with her for most of her life.

The dog is death. Her death.

Kate hears the metallic click of the gun behind her.

She's going to die. The only words in her head are, for some reason, *I'm so sorry, Mum.*

Then the beast leaps. Flies towards her across the dizzying space between the buildings. Its shape seems to fill the sky, blacking it out.

Kate falls on to her knees. She raises her arms, perhaps in a hopeless attempt to protect herself from the animal. Or perhaps to welcome it. She closes her eyes.

A long inhuman scream splits the night.

But it's not Kate's scream. It's not her agony.

She turns, dazed because she is still alive.

The dog has the gunman down on his back, tearing at him, its thick whip of a tail thrashing. Dog and man are a single writhing shape, howling and snarling. Then the man's right arm emerges. The hand still has the gun in it. He shoots the dog, twice, up through its body. Kate clearly sees the points in the dog's back where the bullets exit. But no sprays of blood. And the creature is unaffected; if anything, the shots only increase its savagery. It twists its massive shoulders and seizes the man's wrist with its jaws, jerking it as if it were breaking the neck of a rat. Kate hears, or imagines, the fracturing of bones, the parting of sinews. The gun skitters across the roof and comes to rest in a puddle. The dog releases the man's arm and stands over him, panting, as though making a decision. Then it attacks again, going for face and throat. The man's feet pedal the air helplessly.

Kate walks unsteadily towards the death-struggle and stands above it, uncertain. Then she puts her hand on the back of the dog's neck, feeling the soft roll of fat and the hard muscle beneath its fur. She digs her fingers in, squeezes gently.

'Good boy,' she says. 'Good boy.'

Its head comes up, the hot eyes rolling, the murderous mouth gaping.

Although she is very afraid, she runs her hand down to its shoulders, stroking.

'Good boy.'

The dog's body relaxes. It steps away from the man, who is now twisting and rolling from side to side; his cries have dwindled into chokes and gargles. Kate looks down at him, expecting to see rips, wounds. There are none. None at all.

The dog sits beside her, panting, its red tongue steaming.

The night fills with a heavy throbbing. For a moment Kate thinks it is the hammering of her heart. Then a helicopter slides sideways into the sky and drenches the roof in harsh light. A hugely amplified voice speaks to her from above; she cannot make out the words. At the same instant, four armed officers burst on to the roof.

One of them thinks he sees a dark shape poised on the parapet as if about to leap. He aims his weapon, but there's nothing. The only persons on the roof are PC

Kate Callan and, just a few paces from her, a man lying with his face in his hands, shaking and sobbing like someone waking from a nightmare.

THE BLOOD LINE

'For now we see through a glass, darkly; but then face to face:
now I know in part; but then shall I know even as also I am
known.'
1 Corinthians 13:12

Jamila Gavin

THE BLOOD LINE

CHAPTER ONE
Rosie and Doug

The Mickledean Parish Workhouse was known as a house of dread. For nearly three hundred years it had been a place of last resort for those who had been abandoned, orphaned or fallen on hard times.

It was set back from a narrow country road that tunnelled down from the wooded hills, and shielded from the good inhabitants of the village by a long row of shimmering poplars – as if it wanted to hide its shame – for it was built in shame for those who would inhabit it in shame. It was certainly out of sight of Mickledean Manor which was also hidden high among the woods above the village, nestled in exclusivity, uncontaminated by the lower orders below. Yet both houses were linked: the one for the destitute; the other for the wealthy.

Since the early twentieth century it had ceased to be a workhouse, but though it had been on the market for years, no one would buy it. Would they not also be buying the sin and sorrow soaked into the stones, and the desperate spirits who many still heard wailing on the back of the wind whistling down the valley? Some even claimed to have seen the dreadful Dame Flegg – the notorious children's matron from the past – half beating to death some child she had taken against with her thick, oak rod. And there were also tales of a ghostly carriage, drawn by two black horses, which would come galloping out of the woods at night, past the old workhouse and up to the gates of the manor.

Then Rosie and Doug came along.

They were a young, newly married couple from London – eager to build a home together and set up a business in landscape gardening. It was Rosie who fell in love with the tumbledown house and persuaded Doug that they must live here, only half taking in its history which the estate agent briefly related, and which all went in one ear and out the other. She loved the name of the village, Mickledean, and said it felt like coming home.

It was exciting. They lived in a disused horsebox they had bought, and parked in the weed-ridden vegetable patch while they worked on the house. It was a do-it-yourself job, helped by parents and friends who came and went during weekends or snatches of holidays, and it started with having to clear out a lot of rubbish.

Anything worth taking had been taken, or scattered by children breaking in for larks, but lying beneath some old sacking they found a mirror in an octagonal oak frame, its glass layered with dust, but unbroken. Doug was about to chuck it on the rubbish pile, but Rosie said, 'No! Keep it!' and, as she rubbed a rag across its surface, it caught the sun and sparkled. 'Hey, look. It's a fine old mirror. It's good to have some link with the past. We can varnish it up and find a place for it.'

Gradually the workhouse began to resume its shape again and become habitable, and its reconstruction seemed also to reassemble people's memories. Locals took to strolling up the road to stand and watch its progress. The older villagers would recall the stories they had been told by their parents and grandparents. 'Do you remember old Flossie who died a year or two back? When 'er da died in a river-barge accident, 'er mum and eight kiddies were taken into the Mick!'

That's what they used to called it – the Mick – which could sound like the Nick or old Nick, the devil.

Sometimes at the local pub Rosie and Doug learned more stories, not just about their house, but about the link between the old workhouse and Mickledean Manor up above the village.

Well they weren't a proper stories, with a middle, a beginning and an end. People screwed up their faces as they tried to recall exactly what the details were. It was more like a rumour; a rumour which had lasted nearly three hundred years.

'My grandma told me,' said an old villager, 'that one of the young Mickledeans, Edmund Mickledean, worked for the East India Company in the seventeen hundreds, and went out to India. They do say,' he continued in a low voice, 'he made friends with a local rajah and married his daughter. He never wanted to come home; he was happy out there, and soon had a son, followed by a daughter. But the rajah got involved in a war between the English and the French, and got thoroughly beaten and his lands taken away; then Edmund's wife died. So what does he do? He keeps the boy with him in India, but puts his daughter – barely five years old – on a ship, and sends her home to England, thinking his family could look after her here in Mickledean. That should interest you, eh?' he said meaningfully, looking at Rosie's olive skin and Indian dark hair.

It did interest her. She did have Indian blood, though was a bit vague about her own history. Her mother and father had both looked as English as English could be, but Rosie was born dark – like a reminder that you can't get away from the past – she had had a great grandfather who had been out in India in Victorian times. No one in her family had been keen to talk and would brush aside her questions, and she had thought that one day she would track it all down.

But what was the link between the manor house and the workhouse?

'Ah, well!' people nodded and looked at each other as if ashamed that any of their kind could be so heartless and unchristian. 'Edmund died out in India, and the Mickledeans here lost a packet of money in the South Sea Bubble financial scandal of the seventeen-twenties. By the time the child was delivered to the manor, it was boarded up, and the family gone. No one wanted to take her on, so they put her in the workhouse.'

'Here?' exclaimed Rosie. 'In our house?'

'That's it! Suppose they thought she would be collected in due course, but no one ever came for her. Perhaps his people never got the news that Edmund had sent a child over. After a while the manor was bought by another family, and the girl was soon forgotten.'

Rosie was silent. Her mind connecting back to the past, reliving the arrival of the little girl perhaps being brought by coach down that winding road, past the workhouse, through the village and up into the woods on the other side. She grieved at the thought of this child so abandoned by the world, and couldn't help feeling that, somehow, she and Doug finding this place and rebuilding it was like fate. It was meant to be. Her heart crossed three hundred years of time, and cleaved to the little girl who had lived there – and—'What became of her?' she asked.

The villagers shrugged. 'Who knows. Probably died within a year or two, as most of them did, from typhus, cholera or God knows what.'

'And her brother?'

They shook their heads. 'There was never any further connection with India again to our knowledge,' they replied, 'and Mickledean Manor hadn't had a Mickledean in it since the family were bankrupted and had to sell. Various families lived in it after that until, a few years ago, a certain Charles Mickledean bought it back into the family. But he still hasn't moved in and the old house is in a right state.'

At last, Rosie and Doug transferred from the horsebox into their new home. Five rooms long and three storeys high – its shape was the only reminder that it had once been the old Mickledean workhouse. Doug proudly chiselled out a piece of stone to embed in their wall with the new name: 'Meadowsweet House'. Some of the villagers shrugged cynically: 'Near a meadow it may be, but sweet? Never.'

Rosie found a place to hang the old mirror in an alcove on the third floor. She took a damp cloth to give the mirror a final wipe and had the strangest feeling another face looked back at her, through her own image. 'Trick of the light,' said Doug in a matter-of-fact voice, when she told him.

They set to work landscaping their garden so that people would see how good they were; creating borders, flower beds, herb gardens and vegetable areas, and then they put up a notice board advertising themselves as LANDSCAPE GARDENERS.

But from the moment they moved from the horse-box into the house, Doug noticed a change in Rosie. She did less and less, barely helping Doug with the house and garden – and there was still so much to do. From a sunny-natured, warm, smiley person, she became short-tempered, distant and preoccupied. Frowns began to scour creases across her brow and, at night, she became restless, her sleep disturbed by terrifying nightmares.

Asking questions about the little girl from India three hundred years ago led Rosie to enquire more about her own family. She wanted to know more about her own Indian blood: how it all came about; what relatives might she still have in India? She began trawling the internet, anything to do with tracing past ancestors.

At first Doug was light-hearted about it all, only too glad that whatever had disturbed Rosie was taken over by this new interest. He didn't complain when the kitchen table became totally covered with notes and print-outs, dominated by a large sheet of paper on which she was assembling a family tree instead of working on designs for gardens. But after a while he grew concerned. She was becoming obsessive, almost secretive, spending hours on the computer going to various websites looking up her family name, Walker.

That's how she found Freddy and his mother, and how Freddy came to Meadowsweet House.

CHAPTER TWO
Freddy

His room was on the third floor at the top of the house. Freddy had reached it by climbing two flight of stairs, almost as steep as ladders, dragging up his sports bag that contained everything he possessed.

'This is your room,' said Rosie. 'I left it fairly bare for you to fill up with your own things. I hope you like it. Look! You've got a view right across the meadows and the river, and you get the morning sun.'

Freddy made no comment. To him, a city boy, it seemed alien. He was used to an urban landscape: the ripples of roofs of housing estates, multi-storey buildings and supermarkets. And Meadowsweet House was so different from the one-bedroomed flat he and his mother had lived in.

'I'll leave you to unpack,' Rosie said. 'Supper will be in half an hour. I expect you're hungry.'

Freddy wasn't hungry. He felt sick.

Rosie was somehow related to him. He knew she'd made a hobby of tracing back her family roots and had come across him and his mother. First Rosie had written a letter, but because his mother had slid into one of her depressions she hadn't answered it and, soon after, Freddy got taken into care again while his mother was admitted into hospital for treatment. Then came another letter – 'just in case you didn't receive the first.' It was a nurse who persuaded Freddy's mother to reply. 'After all, she says you're related. We all need family – and who else have you got?'

Rosie had written back immediately. *Why don't you send Freddy to us until you're better?*

Everyone thought Rosie and Doug were the perfect solution. 'You're going to your own flesh and blood,' whispered his mother hugging him tightly. 'It's a miracle.'

So here he was with his own flesh and blood. His mind tumbled with angry thoughts. He unpacked his clothes and shoved them untidily into the drawers. It meant nothing to him that they were supposed to be related. There had only ever been him and his mum.

Having randomly stacked his few books and CDs on to the shelves, and some folders from school projects into his desk, he extricated Monty, his faded bedraggled monkey, dressed like a little Indian rajah in his once bright-red jacket, his worn-out shiny green trousers and a silken turban wrapped round his head. Freddy propped Monty on the chair, draped his jacket over him and went down for supper.

Doug appeared. 'There you are, Sunny Jim!' he hailed him cheerily.

'You know what, Rosie!' exclaimed Doug. 'Perhaps you're right about you and Freddy being related. Just look at you both!' Rosie and Freddy appraised each other, sharing the dark brown hair and olive skin, the large brown eyes, the longish nose and full lips.

'No "maybe" about it!' exclaimed Rosie, giving Freddy a warm hug. 'Later I'll show you the family tree I've been drawing up. I'm sure it will soon fill up with other relatives belonging to you and me. Doug's bored stiff with it all – but perhaps, now you're here, he'll take an interest. We'll go up to London soon and show it to your mother. I hope you managed to find a place for everything in your room,' she chattered on, and Doug felt relieved to see her more animated than she'd been for a long time and hoped that Freddy would restore Rosie to her old happy self.

Later, when Freddy went up to bed, Monty was gone.

He couldn't believe it. He had never ever lost Monty before. He was the one thing Freddy had owned from the time he was a baby and had lived with his mother – before he was taken into care. Monty was the one thing he had refused to be parted from even though now he was nearly ten. Monty was always close to hand, and Freddy still took him to bed, though hiding him so that no one would laugh and call him a baby, as one of his foster fathers had done.

He had placed him on the chair, he was sure of it. Yes, he'd covered him with his jacket as he didn't want anyone to mock him for still having his manky, frayed, sucked and hugged cloth monkey. So he knew he wouldn't have been careless or forgotten him in the move. The jacket was still there, but not Monty.

It was a small-ish room with just a bed, a chest of drawers, a built-in wardrobe, a desk with a computer and a chair. So how could he not find him? He turned everything over and over, went through all the drawers he'd only just filled; opened his suitcase again and again – as if somehow he could have missed seeing him. He looked under the bed, behind the chair, behind the drawers, in the wardrobe, on the book shelves, even in the bathroom and toilet.

Finally, feeling bewildered and bereft, Freddy went to bed.

When he awoke the next morning, the first thing he saw was Monty, sitting on the chair exactly where he had left him. Freddy leaped from his bed and clutched him in his arms. 'Where were you?' he whispered.

'Breakfast in ten minutes!' Rosie called from two floors down, and Freddy hurried along to the bathroom, taking Monty with him.

'Are you my brother?' a child's voice asked, like a breath down the chimney, or leaves brushing against a windowpane.

He spun round. 'What? Who said that?'

But there was nothing. Just the old mirror in its re-varnished oak frame, hanging near the north-facing window; reflecting the hills, a winding road and the roofs of an old house peering through the tops of the trees.

He washed and dressed then, hiding Monty at the back of his wardrobe, went downstairs for breakfast.

'Does anyone else live here?' asked Freddy.

'No – it's just the three of us,' laughed Rosie, 'though we live in hope we might have children one day.'

'Why do you ask?' Doug wondered.

'I thought I heard someone else's voice.'

'It was the same for us,' said Rosie. 'I'm sure I—'

But Doug interrupted her quickly with a warning look not to disturb the boy. 'When we first came,' he laughed, 'we thought we could hear things. We're town folk too, you see, trying to get used to the silence – yet it's not silent. An old house is always full of creaks and groans, and shifting and rustling. Sometimes it's the wooden floors or the water pipes, and other times it's the wind in the chimney or the trees outside, or night creatures. So take no notice. You'll get used to it.'

After breakfast Rosie spread her roll of paper across the kitchen table where her family tree was spreading its branches, and he saw his and his mother's names added to it. He had to admit it was quite exciting.

'Look!' She stabbed her finger at one of the branches. First I found John Walker, a major in the British army posted to India in 1855. He's the link to both of us.

'Yeah! Walker's my name,' Freddy exclaimed. 'Freddy Walker!'

'And I'm a Walker too. I'll show you how we're

related!' She traced her finger along the branches: 'Major John Walker, Afghan Rifles, 1855-68. He fought at the northwest frontier! Then he left the army and went into business in Calcutta. He married an Indian lady, a certain Rukmini Biswas. See!' said Rosie, pointing to the three lower branches. 'They had two boys and a girl. The boys were sent to England to be educated. One returned later, but the other stayed on here and became a doctor. We're both part of that branch and that means we both have Indian blood in us. Once I made that discovery, it was easy to find you and your mother – except there is a blip I can't quite work out.' Rosie sank into an intense silence, and seemed to forget Freddy was there as she crouched over the table, tapping her pencil.

'Hey, Freddy! I think we'll leave her to it. I've got to go into the village. Want to come?' interrupted Doug softly.

Over the next few days Freddy tried to settle in, but other small things kept happening which caused Rosie or Doug to 'have words' with him. 'Freddy, dear, do make sure you turn the taps off properly after you've washed. I've found them running two days in a row. Mustn't waste water, you know.'

Though Freddy was sure he hadn't left the taps running, he didn't argue.

'And try not to unravel so much toilet paper. I found it trailing across the floor. Be a bit more careful, yes?'

But he hadn't unravelled toilet paper across the floor – his previous foster homes had taught him that. Then there was Doug's favourite paintbrush. It was missing from his studio, and they found it in Freddy's bedroom. 'Did you want to paint a picture or something?' asked Doug. 'You only have to ask, you know.' But though Freddy protested his innocence, he didn't feel they believed him.

One night Freddy woke in a shivering panic. Where was he? He had a strange feeling of not sleeping in a proper bed, but on something unbearably hard, covered only by scratchy sacking. It felt bitterly cold. Around him were sounds of whimpering, pitiful cries, and it seemed that his whole room was lined with wooden pallets on which restless children itched with fleas, and there was a terrible smell of filthy clothes and unwashed bodies. Somewhere in this stinking darkness, a child moaned out a song which struck a distant memory in him. Someone had sung it to him once.

So jao, so jao,
Little Freddy sleep now.

A dark brown face leaned over him singing tenderly.

But when he sat bolt upright staring around, he was alone. All was quiet, and he was relieved to find he was in a bed after all, and faint moonlight splattered dark shadows across his cosy duvet.

Clutching Monty to him, he went to the window and looked out across the dark meadow with the river glittering like silver ribbon. He felt desperately lonely, and wondered about running away. He hated it here. Hated it, hated it. Bitter tears fell, soaking Monty's jacket. Even if they were blood relatives, Rosie was weird, and Doug – well he was OK, though always working. This wasn't home; could never be home, not without Mum.

After a while he was overcome by sleepiness, but he needed the loo. He tossed Monty onto his pillow and opened the door. He was instantly struck by a chill draught of air. It was shivery cold and dank, as if the walls had never known any heating. He almost risked not going, but then knew he must and hurried down to the bathroom. He peed, and was about to return to his room when he heard a noise in the corridor: a scuffling sound like children's feet, and a flurry of hushed whispers.

'Are you my brother?' a voice hissed through the door. 'Can we go home now?'

Then came the sound of something tapping determinedly down the wooden floors of the corridor. *Tap, tap, tap* . . . it came nearer and nearer. *Tap, tap, tap* . . . getting closer and louder. 'I've got to go! She's coming!' wept the voice.

Surely it was Rosie or Doug. 'It's me!' Freddy cried out, but not daring to open the door. 'I just wanted the loo.' The tapping ceased.

'Doug? Rosie?' He called again. There was no reply.

Then the tapping started up more fiercely. It was close now; nearly outside the bathroom door; terrifying; menacing. *Rattattat!* Surely it would wake the house? If it were Rosie or Doug, why didn't they speak; ask if it were him?

It's me, Freddy! But barely a squeak broke out of his strangled throat.

He heard a swish of skirts and the high-pitched scream of a child.

Rattatap tap. The bathroom door was struck with such ferocity, Freddy thought it would crack open. 'Go away! Please go away,' he wept, backing to the far wall. And it did. *Tap, tap, tap.* Down the wall of the corridor, further and further away, until the sound diminished to silence.

He waited; who knows how long? He crept to the door and pressed his ear against it; listening. Silence. Slowly he prised it open just a little, holding his breath as if to stop his heart leaping about. He peered out. *Aaah!* His mouth opened soundlessly in terror. A woman stood before the mirror. 'Rosie?' Yet the more he looked, the more she transmogrified into a figure more matronly: her clothes were odd; a floppy bonnet tied with ribbons under her chin, full skirts falling to her booted ankles, and a large ragged shawl which enveloped her shoulders. She leaned forward heavily on a stick.

Help! Help me! he screamed inside. But his bones were rigid; his skin as cold as ice. The woman's head turned, but she had no face. Her bonnet framed a black void, yet she seemed to look into his very soul.

Rattattat. She thudded her stick, then raised a finger and beckoned him. The command was unmistakable. 'Get in there,' she rapped the mirror.

Energy came from somewhere. Freddy sprang back inside the bathroom, locked the door and stumbled into a space between the bath and the wash basin. His legs gave way and he sank down, his head buried into his arms clutched round his knees.

How long he stayed in this huddle, he didn't know. Was it till his heart had stopped beating like an express train? Or till he was roused by the hunting cry of a night owl? He couldn't tell, except that when he awoke the next morning, he was back in bed.

But Monty had gone again.

'Freddy! Go down to the village,' Rosie suggested the next day. 'You're looking like a typical pale and pallid city boy. You might as well see if you can get to know some of the village children. There's always a group playing football on the green. Go and take a look.'

Feeling homesick, sulky and aggrieved, Freddy followed the road across the meadow. All he could think of was Monty. Where was he? Was it a conspiracy between Rosie and Doug to hide him away. Perhaps they thought he was babyish and unimportant.

He reached a junction; one road ran straight into

the village. The other road ran along the far side of the meadow. He paused, unsure what he wanted to do.

That's when he saw the gate. It was set deep into a grassy bank; a tall iron-wrought gate almost completely hidden by ivy and weeds. Beyond it there was just the semblance of a path going steeply up through trees entwined with creepers and foliage. It looked mysterious and exciting. Freddy pushed the gate, and it opened, just sufficiently for him to squeeze through. It felt like running away, and he thought perhaps he could make a den somewhere inside and live there for a while.

He struggled up a single overgrown path, beating back the undergrowth with a stick. He was so taken with pulling himself free of brambles and finding a way forward, he didn't look up until he reached the top of the incline. Then he almost gasped with surprise. Looming before him was a house of many windows and gables and chimneys — covered in ivy like the gate had been, as if it were in hiding.

'Hah!' said a voice. 'There you are! I thought I spotted someone.'

A tall man dressed in sporting plus fours, wearing bright yellow socks and stout boots, stepped out with a large stick under his arm.

Freddy gave a shout of terror, and immediately turned tail and hurtled down the slope, ignoring the voice which urged him to come back. Slithering, sliding, his clothes being torn by the brambles, he tumbled out into the road and ran all the way back to Meadowsweet House.

Later that afternoon, there was a knock on the door. When Rosie answered it, Freddy was horrified to see the man from the old house.

'I'm Charles Mickledean from the manor over there. I saw your notice. Landscape gardeners, I see. Well I'm sure this young lad will agree that my house is in dire need of landscape gardening, and I wondered whether you would be interested?' Rosie looked questioningly at Freddy and back to Charles Mickledean.

'You know each other?' asked Rosie.

'Oh, we bumped into each other this morning, didn't we?' smiled the old man. 'It's quite easy to stray onto my land with most of the wall and fences in need of repair. I bought the house ages ago, but have only just moved here to live and start trying to restore it to its former glory. Sorry if I gave you a fright, my lad. You were a bit of a shock to me too! I haven't yet got to know many people in the village.'

'I was only exploring,' Freddy murmured, gratefully moving aside for Doug, who came rushing forward enthusiastically to ask the owner of Mickledean Manor to come in.

This could be their first real job!

CHAPTER THREE

The Painting

Charles Mickledean suggested they go and look over the grounds. Rosie and Doug took along their sketchbooks and jotted down all sorts of ideas for restoring the garden. Freddy was free to explore wherever he liked until, after a while, Mr Mickledean invited them into the house. Rosie thought it important to see the garden from inside, and understand what kind of views might be pleasing to the eye.

They entered through the front door and found themselves in a large hall, with a grand fireplace large enough to roast an ox. To the left was the main staircase leading to the upper floors. They stopped on the first landing to look eastwards over an overgrown maze. As they turned to carry on through the house, Rosie gasped with interest. She was staring at a large dusty oil painting hanging above the stairs. It showed an eighteenth-century English gentleman dressed in oriental clothes, seated in a reclining cane chair. Positioned around him was an Indian woman in her finery and two children: a boy of about eight years old, dressed like a little rajah, with a jewelled turban and flowing silk garments; and a little girl of four or five with shiny black plaits beneath a gauzy veil which covered her shoulders, wearing a long

Indian skirt and blouse glittering with sequins and embroidery. Whereas the two adults looked tenderly at each other and the boy's attention was on his pet monkey, the little girl looked straight out of the painting into the eyes of the viewer.

But it was the monkey which, at first, caught Freddy's eye. It looked just like Monty, dressed in a scarlet jacket over green trousers and a silken turban on its head.

'Is that Edmund Mickledean and his family?' asked Rosie intensely.

'No idea!' laughed Mr Mickledean. 'I inherited that painting. Don't know anything about it. It was in my grandmother's attic for years, and passed onto me after she died. I never saw it hung in her house, and I'm not even sure whether I like it or not. I'm afraid I've never taken an interest in family history, but I expect they are Mickledeans. We did have an Indian connection way back, I'm told.'

'She has a sad look,' commented Rosie with feeling.

Freddy found himself staring into the eyes of the little girl, and suddenly it was as if she spoke to him. A thin, quiet voice sounded in his head like the one he thought he had heard when he first arrived. 'Are you my brother?'

When they finally returned home, Doug was almost leaping with excitement. 'This is our breakthrough!

Our first really big commission – and what a wonderful job!' He wanted to get down to work immediately but, to his disappointment, Rosie pulled out her family tree and studied it as if it held her fate.

At supper the silence continued. Freddy felt uncomfortable. Rosie hardly ate anything and Doug looked moody too. They'd been arguing. When her husband had tried to talk about landscaping, all Rosie could talk about was the Mickledean child from India, wondering what happened to her. 'It could be her in the painting!'

'What if it is? She's dead, Rosie. Whether she died here in the workhouse of typhus or something, or whether she survived and became a housemaid in Buckingham Palace, it was three hundred years ago. She's dead.'

'It's just that...' Rosie looked Doug straight in the eye. 'I feel her presence so strongly.' Then she turned her gaze on Freddy so powerfully that, with a shudder, he remembered his dream: the woman with the stick; the woman without a face yet who had seemed to look deep inside him; the woman who had stood in front of the mirror and told him to get in there.

It was with dread that Freddy climbed the stairs to bed that night. The mirror gleamed in its alcove. He tried to run past without looking into it, but something caught his sleeve. He whirled round in time to see a small hand retreating back into the glass.

Instinctively he reached out to grab the hand and, for an instant, he felt as if he did indeed touch cold little fingers. They gripped his and pulled, as though they wanted to tug him into the mirror. He snatched his hand away and leaped back staring at his own wide-eyed reflection and the look of horror on his face.

So jao, so jao,
Sleep my little Esme now...

It was the song from his dream; a small child's voice sang, and it seemed to come from within the mirror. The surface clouded over, but something else was there; faintly glimmering through his own reflection was a little girl and, in her arms, she rocked Monty. But the moment he realised it, she faded away, and even though he rushed to the mirror and slapped his hand over it, all he saw was his own desperate face.

Sleep was impossible. For a while he lay fighting with unease, confusion, fear. Perhaps he dozed after all; sleeping, waking, but sometime in the night, he knew that he must get Monty back.

He threw back his duvet, strode out into the corridor and stood in front of the mirror. As before there was that dank shuddery coldness, but he felt bold and undeterred. He rapped on the glass. 'Give me back my monkey,' he breathed, pressing his mouth close to its surface. His breath created a misty cloud and then he stepped back as a face emerged through the haze.

The image continued to form and grow more solid and complete. He thought he looked at himself: olive skin, dark brown eyes, long nose, black hair, except it was a girl; like the girl in the painting in Mickledean Manor. Yet she was different: she was not wearing glimmering silken garments, with pink and gold threaded slippers as in the painting; she didn't have a string of pearls round her neck, or bangles and gold earrings. Her hair was not beautifully shining and plaited. This girl looked half-starved, and wore nothing but a roughly spun, raw-cotton shift hanging halfway down her bare thin legs. Her hair was unkempt and dull, in knotted tangles down to her shoulders. She held Monty tucked into her neck as if she would never let him go.

'He's mine. Give him back!' hissed Freddy.

She stretched out a hand. He stretched out his. At first his fingers touched only the hard surface of the mirror, then the hardness seemed to dissolve and he touched her fingers.

'Have you come to take me home?' asked the girl.

'No. I want Monty. He's mine,' said Freddy.

She clasped his hand and pulled. He resisted. But as they tugged at each other, her hand became a vice.

Tap, tap, tap . . .

A gasping scream left her throat. 'Take me home!' she wept. She was fading away, but still gripped him. Then the child's fingers were replaced by the old dame's gnarled and bony hand, impossible to escape from. She held up her stick with the other hand and swung it. 'Get in here, you little brat!' she rasped, and tried to drag him through the mirror.

'No!' Freddy yelled. His screams seemed to echo through the walls and up into the timbers of the roof and out into the lane; and mingled with the jangle of harness bells and the sound of horses' hoofs clattering past.

A light came on. It shone fiercely in the mirror, blotting out the images. Rosie pounded up the stairs. 'Freddy? What's going on?'

He stared at her, but no words came out.

'Freddy, did you see something?' demanded Rosie, gripping his face in her hands.

'Rosie, Rosie! The boy's had a nightmare.' Doug appeared at her side. 'He's sleepwalking. Be gentle. Let's get him to bed.'

Freddy hoped Monty might reappear as last time, but two or three days went by and there was no sign of him. Sometimes, when he passed the mirror, he whispered, 'Give me back Monty.' But nothing happened.

Then Doug had to go away to London for two days on another commission.

When he'd gone, Rosie said, 'So it's just you and me, Freddy.'

Pause.

'Just you and me.'

Pause.

Freddy felt a wave of unease.

There was an ominous silence.

'You've seen her too, haven't you, Freddy?'

Freddy shuddered. Rosie seemed almost like the terrible woman in his nightmare.

Fiercely, she pulled him over to the table. The spidery markings on the sheet had spread and spread. Rosie had added branches which went back earlier than her Victorian ancestor, Major John Walker. 'I began looking up the Mickledeans,' she muttered, her fingers fumbling as she riffled through pages of notes. 'I found something vital. Major Walker's daughter married a Mickledean – a direct descendant of Edmund Mickledean's son who stayed back in India in the seventeen-twenties. Do you see, do you see?' She looked crazily triumphant.

Freddy didn't look. He was too afraid, and wanted to flee, but she still gripped his arm.

'The Walkers and Mickledeans are linked.' Rosie was almost feverish with the excitement of her discovery. 'I knew there was something about this place from the moment we came. It's as though I was brought here to reunite our ancestors.' She gazed at her papers again, muttering over and over. 'I found you, now we must rescue her. She's in the mirror.'

'The mirror?' Freddy whispered with dread.

'I first saw that woman's face when I found the

mirror – Maria Flegg. She was the matron when the Mickledean girl was left here in 1723. I looked up the records in the Records Office. But they don't list the girl's name. Her name isn't there.'

'What does Doug think?' whispered Freddy, wishing Doug were here.

'Doug thinks I've got a vivid imagination. Maybe I have. Maybe I've become too involved with the story of the abandoned child. Doug thinks I'm obsessed. He told me to throw the mirror away. I was going to smash the mirror to bits; drop it in the river. I tried, but as I lifted it off the wall, instead of Dame Flegg, I saw the girl, and I was certain it was the Mickledean child who had been brought over from India. So I couldn't destroy the mirror. Not till I'd saved her. Got her out of that place. But that woman's trying to stop me; trying to destroy me.'

Rosie's voice changed: grated and got lower, snarling like a wild animal. 'I rule here. This is my domain.' She thudded her pencil on the table, *rattatap tap*, *rattatap tap*.

Like a change of light passing over the sea when the sun is briefly dimmed by a cloud, Freddy seemed to see the dreadful dame envelop Rosie as she crouched over the table, rapping with her pencil. But Rosie sprang to her feet waving her arms wildly as if to push her away.

'Let me take the girl to where she belongs.' It was Rosie's voice again; plaintive; desperate. 'But how do I rescue a ghost?'

'So she *is* a ghost,' stammered Freddy, trying to back away.

'Ha!' Rosie grabbed him so tightly it hurt. 'I knew you'd seen her.'

'Is she really a ghost?'

'They all are. Poor wretched creatures – Dame Flegg too. It was a cruel time – and they couldn't help what they became. But Dame Flegg is trying to become me. I feel it. She's trying to take me over and stop me from saving the girl, because then she knows I'll destroy her.

'Sometimes I feel I've become Dame Flegg already. Save the girl, Freddy! She'll listen to you.' Rosie let him go, and slumped over the table.

Freddy retreated step by step. 'How?' He reached the back door.

'By calling her name.' Rosie put her hands to her head and dragged her fingers through her hair. 'But I don't know her name!'

Freddy fled silently away. He went down to the river and sat beneath an old willow tree, his back hard up against the trunk as if seeking comfort from it. Time flowed with the water, and he thought of the blood flowing in his veins; where it had come from, where it was going. He rocked gently, humming the old lullaby to himself. He slept and dreamed. A gentle dark face leaned over him singing:

So jao, so jao,

Little Esme sleep now.

Esme? No. His name was Freddy. Who was Esme?

Among the willow leaves trailing in the water, a little girl's face floated just under the surface. 'Esme?' The face sank from sight. That's what the girl in the mirror had sung. Was that her name? Freddy ran back to the house.

'Rosie!' he rushed into the kitchen, then stopped. All was quiet. She wasn't there, though the family tree was still spread out on the table. 'Rosie?' he called again, moving swiftly to the living room, the study and up to the first floor. There was no sign of her.

Filled with a deep fear, he climbed to the second floor and stood at the bottom of the stairs leading to the third. It was deeply, horribly silent; yet it was the silence of willow leaves trailing in rivers; the silence of the bottom of deep oceans; the silence of blood surging through his ears – a roaring silence. He knew he must go upstairs.

'Rosie?' he whispered hoarsely. No one answered. Above him, a child began to sing.

'*So jao, so jao,*
Little baby sleep now.'

'Come up, Freddy,' Rosie called.

Like a sleepwalker, Freddy climbed to the third floor, singing as he went.

'*So jao, so jao,*
Little Esme sleep now.'

The figure stood before the mirror. Was it Rosie or Dame Flegg? A bonnet enclosed her head, and the full skirts which fell to the ground made it look as if she floated. She leaned forward on her stick and turned her faceless void to him, that deep, black hole which seemed intent on sucking out his soul.

But it was Rosie's voice which called him. 'Her name, Freddy. She'll come to you if you call her name.'

'Get back in there,' came a different voice, harsh and cruel. The dame's hands gripped him.

'I'm losing her, Freddy! I don't know her name!' Rosie was howling, as hands pushed him till his face was pressed up against the glass.

'*So jao, so jao,*
Little Esme sleep now.'

He muttered the words over and over, his breath misting the glass and seeming to drift through it.

'Esme!' Freddy yelled from the depths of his stomach. 'Rosie! Her name is Esme!'

He shouted the name over and over again. 'Esme, come!'

From within the dark reaches of the mirror, the girl appeared. She was rocking Monty in her arms like a baby. 'Are you my brother? Have you come to take me away?' she asked.

'Get the mirror, Freddy!' It was Rosie's voice. 'For God's sake take it off the wall. Get it out of here. Take Esme to the manor!'

Freddy wrenched the mirror off the wall and, as he turned to go down the stairs, he saw two people now before the blank space on the wall; the dame and Rosie in a deadly embrace, as they fought for each other's soul.

The road wound as thin as a silver thread. The evening sky spread for ever, vast as an ocean, the roofs of the manor visible now, bobbing among the trees like a galleon. Thundering hoofs and a furious jingling of harness bells bore down on him. The road was too narrow to stand aside and the banks of the lane too high for him to climb out of the way. He ran and ran, till the pounding horses and the crunching wheels overwhelmed him, hurling him to the road, the mirror clutched to his chest. From Meadowsweet House came a shriek which set the rooks wheeling in an arc like a shower of arrows.

Charles Mickledean caught the boy in his head-lights, driving back from the town, running as if the hounds of hell were after him. He saw him stumble, yet so keen to protect the mirror that, when he fell, its face was clutched to his chest, unbroken.

As he drove the boy to the manor, a figure emerged from Meadowsweet House. Rosie, her face thrown joyfully up to the stars, threw her arms wide as if to embrace the universe.

The mirror hangs near the old painting in Mickledean Manor; just a mirror now, and the only images are reflections of those who pass by, or pause to stare into the glass, as it did when Doug came back from London, bringing Freddy's mother, and they all visited Mickledean Manor.

Rosie smiles again; at peace now. The Mickledeans and Walkers together; a blood link which finally united them. She completed the family tree and put it away.

But at a certain angle, the mirror reflects the little girl in the painting. No one notices except Freddy. Esme now holds, half hidden in her Indian veil, a cloth monkey, in a faded red jacket, worn-out shiny green trousers and a silken turban wrapped round his head. It's Monty, but Freddy doesn't mind. He doesn't need him any more. After all she could be his sister. She looks out of the painting, straight into his eyes. There is a smile; sad? Yes. But she has at last come home.

So jao, so jao,

Little Esme sleep now.

THE GHOST
IN THE
MACHINE

Eleanor Updale

THE GHOST IN
THE MACHINE

Hello? Hello? Can you hear me over all this din? I'm ready now. Don't close the file. Don't turn down your speakers. This is really important. Please listen. I'm going to try to stay calm and tell you everything, right from the beginning, even though I'm really scared, and I don't know how much time I've got. If you can't make head or tail of this, please pass it on to someone who understands computers. Or ghosts. Or both. Somebody, somewhere will know what to do. Don't switch off. This isn't a joke.

I should tell you who I am. This is Hari Patel. Or at least I was Hari Patel. You probably haven't heard of me. Even if you have, no doubt you think I'm dead. Well you're right, I suppose. I am. But I'm in real trouble. I need your help.

It shouldn't be the ghost who's frightened. That's the first thing they teach you at Ghoul School. Or at least I guess it must be. I was late. Yes, I know. I know. Typical. Anyway, I missed the introduction. Maybe that's why I'm in this mess now. It was all my own fault as usual. The paranormalmedic who picked me up from the curbside was trying to do his job. I feel bad about him getting into trouble for failing to deliver me on time, but somehow my Totalplayer was still working after the accident, and even though I was dead, I had to carry on with the game. It was Warjammer, and I was just on the verge of breaking through to Level Ten. Nothing else mattered to me then. Anyone out there who's into gaming will understand.

That's why I was killed, by the way. I wasn't looking when I stepped into the road. Or listening. I had my earphones in. That's the great thing about the Totalplayer 9: you can have every program running at once: phone, emails, pictures, games, music. My tracks were on shuffle, and the machine had just selected a rubbish rap by some girl group on an album my little sister gave me for Christmas. I don't even like that song, and now – just as I'll never wear any other clothes – I'm doomed to have part of it running through my head for ever. It's not surprising that some of my thought processes have gone haywire. Yours would too if they had *This is a visit from the Spirit. It ain't easy being dead*, hammering away in the background all the time.

Still, in a way I was lucky. I didn't feel a thing. In fact, I've only just found out that I was hit by a lorry. It was carrying medical supplies to the local hospital. Saving lives and taking one at the same time. In other circumstances I might think that was funny.

So, anyway, the paranormalmedic was taking me to Ghoul School, rather than Heaven, because I was so excited about what I was doing when I died. That's how you become a ghost. You have to be in a state of high emotional charge when your heart stops. Otherwise you just slip straight through to Eternal Rest. We ghosts are in Limbo: a sort of 'cooling area' while we get fit for Heaven. You don't get held in Limbo if you just dwindle away quietly after a peaceful life, or a long illness bravely borne; or even if you are killed violently, but don't see it coming, and so don't feel the horror. The old stories are true. There are a lot of ghosts with their heads tucked underneath their arms – the last seconds before execution being about as nerve-wracking as you can get. But it doesn't have to be physical excitement that stops your soul from melting into oblivion. Seething anger or great misery can be just as powerful. So the tales of ghouls moping about wringing their hands and wailing are accurate too. But we don't wear sheets. We look just how we used to look, at least to each other. I'm turning on the webcam now. I'll attach a picture to this message. You'll see what I mean.

I can tell what you're thinking. If I'm just some sloppy kid who stepped carelessly into the road because he was distracted by a stupid game, why have I been made a ghost? You're right. Normally I wouldn't have been taken to Limbo. I would be in Eternal Rest with the other accident victims who were knocked unconscious before they had time to think. But Warjammer changed all that. You see, just as my human body was killed, my virtual self was under maximum threat. There were Zargs with their lasers to the right, Thargs with their axes to the left, the timer was ticking towards zero and I had used up all my reserve power fighting off the Heralds of Doom in Level Eight. In the corner of the screen a warning flashed bright orange. The portal to the netherworld was beginning to open beneath me. I had only seconds left to slay the Dargeron, or vacuum forces would suck me into the abyss (and back to Level Five). My hands were so slippery with sweat that my thumbs kept sliding off the buttons. I was terrified. So when I was accidentally plunged into the real Netherworld, with the paranormalmedic dragging me on and insisting that he had to deliver me to someone he called 'the Professor', all my emotional juices were pumping. I was still battling to survive: dodging and diving from virtual threats. My mortal and cyber wires were crossed.

The paranormalmedic turned up long before the real ambulance men. I thought at first that he must be on his way to a fancy-dress party. His uniform was like something out of a history book: all shiny buttons, leather straps and feathers in the helmet. It was soon clear to me that he was on special business. He told me his name was Merk, which I suppose might be short for Mercury, but I didn't have time to ask. He scooped me up in some sort of ethereal net. I struggled against it, of course, but though it was so light that I could hardly see or feel it, I couldn't break out. Merk clicked his heels and we started to rise into the air, with him pulling the net behind him. If you could have seen us, we probably would have looked like a stork arriving with a baby – only, of course, we were going the other way. I thought we were travelling pretty fast, but Merk kept complaining that he couldn't get up to full speed. Then he saw me on my T.P.9.

'How come that's still running?' he asked, as if I should have the faintest idea. 'Nothing like that works up here. It must be interfering with the force fields.'

I didn't want to stop. I had only two more Zargs to capture, and then I would be on to the next level. No one I knew had got that far, but I'd heard that you got new lifelines if you broke through. I kept on with the game.

You're expecting me to say that I turned the T.P.9 off when I got to the Pearly Gates, aren't you? Well I didn't, because I couldn't. Something had happened to the electronics, and the switch wouldn't work. And anyway, Pearly Gates? The entrance I went through was more like the door to a power station or an army camp. There were no angels with harps, just a bored bloke with a clipboard, complaining that the paranormal-medic was late.

Merk turned round and whispered to me, 'Hide that thing. We haven't got time to mess about with searches. We're late enough already. I'm going to be in real trouble.'

So I stuck the T.P.9 in my hood, while Merk dealt with the guard.

'It's just a kid who walked under a truck. No need for a check. He's empty-handed. The Professor will kill me all over again if I don't get him to school soon. Sorry you've had to work overtime.'

It did the trick. The guard raised the barrier and waved us through. Soon we were climbing the stairs of a dilapidated building. Clearly this wasn't Heaven. The classroom was like something out of an old black and white film. An assortment of battered and bloodstained people, some of them much too big for the furniture, were seated in rows of wooden desks. At the front of the class stood the Professor: a balding, dishevelled figure of about forty, I guess, wearing a tattered lab coat with chemical stains all over it. His glasses were held together with a grubby strip of old-fashioned Elastoplast – the kind that's made of stretchy pink cloth. He didn't look like someone who was going to change my life – or should I say death?

He was annoyed with me at first. Standing at the blackboard, twirling a piece of chalk as if he were about to fling it in my direction, his snide greeting was worthy of Mr (B.O.) Barwood at my school: 'Glad you have deigned to grace us with your presence, Mr Patel.'

As I went to take my seat at the back of the class, my T.P.9 bleeped. The Professor stopped talking. I took the machine out of my hood and tried to turn it off, but yet again the button had no effect. The Thargs and Zargs were still thrashing it out. Miraculously, in the game at least, I was still alive.

'Bring that thing here!' shouted the Professor, and everyone stared at me as I returned to the front of the class. I was expecting to be told off, and the Professor did take away the T.P.9, but, as he turned his back to shut it in a cupboard, I'm sure that I heard (over the noise of *This is a visit from the Spirit. It ain't easy being dead*) an excited whisper: 'Yes! It's time!'

The Professor called the class to order, and hurriedly ran through the essentials of being a good ghost (stick to the rules: don't reveal any secrets of the Netherworld, be appropriately scary, etc, etc). Since we were all beginners, it was pretty basic stuff. Then he allocated the jobs. The murder victim was sent back to the nightclub where he was stabbed, with instructions to spill drinks and block the toilets so they would flood. The soldier was returned to Afghanistan to warn and encourage his old comrades, and the various miseries were dispatched to haunt the families and business associates who had blighted their lives. The Professor called the sad ghosts 'the Glums'. One drunken barman he called 'the Wine Glum'. The rest of us laughed, though we sensed it was a joke he had used before.

He asked me to stay behind. I was dreading punishment, but he held out his hand. I went to shake it, and that's the moment I accepted that I was now a ghost. Our palms passed through each other. There was no contact, no warmth, no grip.

I was sure I was in for an ear-bashing, though why I should have known the rules of Heaven, or wherever we were, was beyond me. He took the T.P.9 out of the drawer. It was still running.

'I've heard about these things,' he said, 'but I've never seen one working.'

'I'm sorry,' I said, 'I couldn't turn it off.'

'No, no. Don't apologise.' The Professor had a twinkle in his eye now. 'This is a godsend. The only artifacts allowed in here are things invented before the Antebellumites took over. I've been longing to get my hands on something like this.'

'The Antebellumites?'

'Our rulers here. They got the upper hand at the beginning of the twentieth century. They've frozen everything at the stage of development civilisation had reached when they were alive. They don't believe in progress, you see. They say technological development caused all the slaughter down below.'

'Why do they care about that?'

'Well, partly for humanitarian reasons, I'll give them their due. No one likes seeing young people, yourself included, losing their lives. But they're mainly worried about overcrowding here. They don't like sudden surges in arrivals. Every time there's a big war, all our services are stretched to the limit. But what the Antebellumites don't see is the essential illogicality of their point of view. While we've held back on inventions, the world has romped away. Now we're even less equipped to deal with consequences of mass destruction than we would have been if we'd kept up with Earth.'

I listened as hard as I could, despite the constant rapping: *This is a visit from the Spirit. It ain't easy being dead.* I didn't agree with the girls in my ears. If this was death it wasn't so bad. Mind you, I was still trying to work out exactly where I was (like I said, I'd missed the beginning of the briefing). The Professor confirmed my guess. It was a holding station between Earth and Heaven. I could believe what he said about the place being badly run. The window frames of the classroom were rotten and the floorboards creaked as he strode up and down punching at the buttons on my T.P.9.

'Why don't you tell the people in charge that you need to modernise?' I asked.

The Professor guffawed. 'Do you think I haven't? Do you think I'd be confined here, doing this dead-end job, if I'd never challenged them? I'm not even allowed to go haunting any more.'

'Why?'

'Because I broke the rules. I did secret research when I should have been tormenting my former colleagues.'

He could see that I was mystified, and tried to explain. He put the T.P.9 down on the desk and ran his hands up and down his filthy lab coat. 'This is what I was wearing when I died,' he said. 'We're all doomed to stay in the clothes we had on then, and so I can't get away from reminders that I am really a scientist, even though they've relegated me to teaching Reception Class now. It was an explosion, by the way. Took me totally by surprise, but I was sent here because I was in a state of such elation when disaster struck. I thought I'd found the formula for a new fuel to replace petrol in cars. I thought it was going to make my fortune...'

He went into a sort of trance, and I picked up the T.P.9 to make sure that he hadn't put me back in danger. It bleeped, bringing him back to his point.

'Anyway,' he said, 'after they'd rebuilt the lab, I was sent to haunt it. But I couldn't resist using each night to catch up on what my old workmates had done the previous day. I learned a lot about new developments:

airships, radio, even television. I came back with big plans for changing things here.'

'How long ago was that?' I asked, suspecting that he hadn't visited Earth for decades.

'Oh about eighty years,' he said. 'Of course, I've picked up bits of information since then by eavesdropping on the new arrivals who come through. I've heard all about those computer things you have now, but no one's been allowed in here with one in working order. I took a damaged laptop to pieces once. Impossible to fathom how it operated. Just a few tiny electrical connections. No moving parts. Extraordinary.'

I filled him in a bit on the principles behind computers, and he got more friendly and more excited as we talked. Then he dropped his voice, even though there was no one else around.

'This could be our way in,' he said, slapping his knees in excitement.

'Way into what?' I asked.

'Our way of finding a more efficient method of ghosting. One that doesn't involve huge transportation costs, getting everyone to Earth and back every night. Our infrastructure is stretched to the limit. You were late. You should know. Trouble on Superhighway 25, I bet.'

I should have admitted that my T.P.9 had caused the delay, but I was getting caught up by his enthusiasm. When I told him about the internet and he suggested using it for ghostly transport, I was glad to contribute ideas – off the top of my head – about how it might be done. I probably should have been more cautious. I certainly would have been more realistic about my own knowledge and capabilities if I'd had any inkling of what he was going to propose. But when he asked me how much I knew about information technology and electronics, I couldn't help saying (with some truth, actually) that they were about the only subjects I was any good at. He took that to mean I was an expert, and I let him.

The Professor fingered the T.P.9 again. That song was still going round my head *This is a visit from the Spirit. It ain't easy being dead.* I was confused, but glad to have found someone who liked me and seemed excited to talk to me. So I suppose it's not surprising that I eventually went along with his plan.

He was desperate to impress the authorities. 'Just imagine,' he said, 'if this works, it might get me out of this wretched school at last – earn me some extra credits – speed up my transition.'

'Transition?'

'To Eternal Rest. Peace. If you pull it off, you might get there quicker too. We could both short-circuit the line to Paradise.'

'Pull off what exactly?'

'Get into a computer. Haunt someone from inside their machine.'

'You mean mess things up for them. Like a virus?'

The Professor looked puzzled. 'You've lost me there. I'd have to leave that side of things to you.'

Between us we came up with a plan. He told me the science behind ghostliness, and I explained what I could about cyberspace. You could see how he'd become a professor. He caught on really quickly, and made it sound the easiest thing in the world for me to use the T.P.9 to email myself to someone and, once inside their computer, get down to my ghostly duties. The only time he lost patience with me was when I said that the idea of turning me into a digital code sounded like magic.

'There's no such thing as magic,' he insisted as he hovered at the top of the blackboard, filling the last few centimetres of space with calculations. 'There's no magic here, any more than there is on Earth. This is science, pure and simple. We're working with the Laws of Nature, just as I did in my laboratory down there. It's just that the laws are different here, that's all.'

'And what we are doing is trying to combine the two?'

'Exactly,' he said. 'Now. We're all set. Can you think of anyone you would like to haunt?' I could tell this was special treatment. No one else in the class had been allowed a choice. And it was easy for me to decide. I'm sure he could see the light in my eyes as I told him about Grant Mason, or GM as everyone called him at school. I described how mean he'd been to me. In fact, we'd been arguing just before my fatal step into the road. GM never misses a chance to slag off my dad for having to work so hard in the shop. He takes the mick out of Mum's accent and makes fun of my sister's teeth. I'm sure he's bullying my little brother too, sending him texts at all hours. I think Sanjay's been taking him cigarettes from the shelf behind the counter, and maybe even money from the charity box by the till. Perhaps I should have told Mum and Dad about that. It's too late now.

Anyway, you can see why I chose GM. I was really glad to come to GM's – and pretty proud that our emailing plan worked. I can't pretend I wasn't scared when the Professor turned me into a string of electronic pulses so that the T.P.9 would pick me up like a wireless signal, but it felt good sliding through the air, and seeing how my favourite machine worked from the inside. The Professor had to be the one to press the button and set it all in motion. I showed him how to send and open emails on the T.P.9. As I attached myself to the message to GM, I could see him switching back to Warjammer. I hoped he wouldn't lose any of my lifelines. How pathetic that seems now.

The Professor made sure I arrived at GM's during the night (there are some traditions even he isn't ready to challenge). He would have been pleased to hear that my ride through cyberspace as an electronic message was indeed faster and more comfortable than the journey in Merk's net. I slithered out of GM's inbox and looked out through the webcam at his hideous bedroom. GM was snoring under his Arsenal duvet, surrounded by empty cans and dirty plates. It turned out that his computer was really old-fashioned: it didn't even have a flat screen. His life wasn't really the big deal he made it out to be.

I started rummaging through his computer files. There was all the stuff you'd expect to find: spam emails and clips from YouTube. But then I got a shock. He'd filmed me on his phone and saved it to his desktop. As I lay, lifeless, on the ground, he'd stood there – not helping, or trying to see whether there was any hope – just coolly capturing every detail. There were close-ups of the blood, the lorry driver streaming with tears, the ambulance men covering my mutilated face and lifting my body on a stretcher. I could hear GM's heavy, excited breathing on the soundtrack. He was thrilled to see me smashed, contorted and bleeding in the gutter. I hated him more than ever. For a few seconds, right at the start of the film, the picture shuddered and dissolved into disconnected pixels. That must have been the moment that Merk had picked me up in his net and carried my soul away.

I set to work, using the time before GM woke to practise operating the computer from the inside. When he switched on the machine, I walked through the game he was playing and waved at him. It was almost worth dying just to see the look on his face: disbelief at first, and then a hint of horror. He clicked away from the game and checked his emails. I'd written my name in the 'From' box of every one. When he went onto Facebook, it was my laughing image where his photo should have been.

His mother called him. While he was eating his breakfast, I went through his homework making his sums wrong, adding extra spelling mistakes into his English and hiding a sentence of sweary abuse about B.O. Barwood in his geography project. I was loving it. I wasn't doing it to help the Professor, or to get to Eternal Rest more quickly. It was pure fun – better than Warjammer – better than any game I've ever played. As I forwarded the mangled homework to GM's teachers I thought I'd be happy to stay inside his computer for ever.

He came back. He'd had honey on his toast. I could feel his sticky fingers on the mouse. Bangs and flashes started up all round me. He'd returned to the game, angrily zapping at soldier after soldier, each of whom bore my face. His missiles passed straight through me. He spat and swore as I survived every direct hit. I was riding the dragon as it lurched from the cave. Staring into his furious eyes, I could tell that he couldn't, or wouldn't, believe the images they were sending to his guilt-ravaged brain. I flipped the words and pictures on the screen inside out and upside down. He thumped the monitor wildly, like someone trying to get better reception on an old TV. Mrs Mason called again. She was rattling her car keys. It was time for school.

GM was almost crying now. I'd really shaken him. But then he did something that changed everything. If I hadn't been gloating so much at his anguish – concentrating on feeding my voice through the speakers, rather than the track he had selected – I might have bothered to read what he was typing into the search engine. Maybe I could have blocked the results. It was only later that I realised he was looking for an anti-virus program. As his mother nagged once more, he clicked on one at random, using her credit card details to pay for it. He'd obviously done that before – he knew the number by heart. Ticking the box to say he accepted the terms and conditions (without reading them) he picked up his school bag and ran from the room, leaving the virus check to install itself and do its work.

I wasn't worried. I was sure the program wouldn't touch me. I had deliberately integrated myself so firmly into the heart of the operating system that any anti-virus scan would identify me as a legitimate part of the computer. It would protect me rather than destroy me. I congratulated myself on my foresight in securing myself so tightly to the machine. But I wasn't the only person who had tricked GM. The link on the website was bogus. He had unwittingly downloaded a powerful virus, carrying a Trojan and a Worm: the first to harvest GM's personal data and distribute it across the outside world, and the second destined to destroy the component parts of his computer, one by one. It wriggled towards the core files – the type of file to which I was now irrevocably bonded. I had to get out. But how?

Of course, the Professor and I had talked about what to do if there was an emergency – if I had to find my way back to Limbo in a hurry. I'd reassured him that I could do it by forwarding myself to my own email account. I'd given him the user name and password so that he could access it on my T.P.9 and fish me out of the electronic soup. I hurried to GM's outbox, pursued by the deafening noise of the Trojan and the Worm churning through the hard drive. The racket almost drowned out the relentless repetition of the song in my head: *This is a visit from the Spirit. It ain't easy being dead.* I knew I had to act quickly, but I wasn't frightened then. I still felt in control. In just a few seconds I would be on my way.

But suddenly the outbox was crowded. I was squashed in a corner near the door. Just as I was about to push my way through and leave, I realised what was going on. The virus was replicating itself, and trying to forward a message containing its destructive code to everyone in GM's address book. I wouldn't have cared about that, had I not seen the message it was using to carry the infection. The bug had latched onto something in GM's drafts folder. The body of the message was blank, but it carried an attachment, and that attachment was the film of me lying in the road the day before.

I could have jumped from the outbox then. I could have got back to the Professor, told him what I'd learned from the experience and worked with him on refining our cyber-haunting techniques for the future. But I couldn't let myself get away. You see, I'd read GM's list of contacts. I knew he had the email addresses of my brother and my sister. I couldn't bear the idea of them getting that message and clicking on the attachment. It wasn't the virus I was worried about. It was the film. I'd seen those images. I knew how my family would react when they saw how I looked before I was cleaned up by the morticians. Jamila's only eight years old. I could guess what she would do. She would show Mum. I had to stop the infected message getting out. I flung myself across the outbox door, trying to block its path.

And that's where I am now, electronically spread-eagled while the outgoing messages multiply. I think I can hold them back for a while, but I can feel the Worm making its way towards me. It was just a tingle at first, but now it's more like electric shocks. If the Worm manages to loosen me from the chip I've attached myself to, the Trojan might suck me up and bind me into the messages, spraying me out into computers all over the world. How will I get myself back together? Which of the clones will be the real me? Which will contain my true spirit? Will they all have the will and ability to get back to Limbo, or will I be fragmented into millions of pieces, doomed to roam cyberspace for all time? And will I have to watch as my mother views the video?

I can feel the suction of the server and the thrust from the Trojan repeatedly pressing 'Send'. The messages are bashing against me. No one told me that ghosts can feel pain. Maybe it's only electronic ones who can. Perhaps I'm the first. I'm not sure how long I can hold out. If only I could escape this noise. The computer's getting so overheated that the fan has come on, and my own head is still generating *This is a visit from the Spirit. It ain't easy being dead* all the time.

I should never have boasted to the Professor that I knew all about computers. And, of course, I've put him in danger, as well as myself. I don't know what's happened to him. Will he remember how to open an email? Will he have got so absorbed in Warjammer that he isn't looking out for contact from me? Has he been found with the T.P.9, and taken away from Ghoul School to be punished again? Am I all alone here?

I don't know what to do. *This is a visit from the Spirit. It ain't easy being dead.* All I am sure of is that I have to stop my family seeing that film. I want to tell them that I love them, that I'm sorry I wasn't more careful crossing the road, and that I wish I'd used my time as a ghost to find a way to comfort them instead of jumping at the chance to persecute GM.

I want to survive, but I've got to keep this door shut, even if the effort kills me for a second time and sends me into some new, horrible, spirit world. I can't write a message. The Worm has disabled the keyboard. The only thing left is the sound card. And so while I'm here, in case I'm destroyed, I'm dictating this message. I'm going to attach myself, and this voice file, to the Trojan's message in the outbox. I'm praying that if the virus wins, and splatters GM's disgusting video across the internet, someone, somewhere may find out from my message what's happened.

If you are hearing this, it means that the Worm has beaten me, and the Trojan has opened the outbox. If you are listening – if you've received an unexpected attachment and foolishly opened it – please, please, don't watch that film. But if you die and find yourself at Ghoul School with the Professor, tell him where I am: fragmented and duplicated across the aether, and desperate to find my way back. I've tried to put in all the detail I can. There's no way I can tell what will be of use to you. If you know anything about computing – if time has passed, and science has moved on – find a way to rescue me, I beg you.

I'm not sure what lies ahead for me. I'm pretty

certain that it's not Eternal Rest. *This is a visit from the Spirit. It ain't easy being dead.* I'm frightened. Please help me. *This is a visit from the Spirit. It ain't easy being dead.* I've got just two lines of that song stuck in my head, but I know what comes later, at the end of the chorus. The singer's right. *Listen, baby, you don't wanna be a ghost like me.*

Surely, surely, it shouldn't be the ghost who's scared?

SONGS THE DEAD SING

Derek Landy

SONGS THE DEAD SING

Sonia was dead a full week before she came to see me. I'd been at her funeral. We all had. There were a lot of people crying. That was understandable. I'd like to say I stood up straight and cried manly tears, but the truth is I was blubbing little baby tears and doing a bit of high-pitched wailing to go along with it. It was a good thing Sonia was the only friend I'd ever had in the world, or I'd probably have lost the lot of them after that impressive display.

My name's Wayne. When I say I'm the hero of this story, I use the word in the loosest possible sense.

The papers were full of stories about the pretty sixteen-year-old who'd been stabbed through the heart, her body found dumped by the side of the road. 'The

Crime That Shocked Ireland', they said. The Guards were sombre and grim, our brave cops promising swift justice, but Sonia was victim number four over a four-year period, and they had no leads and everyone knew it. Our little patch of the coast, our little Blessingtown, was traumatised, according to the newspapers. They were probably right.

She died on a Saturday, she was buried the following Thursday, and two days later she appeared in my kitchen, shouting into my face. I screamed and jumped backwards, my arms flapping like an ungainly duck. My ankle hit my other ankle and my legs twisted and I collapsed rather awkwardly to the floor.

'*Finally!*' she said, looking at me like it was all my fault.

I made a sound with my mouth that wasn't a word.

It was her. It was really her. Tall. Slim. Long brown hair. Blue eyes. Standing in my kitchen with one leg disappearing into the table.

'Oh my God,' I said.

'Wayne, we have to talk.'

'But . . . you're dead.'

'I am.'

'You're *dead*, though.'

'Yes.'

'But *you are* dead.'

'You can say it a hundred different ways and you'll

be right a hundred different times, but what's the point of that?'

'What's happening?' I asked, getting slowly to my feet.

'I'm a ghost. It's stupid, but there you go. I was killed, then I opened my eyes and I was standing over my own body. It sucks.'

'Who . . . who killed you?'

'Devil worshippers.'

'Seriously?'

'Do you really think I'd joke about my killers? They all wore robes with the hoods up. I didn't see their faces. There were three of them. They grabbed me when I was walking home from work, took me to that old church outside of town and strapped me to an altar.'

'How do you know they were devil worshippers?'

'Because then they started worshipping the devil. It was kind of a giveaway.'

'There are devil worshippers in Blessingtown?'

'Apparently so.'

'That's crazy.'

'No, what's crazy is that you're talking to a ghost.'

I paused to gather my thoughts. That never takes long, as I tend to have very few. 'Why aren't you in Heaven?'

'I don't know if there *is* a Heaven.'

I gaped. 'There's no *Heaven*?'

'I don't know, Wayne. I know that there is *something* we're meant to move on to, but for whatever reason I'm stuck here for the moment as a ... well, as a ghost.'

'Are you haunting me?'

She hesitated. 'I ... actually, I didn't think of it like that, but, yes, I suppose I am.'

'Why me?'

'Sorry to burst your bubble, but you weren't my first choice. I tried getting my parents to see me, then my boyfriend, then three of my friends, and when that didn't work, I tried you. I've been screaming at you for hours.'

'How come I can see you?'

'Apparently there's a rule, that each ghost gets to open the eyes of one person, and one person only, but that person has to be, like ... receptive, or something. It didn't work on the others, but I've managed to open *your* eyes. You're welcome, by the way.'

'I ... I've missed you.'

'That's nice.'

'You're my only friend.'

'That's pathetic.'

'What do you want?' I asked. 'Is there anything I can do to, you know, help you or ... Do you have unfinished business, or something?'

'Unfinished business? Like what?'

'Like ... uh ... actually I don't know. But if what you say is true, then the thing that's keeping you from moving on is the fact that you have unfinished business to take care of, and then you'll be free to, like, float away, or whatever.'

'Float away?'

'Or whatever.'

'Wayne, I don't know what's going on. I was talking to another ghost, and he's been dead for forty years, and not even he knows what we're meant to do.'

'You met another ghost?'

'Hmm? Oh, yeah. He's out in the garden.'

'Will I be able to see him?'

'I told you, I opened your eyes. Come on, I'll introduce you.'

She turned and walked through the wall. I chose the more conventional route of the door, and emerged to see an old man in a tweed suit standing on the grass.

'This is Donal,' said Sonia. 'Donal, this is Wayne.'

'Hullo,' said Donal.

'Uh, hi.'

'Hope you don't mind me being in your garden.'

'Not at all.'

'It's a nice garden.'

'Thanks. You're dead, then?'

He nodded. 'Died in 1965, so I did. Heart attack.'

'I see. And how did you . . . how did you two meet?'

'I went to the graveyard,' Sonia said. 'I figured I needed someone to tell me what to do, and I thought the graveyard would be full of ghosts.'

'It isn't,' Donal told me. '*Hospitals* are full of ghosts, but that's it, really. To be honest, there aren't very many ghosts wandering around anway, and you wouldn't usually find us in a cemetery.'

'Then why were you there?' I asked.

'I tend to get lost very easily.'

'Donal,' Sonia said. 'Wayne was saying something about unfinished business.'

Donal nodded. 'Ah, yes. That's why we stick around. The problem, however, is that most of us don't know what our unfinished business actually is. You're lucky, you see. You were murdered.'

Sonia blinked. 'That's lucky?'

'I'd have *loved* to have been murdered,' the old man said wistfully. 'What I wouldn't *give* to have been murdered. It's clear-cut then, isn't it? You were taken before your time. Your unfinished business is straightforward. Not like mine. I was a teacher. Didn't like it much. Hated it, in fact. But that's where I died, in that classroom, slumped over my desk. It took my students a good half hour to work out that I hadn't just fallen asleep.' He shook his head. 'They weren't the brightest, those kids.'

'Right,' I said. 'But...with Sonia it's quite clear what her unfinished business is, yeah? She has to find her killers.'

'And bring them to justice,' Donal nodded. 'But the only way she can do that is with the help of somebody living. Which'd be *you*, I suppose.'

'What do *I* know about finding murderers?'

'You watch all those shows on TV,' Sonia said. 'So what's the first thing they do?'

I frowned. 'I don't know. I mean...I suppose it would be, like...'

'Yes?'

I sighed. 'I suppose it would be examining the scene of the crime.'

We walked the back roads round the fields and rows of glasshouses. It was weird. Sonia and Donal looked so solid beside me, but then I'd realise the breeze wasn't moving Sonia's hair, or a puddle wasn't rippling when Donal walked over it, and they'd stop being quite so real.

'I never did anything with my life,' Donal was saying. 'I was born here, then moved to England when I was a lad. Enlisted in the army to fight in the Great War, so I did.'

I looked at him. 'You fought in the First World War?'

'*Fought* might be a bit of an exaggeration,' he said. 'To be more accurate, you might say that I hid.'

'You hid?'

'It wasn't easy, finding places to hide on a battlefield. The trenches were the worst. But I managed it. The only shots I ever fired were into the air. I think I may have hit a sparrow once, but I certainly wasn't aiming for it. They eventually shipped me back, and I came home, became a teacher. Wasn't much good at that, either, but at least my students didn't have bayonets fixed to the end of their pencils.'

'We're here,' Sonia said.

I hopped a gate. They walked right through it. There was an old church across the way. It was small, and fire had smudged and blackened the stones that made its walls. It looked like God had tried to rub the whole thing out. It stood in a field of long yellow grass that twisted with weeds.

We walked to it without speaking. We met what had once been a narrow road, and was now just two parallel tracks of dust and dry dirt, leading from the mouth of the church up to an old shed in the distance. There was a chain on the doors with a new padlock, but it was loose enough to push the doors open and slip through underneath.

The first thing that hit me was the smell. Not the smell of death, of splattered blood and decomposing flesh that I was expecting, but of disinfectant. There were no pews, no pictures on the walls and no statues, but there was a large slab of an altar.

We walked forward slowly. The slab was spotless, as was the surrounding area. There was a clear circle of scrubbed cleanliness around the altar that kept the dust back. No sacrificial knives or bowls or candles were on view.

I looked at Sonia. She was staring at the slab, visibly shaking.

'They've cleaned up after themselves,' I said, 'and they've done a good job of it. We should go. Sonia, are you listening? We should go, before they come back.'

She nodded. 'Yeah,' she said, and led the way out.

Back in the sunshine, I looked around. 'This is Colin Sullivan's land,' I said. 'Maybe we should ask him if he's seen anything strange lately.'

'If he owns the land,' Sonia said, 'he might be one of them.'

I stopped walking immediately. Suddenly the sunshine didn't seem so warm. 'Maybe I should confront him in a public place, where there are witnesses.'

'That's what I'd do,' said Donal. 'You don't want to take any unnecessary risks. There's a lot to be said for being a coward.'

I frowned at him. 'I'm not a coward.'

'It's nothing to be ashamed of.'

I glared, then turned and strode off up the hill, towards Sullivan's house. I fully expected Sonia to beg me to reconsider, to beg me not to be so brash and foolhardy and brave. Instead she walked alongside me, head down, mind on other things. Halfway up the hill I started to panic. I waited for Donal to say something, but a quick glance over my shoulder told me he'd forgotten what was going on. Now I was really panicking. My legs started to wobble.

'Your legs are wobbling,' said Donal helpfully.

I ignored him, and managed to stagger to Sullivan's front door. I stood there, staring at it. This was a really stupid idea. This was a really stupid idea that was going to get me killed. I turned, ready to walk away, and the door opened.

'Yes?'

I turned again. Colin Sullivan looked at me. The same age as my dad, a bit heavier around the midsection. Big, farmer hands. They didn't look like the hands of a killer, but what did I know? 'Hi,' I said, trying to keep my voice from trembling. 'Mr Sullivan, I'm Wayne Stanley. Could you spare a minute?'

He looked around, then back to me. 'What can I do for you?'

'I was, uh, wondering, actually, about that old church down the hill. I was wondering if you'd, like, ever seen anyone in it or near or...'

His eyebrows came together in a frown. They didn't look like the eyebrows of a killer, but, again, what did I know?

'Church?' he said.

'Uh, yeah. Down the hill, where the road turns off by the stream.'

'Oh,' he said, almost laughing. 'You mean the *chapel*.'

'Right, sure. Chapel, then.'

'What about it? You doing a school project, are you? Old buildings in town? Well, I'd love to let you see it, but

148

it's unsafe, I'm afraid. Falling down.'

'Have you seen anyone in it?'

'In it? No, of course not. Like I said, it's falling down. It's a deathtrap. No one's been in it for years.'

'That's not exactly true.'

'Hmm? It isn't?'

'The inside is clean. Scrubbed clean. And it was done recently too.'

His eyes narrowed. 'Wait— You were in it? That is private property. Do you understand that? If you were even *near* that chapel you were trespassing on my land. And if you were *in* it, that's breaking and entering too. I should call the Guards.'

'Don't mind him,' Sonia said. 'Keep going.'

I took a breath, really hoping he wasn't about to lunge at me. 'Someone has been using the chapel,' I said.

'Nonsense.'

'People in robes. People who—'

Sullivan's hands closed around my shirt and he almost lifted me off my feet. I screamed.

'Hey!' Sonia shouted, lunging on instinct. She passed right through Sullivan as he stared at me, teeth gritted.

'Do something!' she shouted to Donal, but he just stood there looking surprised.

My attention was firmly on Sullivan as he leaned in. 'It's not safe. You don't know what you're asking. Go home. Forget about this.'

'I'd like to,' I gasped.

'Ask him who they are,' Sonia demanded, and I tried to pull his hand away so I could breathe.

'I already know enough,' I gurgled. 'I know they're in that chapel to worship the devil.'

His face slackened, went pale, and he released me and stepped back. 'How do you know that?'

'Ha!' Sonia yelled triumphantly. 'Progress!'

'I just do,' I told Sullivan, my voice still a little strangled. I really needed to pee. 'Who are they?'

He shook his head. 'I don't know, OK? I was out walking my dog one night and I saw a light, went to investigate, got there in time to see them drive off. The next night I found my dog's head on the bonnet of my car. You don't want anything to do with these people, Wayne. Leave them alone.'

'How often are they there?'

'I don't know. I don't even look in that direction any more. I certainly don't walk down there. Wayne, it's not safe. Please, I'm begging you. Forget about this.'

'These people killed Sonia Keane.'

Sullivan froze. 'What?'

'Yeah,' Sonia said in his ear. 'How'd you like *that*, huh? That shut you up.'

'They killed Sonia,' I said, 'and they probably killed those three other teenagers they're talking about on the news.'

Sullivan seemed to visibly shrink. 'How do you... how do you know?'

I hesitated, looked at Sonia, who shrugged. I looked at Donal.

'Tell him it's top secret,' he said.

Sonia made a face. 'Don't say top secret.'

'That doesn't matter right now,' I said. 'If I go to the cops, will you back me up?'

'Yes,' Sullivan sighed. 'Yes, I will.'

Sonia looked at me. 'You go on. Talk to the cops. We'll catch up.'

I raised an eyebrow.

'I want to stick around to see if he makes any calls after you've gone,' she explained. 'If he doesn't, we'll meet you at the police station.'

'What are you looking at?' Sullivan asked.

I smiled at him. 'Nothing. Nothing, I...I was thinking. That's what I look like when I think. I'm going to go talk to the Guards now. I'm sure they'll be in touch.'

I turned, walked away. When I heard the door close, I looked back. Sonia and Donal walked through the wall. I was really starting to envy that ability.

Half an hour later I arrived at the police station. A uniformed Guard stood on the other side of the hatch, writing.

'I'd like to speak to someone about Sonia Keane's murder,' I said.

The cop looked bored. 'We are still no closer to finding her killer, but we are following up on multiple leads. The Blessingtown Station isn't even handling the investigation anymore. All the detectives are in Balbriggan.'

'No,' I interrupted. 'I'm not here to ask about it, I'm here to help. I know where she was killed.'

He looked at me with something approaching interest. 'Well then. Looks like you're going to have to give a statement.'

He disappeared from the hatch, and a moment later a door opened and he beckoned me through. The inside of the police station was a bit of a disappointment. There were desks and a photocopier and a bulletin board with notices for cake sales stuck on with red pins. I sat on a rickety chair and the cop sat the other side of the desk and took out a pen. I gave him my name and details, and when he was satisfied he looked up.

'I'm Sergeant Rourke,' he said. 'Is this a confession?'

'No.'

'It'd be easier if it was.'

'It's not, though.'

'It'd save a lot of time.'

'Sorry.'

A phone rang in another room. He looked at me for a moment, perhaps judging if I could be trusted not to steal anything. 'Stay here,' he said, getting up. 'Don't move. And don't touch anything. I know where everything is.'

Rourke hurried out, and I heard him answer the phone. I sat there quietly.

Very, very gradually, I became aware of someone standing in the corner of the room. I didn't look. I didn't turn my head. I kept my eyes fixed on the desk. My heart sped up and my hands turned clammy. My flesh shivered and my stomach felt queasy.

The dark shape moved slowly in my peripheral vision, walked over to me. Still, I kept my head down. It walked through the chair beside me, stopped and put its hand on the desk. Its hand was blackened and withered, like the dried-out husk of a corpse long buried. Its fingers tapped the desk. I desperately wanted a drink of water. I desperately wanted to pee. I dragged my eyes up, from the withered hand to the sleeve of the robe, to the shoulder and the hood and the dark face beneath. The dark ghost looked at me with lidless yellow eyes.

'Summon her,' he hissed.

I couldn't speak. My mouth was dry as a desert.

'Call the dead girl's name,' the dark ghost said.

I heard footsteps. Rourke. He came back in, sat on the other side of the desk, picked up his notepad. He didn't even glance at the ghost.

'Now then,' Rourke said, 'you have something to tell me?'

'Summon her,' said the dark ghost.

I moved. I finally moved. I shook my head defiantly.

'No?' said Rourke. 'You don't have anything to tell me? Are you wasting my time? Because any time wasted here with you is time that I could be spending standing over there at that hatch filling out forms. They are important forms that need filling out.'

The dark ghost went round to Rourke, bent down and whispered something in his ear. Blood started running from Rourke's nose.

'Oh,' he said. 'Good God.' He stood, hands up to stem the flow, the blood dripping through his fingers. He hurried out, cursing as he went. The dark ghost stood there and kept his yellow eyes on me.

I ran.

It took me ten minutes running full tilt to reach my house. I barged into my room, dropped onto the bed and tried to remember how to breathe properly. An hour later, Sonia and Donal walked through the wall. I screamed.

'Boo,' said Sonia. 'You were supposed to wait for us at the police station. Where'd you go? We waited around Sullivan's house for fifteen minutes. You know what he did? He sat on his couch with his head in his hands, and then he went to the loo. We left pretty soon after that.' She frowned. 'What's wrong? You look like you've seen a ghost, and not a hot ghost like me.'

I told them what had happened.

'I've heard about things like that,' Donal said. 'I think it's a Soul Eater.'

'Is that anything like a sword swallower?' I asked.

He ignored me. 'It's a ghost but it's also ... *not*. It straddles life and death.'

'Why is it after me?' Sonia asked.

'It needs you to feed on.'

Sonia blanched. 'It wants to *eat* me?'

'It's how it survives. It needs young fresh souls. Strong souls. The longer you evade it, the hungrier it will get, and the more desperate it will become. This thing is very dangerous. You don't want to be anywhere near it.'

'What can it do? I mean, I'm already dead.'

'There are fates worse than death, my girl. There is the afterlife, there is existence as a ghost, and then there is oblivion. There is nothing. I've seen it happen. We can be trapped, you see, bound to our bodies until our bodies turn to dust. We can be trapped with salt, or with iron. An iron spike, hammered into the body will tether the spirit to the physical form. And when a body turns to dust, the spirit that is bound to it fades. Even the dead can die. But a Soul Eater? A Soul Eater needs none of these tricks. If the Soul Eater gets you, you'll be lost for ever.'

'Wow,' she said. 'That's depressing.'

'It was wearing a black robe,' I pointed out.

'So?'

'Well...you know...a black robe, like the robes the devil worshippers wore.'

Sonia's eyes widened. 'You think they're working together?'

'Even though I have absolutely no basis for it...yes. Yes I do.' I stood up suddenly. 'We're not safe.'

Sonia arched an eyebrow. 'You're just figuring that out?'

'No, I mean, we're not safe *here*. What if the dark ghost knows where I live? And if it *is* working with the devil worshippers, then it could tell them that I'm involved, and *they* might come for *me* while *it* comes for *you*.'

'Nobody ever wants to come for *me*,' Donal muttered.

'I know where we can hide,' Sonia said. 'Tell your folks you're staying at a friend's house and pack some things. Food. Water. And a sleeping bag.'

'Are we going camping?' I asked.

'No,' she said. 'We're going hunting.'

I opened the chapel doors as much as I could and slipped under the chain. I went to the back, behind the altar, and up a few steps to the wall, and unfurled my sleeping bag in the dark. I took my shoes off and laid them beside me.

Sonia walked through the wall. 'No one around,' she said. 'Donal's doing a second sweep of the perimeter. That's what he called it, anyway. I think he just likes walking in circles.' She came up the steps and sat beside me.

'Why don't you sink through the ground?' I asked.

'I don't know.'

'Why don't you float into the air?'

'That's another thing I don't know.'

'What are we going to do if we see the Soul Eater?'

She shrugged. 'Donal said iron hurts ghosts, right? So we hit it with something iron.'

I sat with my back against the wall. She brought her knees in, folded her arms on top of them and rested her chin on her arms. My eyes had adjusted to the gloom, and I could pick out the shape of the altar on which Sonia had died.

'It was awful,' she said quietly.

I had no words to comfort her, so I didn't say anything.

'They carried me in, and I was kicking and screaming and cursing. I almost got away, but they grabbed me again, tied me down. I didn't understand what was going on, you know? As soon as I saw the knife that one of them had, I figured it out. I started crying.'

I didn't say anything. Just waited for her to continue.

'I begged them. Can you believe that? I actually begged them not to kill me. Didn't make any difference, obviously. I have never, ever, felt so alone and helpless. And it all happened there. On that slab.'

She was looking at it, couldn't take her eyes off it. I felt the anger flow through me and I stood up.

'What are you doing?' she asked.

I strode over to the altar and curled my fingers under the slab.

'Wayne, don't.'

I heaved.

'Wayne, someone will hear.'

I strained. Sweated. Grunted.

I took my hands away. It hadn't moved. Hadn't even budged. I returned to my sleeping bag.

'That was very impressive,' Sonia said.

I zipped up the bag and lay down. 'Shut up,' I said, and Sonia started laughing.

I woke up the next morning to find a man standing over me.

'Well well,' he said, 'look what we have here.'

I tried to spring up but my sleeping bag kept me down. I lunged sideways and rolled away from him as fast as I could, down the steps and across the floor like a deranged caterpillar. Another man was waiting there and he stopped me with his foot.

'I have foiled his ingenious escape,' he announced, chuckling. I recognised him. It was Mr Mallon. He owned the pharmacy on Main Street.

I couldn't see Sonia or Donal. I tried to unzip the sleeping bag but Mr Mallon stood on it. I kicked and squirmed uselessly. The other man came over. I'd seen him around town but didn't know his name.

'Hello, Wayne,' he said.

I stopped squirming. It was becoming undignified. 'You killed Sonia Keane,' I said, just to make sure they were who I thought they were. 'You killed those others too.'

'See that, Tommy?' Mr Mallon said. 'The boy's a detective, is what he is. We should be quaking in our boots right about now.'

'Is that what you are?' the man called Tommy grinned at me. 'A detective? Are you here to arrest us?'

They laughed together, and I seized my chance. I wriggled out of the bag, tripping over myself as I burst free. This made them laugh harder.

'You'll never get her,' I said.

Mallon wiped the tears from his eyes. 'Get who, lad?'

'Sonia. You'll never catch her.'

The laughter faded, and the two men glanced at each other.

'What are you talking about?' Tommy asked. 'She's dead, you little weirdo. She's been dead for a week.'

'I know that,' I retorted. 'I mean her ghost. You'll never catch her ghost.'

They stared at me.

'Right,' said Mallon. 'I think the lad really has snapped.'

I frowned. 'You don't... You don't know about that? You don't know about the Soul Eater?'

'We should tie him up,' Tommy said to Mallon. 'See what Colin has to say about what we do with him.'

'Colin Sullivan?' I asked. 'He's involved?'

'Involved?' Mallon laughed. 'He's the Arch-Deacon. He started this whole thing. He showed us the power of Satan, he showed us the rewards we could get. One fresh soul a year, that's all he asked.'

'A soul a year,' I said. 'So you've been at this for four years, and what have been your rewards so far?'

'Wealth, lad. Wealth and power.'

'You don't look especially rich. And how powerful can you be, running a pharmacy?'

Mallon's smile dimmed a little. 'We haven't...we actually haven't seen the rewards yet, but they are coming.'

Tommy nodded. 'They're coming. Colin told us that Satan was very happy with our offerings. Any day now, he said.'

'Oh my God,' I said. 'He's lying to you.'

'I think,' Mallon said, 'you're going to have to work a little harder than that to plant the seeds of doubt in our minds.'

I shook my head. This was all making sense now. 'You haven't been worshipping the devil.'

'Pretty sure we have,' said Tommy.

'Sullivan doesn't care about that. He's been using you to catch and kill those people. This was never about the devil, it was always about him. He's working with the Soul Eater. He's feeding it.'

'I don't even know what that is,' said Tommy.

'He's making it up,' said Mallon.

'Making what up?' asked Sullivan. He walked into the chapel behind them, never taking his eyes off me.

'You'll never catch her,' I told him.

Sullivan looked at me, didn't say anything. Tommy glanced at Mallon, then back to Sullivan.

'He was saying that we're not really worshipping the devil,' Tommy said. 'Can you imagine that? Comes in here, says that to us.'

Sullivan shrugged. 'He's scared. He'll say anything.'

'That's what I thought,' Tommy said, nodding. 'Because it's coming, right? The rewards? The money and the power? Only, I'm behind on a couple of bank loans, and I really need it all to happen in the next few weeks.'

'Yeah,' Mallon said. 'The pharmacy hasn't been doing that well lately, to be honest, and it looks like I'm going to lose my seat on the county council. I've really been relying on the boost of power to see me through to next year.'

Sullivan sighed. 'I understand that you both have a lot of pressure on you,' he said. 'But so long as we keep up with the sacrifices and we do all the chanting and praying, the devil will sort us out.'

Mallon chewed his lip. 'Yeah. Yeah, OK. What's a Soul Eater, though?'

Sullivan snapped his head to him. '*What?*'

'A Soul Eater. The lad says you're working with one.'

'Does he, now?' Sullivan said, turning back to me.

'Well...aren't you the one with all the surprises today? All these fancy words and notions. I bet you're even seeing ghosts, are you? Are you seeing the ghost of Sonia Keane, eh? Maybe you could call out to her. Do you think you could manage that, eh? Just summon her, there's a good lad.'

I stared at him. 'You,' I said. 'You're not working *with* the Soul Eater. You *are* the Soul Eater.'

'Uh, Colin?' Tommy said. 'What are you two talking about?'

'You'll never get her,' I said.

'I'm confused,' said Tommy.

Sullivan grabbed my shirt, pulled me close. 'Summon her.'

My knees were trembling and I needed to pee again, but I did my best to match his gaze. 'It wouldn't do any good,' I said. 'She's not around to hear me. I don't know where she is.'

Sullivan smiled. 'See that? You don't know everything, do you? She *chose* you, sunshine. You're bound to each other. All you have to do is scream her name and she'll know where to find you. So...scream.'

'Wait a second,' Mallon said. 'So *have* we been worshipping the devil, or haven't we?'

Sullivan shoved me back, and turned to the other two. 'All right,' he said. 'Fine. So I kind of fibbed. No, we haven't been praying to the devil. As far as I know, the devil doesn't exist. I just needed two more people to complete the ritual. Tommy, I'm afraid you're going to lose your house. Michael, you're not going to be on the county council next year. On the plus side, you have both helped me murder four teenagers in the last four years, so shut up and do what I tell you.'

Mallon and Tommy stared at him, open-mouthed, but he was already returning his attention to me.

'She's led me on a merry chase,' he said. 'They don't usually escape, you see. I kill them here, with the two geniuses in front of you, and their ghosts hang around. They're too confused to do anything else. That gives me loads of time to send my co-killers away to dump the body, and then I can feast. I swear, the ghosts are almost grateful when I eat them. At least their fear ends.'

'But Sonia didn't hang around,' I said.

'She ran,' Sullivan laughed. 'Just took off. One moment she was there, the next...gone. I was annoyed, I don't mind telling you. I was so looking forward to her. And now, once again, I'm this close to having her.'

'But she's not alone any more. She has a protector.'

Sullivan laughed. 'You mean that old man? You think he poses any kind of threat? The most he could do is slow me down and let her run off again. That's why I didn't go for her when all of you oh-so-politely turned up at my door.'

'OK,' Mallon said, 'let's all just take a moment, calm down and start making sense. Can we do that?'

And then Sonia and Donal ran in through the wall.
'Run!' I yelled.

Tommy and Mallon spun round, but failed to see what myself and Sullivan were looking at.

Donal wavered, halfway between staying and running away, but Sonia didn't look the slightest bit intimidated.

'You're the one who killed me,' she said to Sullivan.

'Indeed I am,' Sullivan answered.

'Who are you talking to?' asked Mallon.

'You need to eat me to survive, don't you?' Sonia continued. 'You need to devour me, the same way you devoured those three other souls.'

'More than three,' Sullivan chuckled. 'I've been doing this since before anyone in this chapel was *born*. It's going to take more than an old man, a silly little girl and her incompetent sidekick to stop me.'

I took offence at that, but kept my mouth shut.

'OK,' Tommy said, 'I think we're missing out on a whole chunk of this conversation.'

Sullivan smiled. 'I'm going to enjoy eating you.'

'No,' Donal said, 'you're not.' He stepped forward until he stood between Sullivan and Sonia. His chin was lowered and his fists were clenched. 'I've run away from every battle I ever had to fight. But not this one. This is a good girl. She has a good soul. And I will be damned if I'm going to let you take her.'

Sullivan sneered. 'Get out of my way, old-timer. I

don't eat souls as decrepit as yours.'

'You want the girl?' Donal asked. 'Over my dead proverbial body.'

Sullivan took a step towards him, and suddenly Donal faltered and looked up. 'Can you hear that?'

'What?' Sullivan growled.

'Singing,' Donal said. 'Like a choir.' He started to hum.

I looked at Sonia, but she didn't seem to know what Donal was playing at any more than I did.

'Oh,' Donal said. 'Oh dear.' His skin started to glow, and he looked at me. 'I've figured out what my unfinished business was. I needed, for once in my existence, to be brave, and now I'm off to the afterlife. This could not have happened at a worst time.'

His skin glowed with a golden luminescence, so bright I had to shield my eyes. Then it burst, like an exploding sun, and when I blinked and looked back, Donal was gone.

'Ah, bloody hell,' Sonia said, then she turned and ran straight through the wall.

Sullivan laughed, and changed.

It was like his body expanded, then snapped back into place but as something different, as the black-robed dark ghost, and Mallon and Tommy cursed and jumped backwards.

'Where the hell did he go?' Tommy screamed, spinning in circles as the dark ghost disappeared through the wall after Sonia.

Mallon stumbled forward, waving his arms in the space where he had seen Sullivan vanish. 'Colin?' he called. 'Colin, are you invisible?'

I bolted.

I was halfway to the door before either of them even realised what was happening. They shouted at each other and started after me, but I was bursting into the sunshine, running as fast as I could and wishing I was still wearing my shoes. I saw Sonia sprinting across the field, the dark ghost right behind her.

I veered off the trail and ran after them both. Behind me, Mallon and Tommy were using up a lot of valuable running-energy by bellowing threats. I didn't look back.

Stones dug into my feet as I ran, and I quickly lost my socks to the muck. Sonia led the dark ghost towards one of Sullivan's sheds. I wondered if ghosts got tired. They certainly didn't look like they were going to slow down anytime soon.

I heard an engine and looked round. Mallon and Tommy were in a jeep, speeding after me. I made a little sobbing sound and changed direction yet again, running for the paddock to my left. As I neared, I saw in my mind what I wanted to happen. I wanted to grab the iron gate with one hand and leap athletically over. That's what I wanted to happen. Reality, unfortunately, had other ideas, and the combination of my fatigue, the muck that was dragging me down and the fact that I had never come even remotely close to any respectable display of athleticism, resulted in me grabbing the gate with one hand and hurling my crotch against it really, really hard. I gasped, curled up on the top bar and toppled over the other side.

The jeep slid to a stop and Tommy was the first one out, laughing so much he could barely stand. I picked myself up and struggled onwards across the paddock. I glanced back to see Mallon approaching the gate, doubled-over, as Tommy staggered to join him. I picked up speed and ran towards Sullivan's house.

The front door was locked, so I picked up a brick from a pile at the edge of his garden and hurled it through the window. It smashed really well, I used another brick to clear the jagged edges, then I climbed through. I went to the kitchen, searched for the phone, grabbed it and dialled the operator.

'Get Sergeant Rourke in Blessingtown,' I told him. 'This is Wayne Stanley. I'm at Colin Sullivan's farm and Sonia Keane's killers are here! Tell him to hurry!'

I dropped the phone and ran to the other end of the house. I could hear Mallon and Tommy cursing each other as they climbed through the window I'd smashed, but I was already climbing out another one.

I ran for the shed.

I slowed as I neared, trying to get my breathing under control, and sneaked to the door. The shed was lined on three sides with workbenches overflowing with tools and equipment and machine parts. The dark ghost had his back to me, and was closing in on Sonia.

'Stop,' Sonia said. 'You hear me? Just, just stop. Wait. Please.'

'But I'm hungry,' said the dark ghost in that dreadful whisper.

'You stop right now,' Sonia said, 'or I'll run and disappear and you'll never see me again.'

'Then I'll punish the boy,' said the dark ghost. 'Punish him until he screams for you. You'll come back. You'll come back for him.'

'I know,' Sonia said. 'You've won, all right? To be honest, I'm sick of this. I just want it to be over. I don't want to feel anything anymore. You can have me. But you need to promise me something.'

The dark ghost tilted his head.

'You have to promise to let Wayne go,' said Sonia. 'Let him go free and unharmed. If your friends don't agree, frame them for the murders. I'm sure you can manage that, right?'

'Maybe,' the dark ghost said.

'All he wanted to do was help. I'll give myself up to you if you swear to leave him alone.'

The dark ghost looked at her, and nodded. 'I swear.'

Sonia looked at him, and nodded too. 'OK. OK.'

I stepped in. 'Sonia,' I said. 'Don't do this.'

The dark ghost turned his head to me, those yellow eyes smiling.

'I'm sorry,' Sonia said. 'But we're bound to each other. If I left, you'd be trapped. Just like Donal said.'

I looked at her. 'What?'

'Just like Donal said,' she repeated. 'I can't do that to you, Wayne. This is the only way you won't be trapped. I don't want to see you turn to dust and fade away.' She looked me straight in the eyes, and I got the feeling she was trying to tell me something. Something clicked in my head, and suddenly I knew.

'Oh,' I said.

She smiled.

Tears came to my eyes. 'I love you too,' I said.

Her smile dropped, and she glared at me. Nope, that wasn't it.

'I hate long goodbyes,' the dark ghost said, and he stepped towards her, and then gasped as I rammed the sharp point of the crowbar into his back. I may be slow, but I always get there in the end.

I tried to trip him up but my leg passed through his, so I went back to gripping the only thing that could touch him, and attempted to force the crowbar all the way in. The dark ghost screeched and hollered.

'The hammer!' Sonia shouted.

I looked round, grabbed the hammer and slammed it into the curve of the crowbar. The dark ghost fell to his knees, and I hammered again, and again, and the dark ghost ballooned out and snapped, becoming Sullivan once more.

Blood dribbled from his mouth, and he fell forward into the dirt.

I stepped away, staring down at him.

'Took you long enough to figure out the plan,' Sonia said.

I looked at her. 'This was a plan?'

'Of course. You think I happened to lead him into a shed full of sharp iron and metal tools by *accident*?'

'I think it was fairly flimsy, as plans go.'

'It worked, didn't it?'

'Barely.'

'And whose fault is that?'

I shook my head and walked back to the door, stepped out and froze. 'Damn,' I said.

Mallon and Tommy were running down the hill towards me, big kitchen knives in their hands. I backed up.

'You hear that?' Sonia said.

I spun to her. 'No!' I said. 'You can't leave! Not now! Ignore the singing!'

'Singing?' she said, raising an eyebrow. 'Who hears singing? I hear sirens.'

And now I heard them, sirens filling the air like a celestial choir. Two squad cars powered over the hill, and Mallon and Tommy reduced their run to a leisurely stroll, dropping the knives to the grass as they did their best to wander innocently away.

I sneaked out the back of the shed, ran round the small hill and trotted up from behind as Mallon and Tommy were bundled into the squad cars.

'They killed him!' I gasped. 'Mr Sullivan! They had an argument and they killed him! His body's in the shed with a crowbar through it!'

Sergeant Rourke looked at me, and frowned suspiciously. 'You,' he said.

'If I were you,' said Sonia as she stood beside me, 'I'd give myself up until you get all this all sorted out.'

I raised my hands above my head. 'That's probably a good idea,' I whispered.

I was released from custody the next day, once the cops were sure I had nothing to do with the murders. After twenty hours of denying all knowledge of virtually anything, Tommy was the first to crack, and blamed Sullivan and Mallon for dragging him into devil worship. Mallon hit back, claiming that Tommy had been the one to start the whole thing. Finally, realising it was best to blame the dead guy, they both admitted their roles in the crimes but told the cops that Sullivan threatened to kill them if they didn't co-operate with his evil deeds. Then each of them tried to claim credit for finally putting a stop to Sullivan's murderous rampage.

The news reports were calling me a hero. I probably didn't enjoy it as much as I should have. My thoughts were on something else.

'Your business is finished,' I said to Sonia, the day after Sullivan's remains were cremated. The sun was setting and we were outside in my yard. I was sitting on an old tree stump that had been there since we were kids, and she was kneeling beside me. 'Does that mean you'll be going now?'

She shrugged. 'I suppose so. That's what happened to Donal. You could see his face, couldn't you? How did he look? Was he scared?'

I shook my head. 'He looked relieved. Happy. Peaceful.'

'I don't know if I want to go,' she said softly. 'This is all I know. All my friends are here, all my family.'

'But you can't talk to any of them,' I pointed out. 'You can only talk to me.'

'Yeah,' she said, eyes on the ground, 'well, that's not so bad.'

I smiled a smile she didn't see. 'You're scared.'

'Wouldn't you be?'

'I'd be terrified.'

'I want to stay,' she said, 'but I can't. Maybe you only get one chance to move on. If I don't go, I might be stuck here for eternity.' She looked at me. 'I owe you . . .' She laughed. 'I was going to say, I owe you my life, but, I don't know, maybe I owe you my death, instead. Whatever it is I owe you, Wayne, thank you. Thank you so much.'

I looked at her, and couldn't help the smirk that rose

to my lips. 'Are you saying I'm your hero?'

'Oh, for God's sake.'

'You are, aren't you? I'm your hero. You think I'm great.'

'Are you quite finished?'

'Shush now, your hero is talking.'

'You're such a goon.' Her gaze flickered somewhere over my head. 'Ah,' she said. 'There it is. The singing.'

She got to her feet and sang along with the music she heard. Her voice was sweet, lilting, and tears came to my eyes. I didn't bother hiding them. I stood up, watched her take a few steps.

She turned. Her skin started glowing. 'Have a good life, you hear me? Try not to miss me too much.'

In spite of myself, I grinned. She grinned back, then she turned so bright I had to look away.

THE BEACH
HUT

Robin Jarvis

THE BEACH HUT

It was such a baking day that even Bram's hair was hot. He patted it curiously and let out a marvelling, 'Wooooaaahhh!'

Eating ice cream was more of a race than a treat, because it dribbled over the cone and down his hand and arm the moment it left the van. He tried licking his arm afterwards, but the taste of the sun block his mother had whitewashed him with soon stopped that.

Grown-ups were lolling about like half-deflated balloons, grunting and sighing about how uncomfortable it was, whilst dogs anchored themselves in the shade, panting mechanically, their tongues dangling like strips of boiled ham. The only thing that made the roasting August afternoon bearable was the breeze that blew in off the sea, but even that was warm.

Bram was poking about rock pools and savouring the cool water around his ankles. He peered into his yellow plastic bucket and wished he'd been able to find more than one solitary crab.

Then the boy shielded his eyes against the glare of the sunlight that bounced off the waters and squinted along the shore. Almost every one of the brightly painted beach huts was in use today. Their double doors had been flung open and people, deck chairs, barbecues and picnic baskets spilled out down the beach.

The hut belonging to his Aunt Pat was the nearest. It was painted yellow and cream, and he could see his mother's robust legs poking out. The rest of her was parked squarely inside. A little distance away, lying on a pink towel, was the body of his older sister, or at least it might have been – the brim of the hat she was wearing was so big, it could have been anyone.

Bram decided he was thirsty, and as much in need of company as the crab in his bucket, so he left the pools and made his way back.

'Look what I found!' he declared proudly as he ran up to his sister, holding out the bucket.

Mel raised her head and the enormous straw hat tipped back. She was engrossed with her mobile phone. All she ever seemed to do nowadays was text her friends. She didn't have time to play with him any more. At thirteen and a half she thought she was too old to hang around with her ten-year-old brother.

'Eew, gross!' she said, pulling a face.

Bram shrugged and trotted up to the beach hut. His mother put a finger to her lips as a signal to be quiet. His Aunt Pat was inside on the bunk, resting. Aunt Pat was having a baby. It was due any time soon and she was really suffering in this freakishly hot weather.

'I got a crab!' he whispered to his mother.

'Lovely,' she whispered back. 'But don't bring it in here, dear – it'll smell and you know how queasy poor Pat is at the moment.'

Bram leaned into the hut and glugged down a glass of water. He loved this funny wooden shed by the sea. It had everything you could want: a little sink and a pump that pulled water from a container, a Calor gas ring to boil a kettle on or fry bacon and eggs, and a paraffin heater to warm it in the winter. There were shelves to store the rare finds of seashells, a dried starfish, special pebbles and a smaller shelf for books where two lanterns served as book ends. Brightly coloured crockery covered the far wall and Aunt Pat had decorated the whole of the inside with wallpaper that matched the curtains tied back behind the windows in the doors.

He wasn't so keen on her choice of décor. He'd have preferred something blue or a jungle green but, from the first moment Bram clapped his eyes on this beach hut, he wanted it as his very own den. He wanted to live in it, to be a creature of the shore, to exist right on the edge of the beach. To sleep in it at night and hear the sounds of the sea in the dark, then wake up with the gulls at dawn, fling open the doors and go dashing into the surf to bathe, before cooking himself a delicious breakfast. He had begged and pleaded with his mother and his aunt to let him do this but they were horrified at the idea. No one was permitted to sleep overnight in a beach hut. It was against the law. It wasn't safe. Earlier in the summer, vandals had set light to one of the huts and burned it down.

Bram was told to forget about that idea completely and forbidden to mention it again. But it smouldered in his thoughts, and the yearning grew daily in his heart until he had to give in to it. He had to try it just once. No one need ever know. In fact he had already stolen the spare key, although he preferred the word 'borrowed'. Tonight was going to be the big night. He couldn't wait.

A sleepy moan disturbed his thrilled anticipation. Aunt Pat was lying on the bunk that ran along one wall, the very bunk that would be his bed that night. He couldn't stop himself from grinning.

'Hello, Bram,' her floppy voice drifted from the shade as she stirred. 'Tell this baby to hurry up, would you? I can't stand much more of this. She's kicking about like a whole rugby team in there.'

The boy chuckled. He had never seen anyone with a tummy that big. The baby was going to be a whopper.

'Come out and play!' he addressed his aunt's belly. 'I want to see you!'

Aunt Pat tapped her tummy wearily. 'You listen to your cousin,' she told it before drifting off into an uncomfortable doze again.

'You should put your sun hat on,' his mother cautioned. 'Are you OK? You looked a bit lost on your own over there.'

'There's no one to play with,' he replied with a shrug. 'The other boys here are either too old or too little.'

'Oh, poor Bram,' his mother said. 'Maybe you'll find a friend before the end of the summer. Still plenty of time.'

He nodded slowly but wasn't hopeful. They'd been here over a week now and he hadn't found anyone to share his days with. He looked glumly at his sister. A text beeped in and she giggled under her hat as she read it and responded.

Bram turned and started down the beach again.

'Where are you going?' his mother asked. 'You haven't put your hat on!'

The boy held his bucket aloft.

'Putting my crab back,' he answered over his shoulder. 'I think he's lonely.'

His mother watched him return to the water's edge. 'Bless him,' she murmured with a sad, understanding smile.

'Oh this day is like an oven,' Aunt Pat groaned as

she shifted drowsily on the bunk. 'This baby's going to come out looking like a roast chicken.'

Later, back at Aunt Pat's house, Bram had to be very careful he didn't betray just how excited he was. Even though he felt close to bursting, he had to pretend it was any other normal evening. But it wasn't.

The time dragged by. He went to bed and then spent several impatient hours waiting for the rest of the household to settle down. When it had been completely quiet for twenty minutes, he shone a torch on his watch and saw that it was past eleven o'clock.

As silently as possible, he got out of bed. He was still fully dressed, right down to his trainers. Carefully he picked up the rucksack he had packed in secret, crept down the stairs and then stole out of the front door.

Once outside Bram started running, racing back to the beach. Fifteen minutes later he clambered over the sea wall, out of breath but deliriously happy and immensely proud of himself.

He hurried to the beach huts, stopping when he reached Aunt Pat's. His hand was shaking as he lifted the key from his pocket to put in the lock. This was a very daring thing to do. In fact it was criminal. If anyone ever found out he would get into so much trouble. The boy chuckled to himself, entered the hut and closed the door behind him. He had done it!

He stood in the pitch-blackness within for a little while, not quite believing he was really here. Then he moved forward and banged his knee against a folded deck chair.

Bram removed his rucksack and took out his torch. He shone it around to find the shelf where the lanterns were kept and then in the cutlery drawer to seek the box of matches. Soon the inside of the hut was aglow with the small flames of two tea lights in the lanterns. Bram let out a contented sigh and tucked into the packet of crisps he had brought along, washing them down with a can of fizzy orange. This was just how he'd imagined it would be – a perfect den of his very own.

Sitting on the bunk he heaped cushions at one end for pillows, and took a small brass travel clock from his rucksack. Its steady tick was reassuring and he set the alarm for half-past five. That would give him plenty of time to tidy up and get back to the house before anyone was awake.

He put the little clock on the shelf with the lanterns, removed his trainers and swung his legs onto the bunk. There was a tartan blanket by the deck chairs and he pulled it over himself, although it wasn't necessary. It just made it even more cosy and snug in there.

Bram put his hands behind his head and stared at the pitched ceiling. The candlelight cast odd shadows from the objects on the other shelf. The ends of feathers became jagged jungle grass and a piece of driftwood was a twisting snake slithering through it.

The sounds of the softly lapping surf began to lull his senses and the hands of the brass travelling clock reached twelve. The salt smell of the sea gradually grew stronger, while the shadows continued to flicker above. He wondered what object could be making the one that looked like a human hand reaching across the ceiling towards him.

'What are you doing in here?' an angry voice demanded suddenly.

Bram jolted upright.

A girl was standing beside the bunk, glaring at him crossly.

The boy stared back at her in shock. She was roughly his own age. Her young face was creased into a scowl and her hands were on her hips. Bram was speechless. Who was she? How did she get in?

'You don't belong here!' she said sternly.

Bram could only gawp back at her. She was wearing a navy-blue sailor's top, matching short trousers – the type that used to be called knickerbockers – and a smart hat of black straw tied around her neck with string and decorated with a ribbon.

'This is my hut!' she told him, frowning even more. 'It's Drusilla's very special, private place and you're trespassing!'

Bram managed to tear his eyes away from her and

glanced searchingly at the doors. They were still closed and locked from the inside. Was there another secret way in? Perhaps some loose boarding at the back?

Finally he found his voice and said indignantly, 'This is my aunty's hut. Not yours, whoever you are. You're the one who's trespassing.'

'It is mine!' she ranted, her voice rising to a shriek. 'Drusilla was here before you, and before everyone. She's been here a long, long time! It's her place! No one but her can come here!'

Bram was about to argue when a sudden realisation flooded his mind. He looked again at her old-fashioned clothes and wondered why it hadn't registered at once.

'Woooaahh! You're a ghost!' he exclaimed, too surprised to be frightened.

'Ghost yourself!' she shouted back.

'No I'm not!'

The girl reached out and pinched him sharply on the arm.

'Oww!' he yelped.

'There,' she told him with a haughty toss of her head. 'I'm not a ghost.'

Bram rubbed his arm. She certainly felt real enough.

'Ghosts are sad and miserable,' she continued. 'And angry too. Drusilla isn't. Drusilla likes to play. She wants to stay here, that's the difference.'

'What are you then?' the boy asked.

Drusilla twiddled with the hat string. 'I'm a spirit child,' she said.

'Isn't that the same thing?'

'Shows how much you know, boy!' she answered hotly. 'I can come and go whenever I want. I'm not tied to no one! Nobody made me, Drusilla made herself. She's not weak.'

Bram paused before he said any more. The ebbing soreness of the pinch was proof he wasn't dreaming but it was difficult to believe in any of this. He was very pleased he wasn't scared, though. He was sure lots of other people would be, even his sister.

'I've never met a spirit child before,' he admitted. 'So I'd no idea.'

That seemed to mollify her and she smiled for the first time.

'It's pretty in here with the lanterns,' she said. 'Drusilla's not seen it so homely. Always dark when Drusilla wakes up.'

She spent a few moments gazing around her and nodded appreciatively. 'She likes the roses on the walls,' she said. 'And the plates and the curtains.'

'My aunty did all that,' Bram said.

'Drusilla's hut hasn't always been so nice. Sometimes it's cold and empty and...' She shivered as though remembering something unpleasant, then picked up a whelk shell and became fascinated by it, putting it to her ear and listening intently.

'Me, my sister and Mum are staying with Aunty Pat during the summer,' Bram eventually added, to fill in the silence. 'She's having a baby and my uncle's away in the army so she's on her own and needed us with her.'

'Drusilla's papa was a soldier,' the girl interrupted. 'He went to fight the kaiser. He didn't come back.'

'My uncle will,' Bram said, touching the wooden armrest of a deck chair.

'They shouldn't make daddies go to war,' she said sadly.

'No, they shouldn't,' Bram agreed.

'Where's your daddy?'

'He works for a big bank in the city. He can't get any time off so had to stay there. He'll come down next weekend, though.'

Drusilla wasn't listening. She had put the shell into the pocket of her sailor top and turned her pale face towards the doors. 'Do you want to come play with me outside?' she asked abruptly.

Bram hesitated for an instant then nodded. It would be wonderful to go exploring the midnight seashore with a spirit child.

He reached under the bunk for his trainers but when he looked up, Drusilla had gone. Bram pulled the trainers onto his feet quickly then unlocked the door and ran outside. Drusilla was there on the beach, her long dark hair blowing gently in the breeze.

'Hurry up, boy,' she said impatiently. 'Drusilla wants to show you.'

'My name's Bram!' he called after her as she went skipping over the pebbles with bare white feet.

The girl ran to the water's edge where she playfully dragged her toes through the wet sand.

'Your shell has no voice,' she said as Bram joined her. 'Every shell should say something. Your shell is empty, but Drusilla knows who can put that right.'

Bram didn't know what she was talking about but it was good to finally have some company, and what extraordinary company! There were lots of questions he wanted to ask her; however, it seemed very rude to ask anyone how they had died, especially if you didn't know them well.

As they walked along the shore, Drusilla chattered airily about how mysterious and wild the seashore at night could be, how it was far more magical and strange than he could imagine. For the moment, Bram was content merely to listen. They skipped flat pebbles along the water to see who could get theirs furthest and she won every time.

Presently Drusilla halted at a pile of limpet-covered boulders, which were shaggy with bladderwrack, and clapped her hands for attention.

'Get up, sleepy,' she said.

Bram wondered what she was doing but, before he could ask, the rocks moved.

The boy jumped backwards and gasped as the boulders shifted. The bladderwrack clacked as it was shaken and fell back like a mop of tangled, bead-threaded hair. Then the topmost boulder tilted, and Bram found himself staring at a weird, wizened face, encrusted with moss and barnacles.

'Woooaaah!' he gasped.

Two dark little eyes on slimy grey stalks poked out from the holes either side of a thin flat nose and pointed in his direction. Then a fleshy, sand-crumbed mouth opened and a gravelly sound rumbled through the pebbles under Bram's feet.

'Don't you pay no mind to this boy,' Drusilla addressed it. 'I found him in my hut.' She took the seashell from her pocket and placed it on the rock beneath the peculiar creature's face.

'Here's one you missed,' she declared. 'It's all quiet.'

A fist of seaweed lifted from between the boulders and dragged the shell down into a hole.

'This is Mr Stone,' Drusilla told Bram. 'At least that's what I call him. I can't pronounce his real name, it's too gurgley and raspy.'

'Hello,' Bram said, not sure whether to hold out his hand or make a bow. 'Nice to meet you.'

The little eyes flicked from one child to the other.

'Mr Stone has been here such a very long time,' she continued in a solemn voice. 'Much much longer than Drusilla. He remembers everything that ever happened, every single day and night on this seashore and he puts those sounds into the seashells for everyone to listen to.'

'Like little iPods,' Bram laughed.

Drusilla looked at him blankly then continued, 'It's usually just the wind and the sea, that's what Mr Stone likes best – the noise of the winter gales blowing over the water. But, once in a while, you get other things.'

'What will my shell sound like?'

The girl wasn't listening. She was gazing out to sea. Then she darted forward, splashing up to her knees.

'Come play!' she called back to him. 'Come bathe and swim.'

Bram scratched his head. She didn't seem able to hold any one thought in her head for more than two minutes. He liked the idea of a midnight swim, though, so nodded readily.

Before running into the gentle waves he looked back at the strange creature she called Mr Stone. The curious face had angled forward into the surrounding rocks once more and it looked like any other group of sea-weed covered boulders.

'Mad,' he murmured to himself. Did that creature really exist or was it a trick? Could Drusilla make him see things that weren't there? He looked at her, running through the surf, giggling and shrieking with careless joy, and realised he didn't mind. This was the best fun he'd had in ages.

'Hurry up, boy!' she shouted, smacking her hands through a wave and flicking a curtain of water at him.

'Chaaaaarge!' Bram yelled. He started to run towards her, then stopped and stared along the shore.

'Who's that?' he asked.

He pointed down the beach. They were no longer alone. Others were here.

It was a group of children. Bram counted seven of them: four boys and three girls. The youngest girl looked about five years old and was dressed in a long nightgown with frilled cuffs. The eldest was a boy who might have been the same age as Mel, Bram's sister. He was wearing striped flannel pyjamas, another wore a long T-shirt down to his knees with a picture of a womble on it, and one of the girls was wrapped in a padded pink, nylon dressing gown.

Their faces were paler than Drusilla's and they dragged their feet heavily as if tired and half-asleep. Bram didn't like the look of them. Their eyes were sunken in dark shadows and, as they shambled closer, he could hear some of them sobbing and weeping.

'They friends of yours?' he asked Drusilla.

The girl shook her head fiercely and wrung her hands. She came out of the water to stand beside him and stared at the approaching children unhappily.

'They're ghosts,' she whispered. 'Look how wretched they are. But where is . . . ?' Her voice trailed off as she peered into the gloom behind them.

'Where's what?' Bram asked. 'What are you look-ing for?'

'The Angry Man,' Drusilla said in a hushed, fearful voice. 'He's always with the ghosts. He herds them and beats them. We shouldn't stay here.'

Bram was glad she said that. The spectral children were nearer now. He could see their wet, lank hair, their blue lips and blackened fingernails.

Drusilla took a wary step backwards then started walking quickly away. Bram followed her and the voices of the ghost children rose behind them.

Suddenly there came a fierce yell and a great dark shape sprang from the shadows by the rocks. It was a tall, burly man. Bram caught a glimpse of a mane of wild black hair and a thick, wiry beard. The man's teeth flashed white as he snarled, and in one of his large hands he wielded a stout stick.

Drusilla screamed and pulled at Bram's arm. 'The Angry Man!' she screeched in terror. 'The Angry Man! Run – run as fast as you can!'

Bram didn't need to be told. They pelted along the shore with the man's raging voice roaring behind them.

'Faster!' Drusilla shrieked when she glanced over her shoulder. 'He's catching us!'

Bram tore across the pebbles. Where could they run to? Who was this Angry Man? What did he want? How could they escape him?

'My hut!' Drusilla shouted. 'We must reach my hut!'

'But we'll be trapped in there!' the boy answered.

'Hurry!' she shrieked.

'Come here!' the fury-filled voice of their pursuer hollered. 'Come here! Come here and I'll stop you – once and for always!'

Drusilla's shrill screams were piercing. Bram saw the row of beach huts ahead. The one at the end, Aunt Pat's, was still glowing with lantern light. If only they could reach it . . .

'I'll send you on your way!' the Angry Man bawled. 'Let me get my hands on you. You'll be sorry!'

He thrashed his stick violently before him. Bram felt the draught as it rushed past the back of his head. That spurred him on even faster. He raced over the pebbles and leaped into the beach hut.

'Shut the doors!' Drusilla yelled, racing in beside him.

Bram slammed them so hard the windows rattled and a plate fell off the back wall. He locked them frantically.

And then the Angry Man was there. He hammered and pounded his fists against the wood, roaring and yelling.

Bram threw his weight against the doors, afraid the man would batter them down. Through a gap in the cheery curtains he saw the spectral, bearded face pressed against one window. He'd never seen anything so frightening in his life. Framed in that mass of black hair, the eyes were wide and round and swivelled insanely in their sockets. Thick tufts of more hair grew from the flaring nostrils and, when that mouth opened to shout, Bram saw only darkness inside where his throat should have been.

'Tell him he can't come in!' Drusilla urged anxiously.

'What do you think I'm doing?' he answered.

'No,' she said emphatically. 'You have to *tell* him. Tell him properly. Tell him to go away. This is a safe place. He isn't allowed in here.'

Bram didn't know what good that would do but he couldn't think what else to try. They were completely cut off and isolated. There was no help for miles.

'OK,' he said.

'Do it!' she pleaded, and the boy could see she was close to tears.

'You listening out there?' he shouted. 'Go away! You can't come in. You're not allowed. This is a safe place!'

The fearsome pounding stopped instantly. Bram peered out of the window again. The horrible face had gone. Everything was silent.

'Is that it?' he breathed. 'Is it over?'

Drusilla let out a great sigh. 'He's gone,' she said. 'You've sent him away. We're safe now. Drusilla thanks you.'

Bram wasn't so sure. He checked again but the beach outside was completely deserted.

'And those kids?' he asked.

Drusilla had picked up a gull feather from the shelf and was twirling it round her head.

'Who were they? Who was he?' Bram demanded.

The girl shrugged. 'Just the Angry Man,' she said. 'He always tries to catch me.'

'Did he catch those other boys and girls?'

She nodded diffidently.

Bram stood away from the window and sat heavily on the bunk.

'That was horrific,' he said, staring at his trembling hands. 'What if he comes back?'

'He won't tonight. Not now you sent him away.'

Even though it was warm in the hut, Bram shivered. Suddenly he wanted to be back at Aunt Pat's house.

Then Drusilla jumped up.

'Let's tell stories!' she cried excitedly.

'I'm not in the mood,' he replied.

'Oh, don't let him worry you. It's all better now. When he chases me, I run back here.'

'Does that happen every night?'

Drusilla gurgled with laughter. 'Course not, silly. Only now and then. The Angry Man won't never catch me.'

'I wonder who he was before... when he was alive. He must have been a raving lunatic.'

The girl pretended not to hear. Then she asked, 'Do you think it will be a girl or boy?'

'What?'

'Your baby cousin.'

'It's a girl, the hospital said. I'm chilly!'

He took up the tartan blanket and wrapped it round his shoulders.

'You're a chilly silly-billy,' she told him.

'My name is Bram,' he said tetchily as he pulled the blanket over his head like a hood. 'Bram Bram Bram Bram!'

'Bram Bram Bram Bram...' she repeated, giggling. 'My new friend Bram. Will you come and play with me again... Bram... Bram... Bram...?'

The boy yanked the hood back to frown at her. But the spirit child was gone.

'Drusilla?' he called. 'Where are you? Drusilla?'

There was no answer, and somehow he knew he wouldn't see her again that night. She had gone back to wherever she had come from.

Bram sat on the bunk again. 'That was...' but he didn't have a word for what he had seen.

He sat up for a while, thinking over everything that had happened, but it had been a long day and an unexpectedly eventful night. Eventually he slid sideways and slept.

Bram woke with a start and his heart was beating fast. Something was outside on the roof. He could hear it scuffling across the tiles. The boy lay on the bunk, frozen with fear. Had the Angry Man returned? Or was it one of those sad ghost children scrabbling around up there, trying to find a way in?

He stared at the windows. The grey light of morning was shining through them. Suddenly the clock's alarm went off. Bram yelped in fright at the jangling din, and the thing on the roof let out a squawk of surprise and flew off.

'Just a gull!' he cried with relief.

And then he laughed, because he felt so foolish.

He opened the doors and looked outside. There were no clouds in the brightening sky, just a rosy glow behind the far rim of the sea.

'Sailor's warning,' he murmured to himself.

Bram spent a few minutes putting the hut in order, folding the blanket and hanging the plate back on the wall. He toyed with the idea of using the little gas stove to cook himself some breakfast but he had forgotten to bring any eggs. He was also too tired for a wake-up swim so he locked the hut behind him and ran back through the town. At five to six he slipped into his aunt's house and tiptoed to his bedroom.

Climbing into bed he thought about everything he had seen. It all seemed so unlikely and dream-like now, but he knew it had really happened and was determined to go to the hut again that night. The memory of the Angry Man didn't seem so terrifying in the daylight. Then sleep crept over him once more.

Mel shook him roughly.

'Mum's called you three times already!' she said. 'It's almost nine o'clock! Wake up, you lazy pig.'

Rubbing his eyes, Bram trailed into the kitchen and ate his breakfast in between yawns.

'Get a move on, dozy,' his mother told him, as she fanned herself with a triangle of cold toast. 'We want to get to the beach before it gets too baking out there.'

An hour later they were at the hut and the sun was beating down.

Bram allowed his mother to plaster him in sun block. Mel took her usual place on a towel with her phone, whilst Aunt Pat retired into the hut and eased herself on to the bunk with a grateful sigh.

The boy wondered what they would say if he told them about Drusilla. They'd think he was making her up to get attention. It was best to keep the spirit child his own special secret.

'What are you smiling at?' his mother asked.

'Nothing,' he answered, pulling away from her as she rubbed the excess lotion over her own arms. 'See you later.'

He ran off along the shore. His mother watched him go, hoping he'd find someone to play with, and chastised Mel for ignoring him this summer.

The girl grunted huffily in reply.

Bram splashed along the water's edge. Holidaymakers and locals who wished to escape the airless confines of the town were wandering on the beach or plonked down on deck chairs. The very ordinariness of them and their noise dispelled the magic he had glimpsed the previous night.

Finally he approached the place where Drusilla had awakened Mr Stone and frowned with irritation. A young couple were sitting close to that pile of seaweed-covered boulders, too close for him to get near. Bram had wanted to examine them and whisper to the strange ancient creature beneath.

'Can't do that with those two snogging there,' he grumbled to himself. He was about to stomp off when he noticed something on top of the glistening bladder-wrack.

'Wooaaah!' he breathed in astonishment. It was his whelk shell. Mr Stone had returned it. He wondered what sound had been placed inside and felt even more annoyed by the couple.

They were so busy kissing they didn't know he was there. Bram twisted his mouth to one side and made his mind up quickly. He darted forward, jumped over them, grabbed the shell then leaped over them again and dashed away.

'Oy!' the man yelled. But the boy was tearing back along the beach.

When he returned to the hut, Bram was out of breath.

'Had a good run about?' his mother asked.

He nodded and swigged juice from a carton in the cool box.

'That's disgusting!' Mel snorted. 'Mum, he's done it again. He's gross!'

'Use a glass,' his mother said wearily. 'None of us want to drink your spit.'

Bram pulled a face at his sister and she immediately texted her friends about how revolting her brother was.

He went inside the hut. His aunt was lying on the bunk, knitting a lemon-coloured cardigan for the unborn baby.

'Aunty Pat?' he asked, 'How old is this hut?'

'Ooh, I don't know,' she answered without looking up. 'I've only had it three years. But some of these huts go way back. Why so curious?'

'No reason,' he said.

His aunt laughed. 'You're very mysterious today,' she said.

The boy winked at her then dodged aside as Mel came into the hut. His sister made a great fuss of pumping water from the tap and filling a tumbler.

'I'm not touching the juice,' she barked at him. 'It's full of your germs.'

Bram left her to it. He wanted to listen to his shell in peace. Stepping into the blazing sunshine again he ducked round the back of the hut and sat on the sea wall.

Not knowing what to expect, he raised the shell to his ear.

At first he couldn't hear anything. The commotion of the crowded beach behind him was too distracting, and a second bout of noisy pumping in the nearby hut signalled Mel was still thirsty. Undeterred, Bram covered his other ear with his free hand and closed his eyes.

Gradually he became aware of a soft sound like a distant roaring. Was it the sea dragging through the shingle? Was it the wind funnelling under tall, wintry waves? Was it the surf breaking against Mr Stone himself?

Suddenly Bram's eyes snapped open. There were voices in that abstract sound. Real human voices!

He could hear children laughing and squealing as they played in the sea. He heard stern governesses scolding them for getting their clothes wet and sandy. He heard a woman calling Drusilla's name.

'Get out of that water at once!' the voice snapped sharply.

'Shan't!' the unmistakable, rebellious tones of Drusilla answered. 'I'm going in farther than anyone. I'm not scared.'

'Drusilla Wilkinson, you come out of there this very instant!'

'Come get me, you starchy old vinegar-face!'

Bram chuckled to himself.

'Just look at you!' the outraged woman ranted. 'You've ruined your best seaside clothes, young lady. It's a mercy your poor departed father isn't here to see how wicked and disobedient you are!'

'Don't you speak about Papa! You're a nasty mean dragon!'

'Graceless child! You shall have to walk all the way home drenched to the skin. There is nothing in the bathing hut for you to change into.'

'I don't care!' the girl cried back. 'I like being soggy. Look how deep I am. It's up to my chin.'

'Come back!' the woman urged, and her voice was now charged with fear. 'You're too far out.'

'I'm a fish!' Drusilla answered. 'I can take my feet off the bottom and—'

'Drusilla!' the woman shrieked. 'Where are you?'

There was a spluttering and frantic thrashing in the waves.

'Help me!' Drusilla called. 'Help—'

'Oh, save her!' The woman cried in horror. 'Someone save her! She's gone under again. Save her! Please! Somebody!'

Bram heard the clamour of voices rise as people raced into the sea to rescue her. He heard other children screeching as the tragedy unfolded.

Drusilla was brought ashore, where they laid her down and desperately tried to breathe life back into her. Someone began an anxious prayer.

After a terrible, long time, a gruff voice uttered, 'No use, missus.'

Then the shell was filled with weeping.

'Let me take her to the hut,' the fisherman suggested. 'Let me lay her down decent. This in't no sideshow for all to stand 'mazed at. Let's place her inside till the police, and what have you, come.'

There was no answer from the distraught woman but Bram heard the crunch of pebbles as heavy footsteps came trudging up the beach towards the hut.

'There now, lass,' the fisherman said. 'You rest easy till they come. No more harm shall come to you in here. I promise. You rest easy.'

'Drusilla!' the woman bawled. 'Oh, little Drusilla!'

Bram lowered the shell in horror. His hands were shaking. He didn't want to hear any more. His face had lost its colour and his heart was racing. Why had Mr Stone put that in there? Why did it make him hear how she had died? He felt sick.

'Have a drink!' Mel's voice suddenly shouted behind him.

The girl threw a glass of water over her brother's head. Bram was so startled he dropped the shell and it smashed on the concrete below.

He stared at the fragments in disbelief for a moment. Then he whirled round and flew at her. It was the most ferocious rage he'd ever been in. He kicked and punched her, and she fled in alarm, yelling for their mother.

'She made me break my shell!' he shouted when his mother had separated them.

'You're mental,' Mel retorted. 'It was only a stupid seashell. There's millions of them.'

'It wasn't an ordinary shell!' he yelled at her. 'It was special. I hate you!'

He tugged his arm free from their mother and stormed over to the towel where Mel had been sunning herself and snatched up her mobile phone. Before anyone could stop him he had smashed it to pieces.

'Only a stupid phone,' he spat vengefully. 'There's millions of them.'

The ensuing row blazed far longer than the sun did that day and Bram was sent to bed early.

Lying in bed he seethed and fumed at the injustice of it all. How could he begin to explain the importance of that shell to them? He was more determined than ever to sneak out again that night, and he waited and waited till the house grew silent.

At half-past eleven he was running through the streets, heading for the beach. Once inside the hut he lit the lanterns, took out the brass clock, sat on the bunk and willed the hands to go round faster. When they pointed to midnight, the briny smell of the deep sea filled the hut and Drusilla was there.

'My friend Bram!' she exclaimed with glee. 'You're

here again. How perfect!'

Bram grinned at her. 'Yes,' he said. 'I'm here.'

'Isn't it exciting? I can't wait to see it!'

'See what?'

'You must know!' she said, clapping her hands. 'It doesn't happen often.'

'What doesn't?'

The girl giggled and hurried to the doors. 'You'll see,' she said and vanished through them.

Bram hurried after her. He pushed open the doors and stared out in wonder.

The beach was alive with enchantment. Wisps of silvery mist were drifting over the sand, spiralling around the groynes, and pouring into the rock pools. Every pebble was glittering as if crusted with diamonds, and a full moon hung heavy and bright in the heavens. But what made Bram hold his breath and shake his head in amazement was the sea itself. It seemed to be on fire. When the small waves fell gently against the shore, they burst with green and yellow flames.

The boy ran down to stare at it more closely. The water was filled with glowing sparks of light. It shimmered and pulsed and cast pale shadows behind him. He had never seen anything so mesmerisingly beautiful. Reaching down he trailed his hand through it, and the lights formed a luminous halo around his fingers.

Bram laughed out loud.

'It's a powerful, magic night!' Drusilla told him. She was standing at the water's edge, the livid glow playing over her young features. 'Anything can happen!'

Gurgling with joy, she ran through the glimmering water. Bram followed, and the mists curled around him. They laughed and played all the way to the rock pools.

'I wish you could be my friend for ever,' Drusilla told him. 'I don't like being on my own.'

'I don't like being on my own, either.'

The girl smiled at him then turned her head to the sparkling sea. An immense bank of fog had moved in over the water, hiding the horizon and the tiny lights were burning brighter than ever.

'Oh, how splendid!' she cried. 'He is here! I didn't dare hope!'

'Who?' Bram asked, peering out at the dense blank fog.

'The king!' she said. 'The King of the Sea is here! I told you it was a magic night, didn't I?'

'I don't see anything,' he said.

'Look there!' she told him. 'That great dark shape rising in the mist. You must see!'

Bram squinted. Out there in the thick fog there may have been a colossal shape lifting from the waters or it may have been a trick of the moonlight on the featureless cloud.

'Can't you hear the sea bubbling and foaming?' she cried. 'Oh, he's so tall. And oh, so mighty.'

'What does he look like?' the boy asked, frantically scanning the wall of grey vapour.

'Like a gigantic, ancient god of the deep, standing proud and majestic on eight legs the size of tree trunks. His thorny shell has grown enormous spikes forming a crown and his robes are made from seaweed. Oh, Bram – he's the most marvellous, magical being in the great big world!'

The boy strained his eyes, trying to make out any of this, but the fog was too impenetrable.

A deep thundering roar came from the heart of the fog bank. It rolled out across the waters and into the August night.

'Oh, Bram!' Drusilla squealed. 'If we swim out to him he will grant us our hearts' desires. He can do anything. I can come alive again. I can be real and play with you. Quick – we must race out to him!'

She darted to the water's edge and ran into the glittering waves.

'Hurry!' she called.

The boy obeyed without question. He wasn't going to miss this. He dashed into the sea and Drusilla took his hand.

'To His Glorious Highness!' she yelled.

'To the King of the Sea!' he hollered.

They lunged recklessly through the waves, and the water flared and shone around them. Bram was so gripped and carried away by the excitement and magic of the moment he didn't pause to think until the water reached his neck and he could no longer feel the sand beneath his feet. They were out too deep and the fog bank was further than he had thought.

'I can't reach him!' he shouted, paddling the water. 'He's too far off. I'm going back!'

But Drusilla would not let go of his hand and she towed him further from the shore, laughing and refusing to listen to his protests.

Bram tried to pull away from her but her small fingers were clasped tightly around his wrist and he couldn't escape.

'Let go!' he cried.

She laughed even louder, and now the sound of it was unpleasant and sinister. Bram swallowed a mouthful of salty water and coughed. He spluttered and looked about them. The twinkling lights had all gone out. The sea was dark and cold, and the fog bank was nowhere to be seen. Every moment saw Bram being pulled further and further out to sea.

'Drusilla!' he yelled, choking as more sea water flooded his mouth. 'Stop it! Drusilla!'

The spirit child ceased laughing and grinned at him. It was a horrible grin. It was cruel and her eyes were pitiless.

'You'll stay with me always, Bram,' she demanded. 'We'll play together on the shore every night. You'll be my friend for ever.'

She lunged forward and seized his shoulders. Then she pushed him under the waves.

The boy kicked and struggled but she was too strong. He couldn't break free of those dead fingers. Down he went, into the silent murk of the sea. Her face was a mask of evil, around which her long hair swirled and billowed.

Bram held his breath for as long as possible, but his lungs were bursting. Finally the spent air exploded from his mouth in a rush of bubbles and he knew it was the end. He stopped struggling, and in that deep, dark ocean he heard Drusilla's girlish laughter surround him. He closed his eyes and sank like a stone.

Then hands stronger than hers found him. He was hauled up – up through the darkness, hoisted from the waves and cast onto the hard boards of a small boat. Large fists punched the sea from his lungs. He arched his back as the life spark ignited once more. Then he rolled sideways and retched up more water.

'You'll live, boy,' a gruff voice said.

It was a voice he had heard before, in the shell. It was the voice of the fisherman who had carried Drusilla's body into the beach hut. And then Bram realised he had heard it even before that.

He turned to see the burly man grip the oars and begin rowing back to the shore. He saw the wild tangle of his hair and the thick, bushy beard.

'The Angry Man!' he murmured, not knowing

whether to be grateful to him or be even more terrified.

The man said nothing. He pulled on the oars till eventually the bottom of the boat scraped over the sand. Then he leaped out and pulled it from the water.

Bram grabbed hold of the side and saw on the beach, waiting for them, the seven ghost children. They hurried to the Angry Man's side and hugged him.

'You left us!' they sobbed. 'Don't leave us.'

The man's forbidding face crumpled into an expression of concern and love. 'I had to go, my dears,' he said. 'Or there'd be eight of you this night.'

'Has she tried it again?' the eldest boy asked.

'Yes, she's tried to drown another. But this time I managed to save him.'

'He's so lucky,' wept the youngest. 'We're all lucky to have you with us, guarding us against her.'

Bram began to understand.

'Drusilla killed all of you,' he said.

The Angry Man put his arms round the ghost children and nodded.

'Twas me she caught first,' he said. 'Not three months after I fished her from the waters and placed her little lifeless body in yonder hut, I saw her shade a-playing in the sea one night when I was out in my boat. Said she wanted a pa, she did. Said as how she was lonely and scared of the dark, and she cried salty tears that made my heart bleed. Then she capsized my boat and held me under.'

Bram shuddered. 'But why the rest of you?' he asked.

'She tires of her toys too quick, too often,' the Angry Man said. 'Weren't long afore the shine wore off playing daughter to me so she went hunting for a brother or sister, promising them all sorts and showing them tricks. Oh, she's slyer than the first snake, that one. She fills young heads with make-believe and fancy shadows till they don't know what's real and can't see the danger they're in. Sometimes I can save them afore it's too late, sometimes I can't, but she always loses interest in her new playmates after the novelty fades and starts hunting anew.'

'Can't you stop her? Get rid of her?' Bram cried.

The ghost of the fisherman gazed up at the stars. 'If I could catch her, that'd put an end to her killing,' he said. 'And we'd all be set free, no longer tied to this shore. But she's too quick and always takes refuge in that old hut where she was placed, where my living self promised she'd be safe. None can touch her in there.'

Bram didn't know what to say. The spectral children clung to the fisherman wretchedly.

'Don't come back here,' the ghost of a thin, seven-year-old girl warned Bram. 'You've escaped. You mightn't be so lucky next time. She wants you, she will lie and steal, and show you miracles and wonders to tempt you back, but it's all false.'

'I'll never come back here at night!' Bram promised.

'Not even the daytime!' the Angry Man told him.

211

'Though she may look like a sweet child, don't be fooled. Her spirit is old and powerful. She's a fiend and evil doesn't sleep when the sun is high. Evil is always watchful and waking.'

Bram thought about the seashell and what he had heard in it that day. It had been another of Drusilla's deceits. She had wanted him to listen to it and make him feel sorry for her. It had worked so beautifully.

'I'll never come here again,' he vowed.

'Then get yourself home before you catch your death of cold,' the fisherman advised.

'Yes,' Bram said, climbing out of the boat in his sopping clothes. 'I'll...'

But the Angry Man and Drusilla's young victims had melted into the air and were gone.

Bram began walking back along the shore. He realised he hadn't even thanked the fisherman for saving his life. He reproached himself but it was too late now and he was never going to set foot here ever again.

Presently the familiar shape of the beach hut loomed ahead. The lanterns were still lit and the doors were wide-open, just as he had left them. It was a sight he dreaded now.

His steps slowed, and he could feel the blood pumping faster through his veins as he grew increasingly anxious. He knew who would be waiting for him in there.

Sure enough, as he drew close, a small figure jumped from the hut and ran towards him.

'Bram! Bram!' Drusilla cried. 'I was so worried! So frightened!'

The boy halted.

'I thought the Angry Man had caught you!' she sobbed.

'You tried to drown me,' he said.

The girl shook her head violently. 'No I didn't!' she swore. 'It was him! I saw him rowing towards us. I tried to hide us, to get away from him. But he pushed you under the water. Don't you remember?'

'You pushed me under.'

'No I didn't. You're my friend! I would never hurt you. Is that what he said? He's a wicked monster. He's a devil! He lies and tries to trap me. Don't believe him, Bram! He doesn't want me to have a friend. He wants me to be all alone out here in the midnight dark.'

The boy entered the hut and wrapped the blanket round his shoulders. Then he removed something from the drawers and took a bottle out of the cupboard.

'You're the monster,' he stated flatly. 'You're the liar. But you can't trick me any more.'

Drusilla stared at him pleadingly. 'Pleeeease!' she implored, her little lip trembling.

He didn't even look at her, and stepped outside. Then her face changed, the soft lines became hard and brutal. It was no use pretending any longer.

'Go then!' she snarled. 'There'll always be someone! Always some stupid child ready to believe in dreams

and fairy tales. It won't be long before I find another.
I'll have a new friend to play with, to go swimming
with – in the cold black sea.'

Bram closed one door.

'I know,' he said. 'You will. You're too evil and
cunning not to. Other children will fall for it, and they
won't be as lucky as me.'

'That they won't!' she snapped, and her eyes were
empty holes in a shrivelled, rotting head.

Bram closed the other door. She sprang onto the
bunk and pressed her horrific face against the window.

'They'll be Drusilla's new friends!' she shouted.
'Drowned and dead, just like her. Frightened pets for
her to toy with and torment.'

Bram locked the hut one last time.

'And some day soon,' he said, unscrewing the cap
off the bottle. 'My unborn cousin will be playing
here. Nothing will stop you pouncing on her. It would
only take a moment. Aunty Pat would turn round and
she'd be gone. You'd have dragged her down to the
sea and held her little head under the water. Not
because you want to play with her, just to get revenge
on me.'

The hideous, worm-eaten face, framed by the
cheery rose patterned curtains, let loose a vile, greedy
laugh.

'Yes!' it shrieked. 'How well you know Drusilla!
The moment that baby is brought here, I'll snatch it

away and hurl it into the deep! What a tiny ghost it will make. *Hahahahahaha* – it will slow the Angry Man down even more.'

Bram nodded. He was strangely calm. He finished what he was doing then threw the empty bottle away.

'You think I'd let that happen?' he asked sombrely. 'No chance. This stops tonight.'

'There's nothing you can do!' the horror bellowed back, causing the glass to quake in the frame.

Bram smiled. 'Yes there is,' he said. 'I'm doing it right now, and what's extra nice is I'm thanking the Angry Man at the same time by giving him the best present ever.'

With that he struck a match from the box he had taken out of the drawer and threw it against the doors. The paraffin he had splashed over the wooden boarding leaped into flame.

'No!' Drusilla screeched when she realised what he was doing. 'Noooo!'

In an instant the brightly painted beach hut was ablaze. It was parcelled in fire and the heat was intense. Bram backed away. He saw Drusilla's small figure silhouetted against the windows as she screamed and cursed his name. Then he turned his back and walked along the sea front, climbed over the wall and headed into town.

When he heard the boom of the Calor gas exploding he knew there would be nothing left of the hut by morning. There would be no refuge for her murderous spirit, nowhere to hide from the kind fisherman. He and the ghosts of the children she had drowned could find peace at last. As for Drusilla, Bram believed she was going somewhere far hotter than a burning beach hut.

Pulling the blanket tighter round his shoulders, he began to run and didn't stop till he reached Aunt Pat's.

THE
PRAYING
DOWN
OF
VAUGHAN
DARKNESS

Sam Llewellyn

THE PRAYING DOWN
OF
VAUGHAN
DARKNESS

Henry Davies – Days in the Life Diary Project

Wednesday 11th April

This is the beginning of our 'Days in the Life Diary Project'. Mrs Preece our history teacher says that we have got to describe our lives for three days. This means we must write down everything about ourselves – where we live, who we meet, what we do, what we eat, the stories we hear, and everything that happens to us. Mrs Preece says that we must hand it in by Friday afternoon, and that the result will be a fascinating historical document and very interesting. Not much interesting really happens, actually. But Mrs Preece says to write down *everything*, even stuff that everyone knows, and include any documents that come our way. So here goes, and do not blame me if it sends you to sleep.

Mum and Dad and me live in a town called Kington in what is called the Welsh Marches, which is where England and Wales meet. England is green and nearly flat, and Wales is browner and made of little mountains. Our house is quite old, on a street in the town, but the mountains rise at the end of the back garden.

Sometimes we go into the mountains, which in summer are green and nice-looking, and covered in larks twittering and all that. But if you go there in winter you can find yourself in a deep valley where the sun never reaches. In valleys like that the frost lies white and icy for weeks, and sometimes you feel there are other reasons for being cold beside the weather. Today we had porridge for breakfast and I went to school and we had sausages for supper and I can't remember what we had for lunch and not much happened.

Thursday 12th April

This morning we had porridge for breakfast. Then I went to school on my bike and there was a visiting author. The visiting author was called Montagu Taplin. He had a scrubby white beard and he smelled like a room where nobody has opened the windows for weeks. He writes stuff about local history, which means what happened round Kington hundreds of years ago. This did not sound too interesting at first, because not much happens in Kington these days, and it used to be smaller than it is now so probably even less happened then.

Montagu Taplin sat at a table in the library and read us a story from a pad of mothy old paper. The story was a bit old-fashioned, but I was surprised at how interesting it was. So afterwards I went up to him, holding my breath because of the smell, and got a photocopy. The story is called *The Praying Down of Vaughan Darkness*, and Mrs Preece said to include all documents in our 'Days in the Life Diaries' so here it is.

Narrative of Montagu Taplin

In a valley of the hills west of Kington stands an ancient house called Hergest Court. It is sited on a low hill frowning over a river, which broadens into a dark mere. Almost six hundred years ago there lived in this house a certain Thomas Vaughan.

Thomas Vaughan was a great lord and a wicked one. He stole money from farmers' chests and wives from their husbands' beds, took children and sold them into slavery, and killed without mercy. In those wild and lawless lands in those wild and lawless times, no-one could prevent this. People came to call him Vaughan

Darkness, and chased him from his house, so he took to the crags and caves of Radnor Forest. And in time they set a hunter called Simon ap John after him.

Simon ap John hunted Vaughan Darkness down in a badger sett, bound him and brought him to Kington. Here he was tried, found guilty of robbery and murder, and (as was the custom of the time) sentenced to hang.

The town of Kington loved a hanging. It was revenge for the wronged. It was entertainment for the curious. And above all it was a lesson for the wicked; or, in the case of Harry Morgan, the said-to-be-wicked.

Harry Morgan was twelve years old, and had been offered by his step-parents to be a monk in Hereford. The reason Harry was said to be wicked was that he did not want to be a monk and live with a lot of old men in a draughty abbey. But his parents were dead, and he lived with his Uncle Davies and Aunt Gwyn, and his Uncle Davies and his Aunt Gwyn wanted him to be a monk because they had their eye on the Hope, which was a farm that belonged to the abbey, and if they gave Harry to the abbey, the bishop (they thought) would give them the farm they wanted.

So Uncle Davies dragged Harry by the ear through the crowd on the day of the hanging of Vaughan Darkness, to show him what happened to ungrateful boys who did not do as they were told.

The people of Kington knew about the plan for Harry to become a monk, and thought it was a good idea, and that being ungrateful was a bad idea, and that he could do with a lesson. The crowd parted so Harry could get a front-row view. Inside a fence of oak palings was a clear circle of cobblestones. In the centre of the circle stood a gallows. Standing on a cart under the gallows was a huge man with a dark and bitter face and a rope around his neck. The other end of the rope was tied to the crossbeam of the gallows.

'There you are, see,' hissed Uncle Davies. 'Vaughan Darkness on the cart at last. They'll whip up the horse, and he'll dangle.'

There was a priest beside the cart, gaunt and blue-nosed in his cassock. 'Darkness, repent!' he cried.

Vaughan Darkness grinned, or perhaps it was a snarl, and fixed the priest with his burning black gaze. 'I'll see you in hell,' he said, not as defiance, but as a matter of fact. The crowd groaned, for in those days hell was real, and burning, and lasted for ever. The executioner whacked the horse with his stick. The cart jolted forward. Harry shut his eyes.

He heard a thump, then the creak of a rope with something heavy swinging on the end of it. When he opened his eyes Vaughan Darkness hung there, dead.

'Behold the results of wickedness, which begins with disobedience,' said Uncle Davies. 'We won't be seeing him again.'

But there, as it turned out, he was wrong.

* * *

The brown earth settled over Vaughan's grave. Winter became spring. And before the grass had its roots well into the mound, strange things began to happen.

Simon ap John the hunter was chasing a stag over the hills when he heard a terrible ripping and snarling from across a ridge. When he went to see the cause, he found all of his hounds with their throats torn out. In the middle of the circle of corpses was a great black dog. When the dog saw Simon it made a horrid bound and sank its fangs into his neck. Simon told this story with his last breath to the shepherd who found him. He added that the dog had had eyes in which red fires burned like the pits of hell. The shepherd passed this on, mentioning that the dead man's wound had stunk of brimstone and corruption; brimstone being one of the chief ingredients of hell fire, with a stink somewhere between burning and bad eggs.

Most people thought the shepherd had made this bit up, and that Simon had been unlucky enough to meet a pack of wolves, which at that time still roved the deep hills of Wales. Then something else happened.

A pedlar was lying at his ease in a hedge. He was watching a carter take a load of straw along the road, and pitying him the hard work of carting. It was a still grey evening, soft, with no wind. The pedlar thought he heard a faint roaring in the hills. The roaring came closer. There was a cracking, like branches breaking in a wind. The pedlar felt a breath of breeze on his face and looked up. He saw a black whirlwind howl down the hillside, whisk cart, horse and carter high in the air, and dash them into the ravine by the road. The odd thing about the whirlwind (said the pedlar) was that it seemed to have threads of fire running through it, red as the pits of hell, and it left behind it a stink of brimstone and corruption.

People believed pedlars even less than they believed shepherds, for pedlars were usually trying to sell splinters of wood as bits of the True Cross, or dog teeth as the molars of saints. They could not check his story with the carter because the carter was in the ravine, crushed under the wreckage of his cart and his horse and the load of straw.

Soon after this, the hangman was out looking after his cattle on Bradnor Hill. A sharp-eyed fowler, snaring larks, saw what happened. Apparently a huge black bull rose out of the ground and charged at the hangman. The fowler saw the hangman run away, the bull chasing him, head down. The head jerked up. And there was the hangman, spinning on a horn like a Catherine wheel on its pin. The bull tossed the hangman into a gorse bush, lifted its gory muzzle and bellowed. As it bellowed the fowler caught sight of its eyes, which he said were red as the pits of hell. When he ran to help the hangman – who, of course, was beyond help, being dead – he could hardly breathe for the stink of brimstone and corruption.

But Harry Morgan did not hear about any of this. For Harry was in the abbey at Hereford with the top of his head shaved bald, learning to be a monk.

At this time it was generally believed that the Devil had a house in Radnor Forest. So people were used to events that were hard to explain, and nobody paid much attention to stories of dogs and whirlwinds and bulls. But at last people did begin to murmur that the hunter who had been killed was the hunter who had captured Vaughan Darkness, and the carter who had been killed was the carter who had driven the cart on which Vaughan Darkness had stood to be hanged, and the man gored to death by the black bull had been the hangman who had hanged Vaughan Darkness. And they began to wonder.

The man who wondered the most was a judge. He wondered very hard, because he had been the judge who had run the trial of Vaughan Darkness and condemned him to hang. The deaths of the hunter and the carter and the hangman made the judge nervous. He soon grew tired of looking under his four-poster bed for dogs and whirlwinds and bulls. So one Thursday he put a holy relic in every pocket, watered his horse at a holy well and rode to Hereford to see the bishop.

The bishop was having breakfast. He looked up from his plate, waving a chicken leg. 'Judge!' he cried.

The judge bowed so deeply that his relics clanked.

'Lord Bishop,' he said, 'we must be rid of the wicked sinner Vaughan Darkness.'

'But he has been hanged, and burns in hell,' said the bishop, taking a mouthful.

'He walks,' said the judge.

'Dear me,' said the bishop. 'We'll have to take care of that. Now, then. Breakfast?'

The judge tucked into a large and delicious breakfast of mutton chops, sausages and three kinds of pie, and started (somewhat greasy) for home.

The road was a stripe of mud that ran through a forest. It was autumn, and the last flies of the year buzzed in low slants of sun between the oak trunks. In a clearing something had died. A cloud of bluebottles rose from the corpse, along with a stink of brimstone and corruption. One of the flies buzzed into the judge's face. He swatted at it, expecting it to fly away. But it buzzed back straight and true. He felt a stinging pain in the soft part of his neck beside his windpipe. The pain got worse and worse until there was nothing else. The last thing he saw as his mind faded were the eyes of the rest of the swarm. They were red as the pits of hell.

Brother Anselmus woke in his cell. A cold moon was peering through the slit window, and a bell was ringing. A monk's life was ruled by bells, and by the vow he had taken to bury his old self, the self that had been Harry Morgan. Harry was a dutiful boy, who kept his promises. But he could not get used to being a monk called Anselmus, and he knew that people had noticed this fact and were not pleased with him.

So he shuddered into the robe of prickly black cloth, and splashed cold water on his face, and tried not to let himself think about how much he hated getting up in the middle of the winter night to go and mumble prayers in a cold chapel.

Someone rattled at his door. A head appeared round it, pitted with shadow by the lantern its owner was carrying. 'Anselmus,' it said. 'Come. The Lord Bishop will see you now.'

This was the Bishop's Chaplain, a very important man who normally would not even have noticed Harry. Harry trotted after him, searching his heart for a sin he had committed dreadful enough to get the attention of a real bishop, and found none except not really wanting to be a monk. Perhaps that was bad enough.

He was still wondering when he arrived in a chamber where the bishop sat. The room was bright as day, lit with twenty candles. The tubby old bishop fixed his cunning eyes on Harry. 'Boy,' he said, 'are you pure in heart?'

'Yes, my lord,' said Harry.

'Then we need you to help us. We are faced with a terrible Thing.'

Harry was pleased to be asked to help, but he wondered why the bishop was calling on him. 'What thing?'

'A Thing of darkness, come from hell,' said the bishop in a deep, solemn voice. 'A Thing that must be summoned and prayed down. We have been watching you with interest. We are sure that you are the boy for the job, Andrew.'

'Anselmus,' said the chaplain.

Harry, thought Harry. 'What job?' he said.

'You will be one of those who travel to Cwm to pray the Thing down,' said the bishop. 'If – that is *when* – you succeed, your name will be great. I know your uncle would like our farm at the Hope. If the ghost is confined,' he said casually, 'we will make sure he gets it.'

The chaplain said, 'He is young. He does not know praying down.'

'Then explain it to him.' The bishop rose and waddled away to bed.

The chaplain sat in the bishop's chair. He did not offer Harry a seat. He said, in the bored voice of a teacher, 'Summonings take place at Cwm because it is a lonely place, and if the devil blasts it, only the Summoners will be hurt. It is done as follows: twelve candles are lit in the church. Twelve priests, nuns or monks stand near them. The Chief Summoner calls the Thing from hell on the stroke of midnight. The Summoners pray the Thing into a bottle and seal it therein with molten lead, and the whole is buried under running water so that the Thing can walk no more. And when the Thing is under the water, the priests and the nuns will be richly rewarded, and your uncle can have that farm he keeps pestering the bishop about.' The chaplain frowned. 'Though, of course, many perish during a praying down. And sometimes if the Thing has eaten enough souls it is content and goes back to hell, and troubles us no more. Well, that's all. Away with you.'

Harry stood staring at the chaplain's tight-shut face. Summon a ghost and pray it into a bottle? So Uncle Davies could have his farm? There was ice in his heart, and his knees tried to knock together.

'Go!' cried the chaplain.

The bishop's people gave Harry a breakfast of bread and a boiled egg, and told him that from now on he was fasting. They led him outside to where two horses were breathing steam in the half-light. The bishop's groom boosted him into the saddle of one of the horses and mounted the other. They rode through the mucky streets and into the forest.

The sun came up and printed the long shadows of the trees over the ground. Harry thought they looked like fingers out to grab him and rode round them whenever possible. At noon the bishop's groom took out some bread and cheese. He did not offer any to Harry. 'You must fast,' he said. 'Orders from the chaplain.' He chewed a bit. 'Not that it will do you any good. The bishop's sending every priest and nun he wants to be rid of to Cwm.' He laughed, mouth open. 'He's promised them money. But we reckon he won't have to spend it, because at midnight you'll be a nice snack for Vaughan Darkness, and that'll be the end of you.'

Sometimes if the Thing has eaten enough souls it is content, the chaplain had said. Perhaps there would be no praying down. Perhaps the Summoners were going to Cwm as ghost-food. Harry shivered, and thought of kicking his horse into a gallop and fleeing into the wood. But if he did that everyone would say he had run away from the ghost that was plaguing them, and nobody would help him, and he would starve. He had a choice, it seemed: starve, or be eaten...

No. The only way out was to summon the ghost, pray it down, and get Uncle Davies his farm. Then he could run away if he wanted to. Let the ghost appear, he thought, pushing the terror into the shadowy corners of his mind. He would pray it down as best he could with the others. And having kept his side of the bargain, he would do as he liked.

On they rode, on and on. The November night came down. The trees thinned, and the land rose, and the road ran into a deep valley. Rags of cloud chased past a pale sliver of moon. At last the sides of the valley drew away and it seemed to Harry that they had come into a bowl of ground surrounded by mountains. He had never been so tired and hungry, or so frightened. Soon, he consoled himself, he would meet his fellow

Summoners. They would help him. They would all help each other.

The moon was setting behind the mountains. The only light out here was a dim yellow glow, perhaps a candle behind a horn pane, in the bowl's centre. Twenty minutes later the hooves clattered on cobbles.

'Off,' said the groom.

Harry slid down from his horse's back, found that his legs would not carry him and collapsed in front of what he now saw was a church gate. Hands pulled him up by the arm and dragged him through. He saw tombstones, the dark shape of a building. Then sounds began to echo around him, and he knew he was in a church, and the hands dropped him onto something less hard than stone, a mat, perhaps; and he went to sleep.

Someone was shaking him. He woke. There was a little more light, and more voices echoing on stone. He was colder even than before. The shaker's face was lit by the yellow flame of a rush light. It had small eyes, and a bulb of a nose, and it gave off a smell that reminded Harry of a wine cellar. 'Come, child,' said a wheezy voice. 'It is time to do our duty to God and the bishop.'

Harry scrambled to his feet. The flames cast shadows: twelve shadows in all, nine monks and priests including him, and three nuns. Some of them seemed to be eating. What about their fasts? But, of course, these were the worst priests and nuns the bishop could find, sent to have their souls devoured by a Thing from hell. His heart sank. These were not good companions for a life-or-death battle.

From somewhere came a high, lost moaning and a scratching like fingernails on stone. 'What's that noise?' he said. His voice sounded higher than he had meant it to.

'Wind in the trees,' said the priest with the bulb nose.

'But the scratching.'

'Twigs on the roof,' said another voice, sarcastic. 'Can it be that he believes in ghosts?'

Laughter from the priests and nuns. Some of it real, thought Harry. Some of it not; the kind of forced laugh you might give if you were trying to persuade yourself not to be frightened of something. He wanted to shout that they should have kept to the rules. But that sarcastic voice would only sneer, and the others would laugh nervously, but they would not argue. Their souls would be eaten, and his with them. He squeezed his eyes shut so he would not cry.

'Let us begin,' said Bulb-Nose.

'Very well, Marcus, your holiness,' said the sarcastic voice, and the others laughed again, and Harry's heart sank still lower.

'Candles, then,' said Marcus. 'Books. What else?'

Another voice said, 'Never mind the mumbo jumbo. Let's get it over with and take our money and go home.'

No, no, thought Harry. They must do things the

right way, or they would be in terrible danger. He said, 'What about the lead?'

'Lead?'

'For melting. And the bottle to put the ghost in.'

There was a silence. Then the sarcastic voice said, 'Well, well, he really does believe. Now listen to me, child. We are here because the bishop wants to be rid of us.' That was what the groom had said. 'But the bishop is a superstitious old fool. We do not believe in being eaten by ghosts. So, at the praying down, Marcus will recite the summons, and, of course, the ghost will not come, and we will tell the bishop that the ghost said sorry and went away, and we will get our pay. I believe in money, not ghosts,' he said.

There was laughter, but the silence in the church seemed to suck it up. In the quiet, Harry was almost sure he heard a voice far, far away, a harsh voice with a long echo. It was laughing too.

Harry told himself it was probably an owl. Ghost or no ghost, getting ready would take his mind off the waiting. 'I'm going to melt some lead,' he said.

'If you must,' said Marcus.

In an alcove in the church wall Harry found a bottle, a little brazier, some charcoal, a saucepan and some odds and ends of lead. He put the brazier on the stone bench that ran down the church wall, lit the charcoal, blew it into red embers, put the lead in the saucepan and balanced the saucepan on the brazier.

'It is time to light the candles,' said Father Marcus, sounding bored. 'Have you quite finished, Anselmus?'

'Coming,' said Harry, hot-faced, blowing the brazier.

The candles stood on the altar, pale as bones. The Summoners walked up one by one, lit a single candle each and went to stand on alternate sides of the altar steps. Harry went last because he was the youngest. The warmth of the brazier had left him, and he was cold with terror. His hands were shaking so much that he could not bring the taper to the candle. The nuns sniggered. He managed on his third try, using both hands. Twelve flames made a cheerful golden glow; but Harry could not help thinking that up in the vaulting of the roof the shadows wriggled in a way that was ... *not quite right*.

Silence fell, broken only by the moan of the wind and the heavy tick of the clock. There was a clunk and a whirring, the first stroke of midnight boomed in the freezing air. Father Marcus held his book to the light of the candles and began to read.

The words were in Latin. Like everyone else in those days, Harry had been taught Latin at school. 'Come up, come up, foul spirit.' Father Marcus paused to blow his nose. 'Visit us, we command thee, that we may strive with thee and compass thee about, and put thy being in this world into a bottle, and thy being in the other world into the Pit. Vaughan Darkness, we command thee to attend us in Saint Michael's holy church of Cwm.'

'Amen,' said the priests and nuns.

The last stroke of midnight died away. The candle flames stood still as golden spearheads and the clock ticked on. A nun said something to another nun. Nothing is going to happen, Harry told himself, warm with relief. Nothing at all—

The church doors burst open with a crash. Wind shrieked in the gargoyles, and icy air flooded up the aisle, bowing the candle flames into flat red lines of fire. The gust died. The doors slammed shut. The candle flames stood straight again and the silence returned.

Harry's skin crawled.

The clock had stopped ticking.

Someone – some Thing – had come into the church.

Harry held his hands in front of his face as if he were praying and peeped between his fingers. A patch of shadow by the door seemed thicker than it should have been. Terror crawled over him like spiders. The shadows drew together. They took on a shape. It was the shape of a man: an enormous man, with huge shoulders and a great black cloak that merged with the darkness behind him. The figure flowed up the aisle and hung over the double line of Summoners like a thundercloud. A voice spoke, so deep that it seemed to come from the vaults under the paving. 'Who summons me?' it said.

Now there was real silence, unbroken even by breathing. Harry saw Father Marcus suddenly start forward, as if one of the nuns had pinched his bottom.

'You?' said the phantom, in a voice full of scorn.

Father Marcus's face was greenish in the candlelight. He lifted the book in his hand and began reading in Latin. 'Avaunt, foul fiend, let thy many sins pursue thee like the hounds of hell into yonder bottle—'

A laugh like vault doors slamming. 'And who are you to tell me where I must go?' said Vaughan Darkness. 'You do not even believe in ghosts, you say. Why should something that does not exist do as you tell it? But perhaps we can make you believe.' The shadowy hand made a small gesture, like one flicking away a fly. Marcus the priest jolted backwards, tumbled up and over the altar and smashed through the east window, his scream fading into the far distance.

One of the candles on the altar flicked out.

'Next?' said Vaughan Darkness.

Through his fingers, Harry saw two of the nuns sidle away into the shadows. Himself, he was too scared to move.

The nuns began laughing, high and mad. Two more candles flicked out.

Another priest stepped forward, mumbling Latin words. The ghost loomed over him, dark and terrible. 'Hmm,' it said. 'Can that be bread and cheese I smell on your breath? Can it be that you have broken your fast?

Aye. Farewell.' A hand of shadow came out, rested above the bald patch on the priest's head, and pressed downwards. The paving slabs under the priest's feet seemed to soften. He sank into the floor, screaming until the screams were muffled by the stones closing over his mouth.

A fourth candle died.

'Some years in the vault will teach him the meaning of fasting,' said the ghost. 'Oh, are you leaving us?'

For six priests and the remaining nun were creeping down the aisle. Now they broke into a run, heading for the doors. The ghost waved a corner of his cloak at them. They fell flat on the paving, like puppets with their strings cut.

It seemed to be getting darker in the church. Harry turned to the altar. Between the fingers of his praying hands he saw the flames of seven more candles die to tiny red coals and vanish.

Eleven candles gone. Only one still burned on the altar. He fixed his eyes on it. It shone pure and clear. He felt its warmth and light flow into him.

The wind moaned in the vaults. The shadow of Vaughan Darkness loomed over him, glaring down with eyes red as the pits of hell.

But in his mind Harry saw the sun bright as the candle, shining from a clear sky on to the green hills of Wales. He heard larks singing, and smelled the grass growing. He saw that this Vaughan was mere death, a nothing, emptiness. So he looked into the terrible red eyes and said, 'Vaughan Darkness, into the bottle with you.'

The eyes flared, but gave out no light. 'The others I destroyed,' said Vaughan Darkness. 'You I will eat.' A red mouth opened in the shadowy head.

But all Harry saw was a filthy rat cornered in a patch of shadow by a hay cart. 'I have fasted,' he said. 'I believe in you, but not in your power, for you are nothing and cannot live in my world. So you have no command over me.'

In his bright hay meadow he bent and picked up the squirming, snapping, red-eyed rat by its scaly tail, and carried it squealing across to the bottle, crammed it in, and took the pan of molten lead from the coals and poured the lead in on top of it. There was a roar and a hiss and a dreadful scream. The great shadow writhed in the light of the last candle. It was a bull, then a dog, then a whirlwind. The whirlwind shrank to become a fly, slow and sleepy in the winter chill. Harry stepped on it. There was a slight crunch, and a wisp of vapour that stank of brimstone and corruption.

He lay down in front of the altar and went to sleep.

They found him there the next morning. The eleven priests and nuns were dead or raving mad. Harry was mad too, they decided. For he declared that he would no longer be a monk. When they asked him why, he showed them a bunch of fresh flowers, the kind you would pick in a hay field in June; though it was November, and a cold one at that. And nobody could make him tell where he had got them.

They took the bottle with Vaughan Darkness stoppered up in it to Hergest Court. They dug a hole in the bed of the mere and buried the bottle in it. Then they covered the place with a great stone, bearing the sign of the cross and a Latin inscription forbidding anyone to move it, ever, and let the water back in to cover it.

As for Harry, he collected his wits and the bishop's reward.

His uncle and aunt died of the plague soon afterwards, and he took on the farm at the Hope, and in time became the father of a large family and lived to a great age, loved by all.

Well that was the story the author told us. I thought it was quite good, but it took me a long time to read. It is supper now. We are having stew, and after that I am going to bed. With the light on.

Friday 13th April

Not much happened today. We had porridge for breakfast and pasta salad for school lunch, which was disgusting. We were supposed to finish these 'Days in the Life Diaries' in the afternoon but me and Craig didn't get ours done because we had to go for our guitar lessons. So Mrs Preece said we could finish them tonight as long as we got them to her house by six o'clock because she wants to read them before Monday. That's OK because she lives near me and Craig.

Anyway, I was biking home when I heard a roar and a clatter and it was Dave. Dave is a friend of my dad's and he drives a JCB 4CX digger and he says that next year when I am twelve he will let me have a go. Everyone rings Dave when there is digging to be done. They even get him to dig the graves in the churchyard. People say, doesn't it spook you? But Dave says a hole is a hole, and what people put in it is up to them.

So Dave slowed down and said, 'Coming for a ride?'

I said, 'Where?' Thinking, not really, because I have the 'Days in the Life Diary' to finish.

But then he said, 'Hergest Court,' and I thought perhaps this is an interesting coincidence. So I put my bike in the bucket and Dave used his mobile to ring Mum to say I would be back for tea, and off we went, me sitting in the spare seat of the cab.

As we drove along I said, 'What's the job?'

Dave said, 'They've drained the mere at the Court, and there's a lot of silty old muck in there that needs shifting and there will be probably be eels.' Dave knows I like catching eels. So we went down Hergest drive and he put the digger alongside the mere, which is only a pond, really, and he started digging out all this black mud, and there *were* eels in it, which was excellent.

I was chasing this big eel through the grass when I heard the digger bucket bang against something hard. So I ran back to have a look. The bucket was deep in wet mud, jerking away at something. 'Stone!' Dave shouted, frowning through the open window of his cab.

It was then that I remembered the stone in Montagu Taplin's story. So I started to yell, 'Stop, Dave!' but Dave could not hear over the noise of the digger, and anyway, Dave thinks a grave is just a hole in the ground, and a story is only a story, so it would have been a waste of breath. He got the bucket under whatever it was and lifted. Up it came; a great big lump of black mud with a stone in the middle of it. The stone looked a bit square, as if someone had shaped it. I really hoped it would not have writing on it. I decided not to go and look, just in case it did.

As Dave swung the bucket to put the load in the dumper truck, something fell out of the lump. Whatever it was winked in the sun like glass. Like part of a bottle, really. And when I went to look at it I saw it was an old, old bottle, broken now. The mud smelled horrible, like a mixture of corruption and brimstone, whatever that is. But I picked up the bits because I thought I'd find out where Montagu Taplin lives and show them to him.

I took my bike out of the bucket and waved to Dave and pedalled off home as fast as I could.

All the way home I was telling myself that Montagu

Taplin's story is only a story. It made me nervous, though, and the only way I could stop myself feeling nervous was to tell myself that it was all a load of rubbish. So I put the bottle bits in the recycling bin and came inside to finish writing my 'Days in the Life Diary'. Craig next door is coming round any minute now and he is going to hand in his 'Days in the Life Diary' to Mrs Preece at her house and he says he will take mine along too.

It is nearly tea time, and Craig will be here any minute, so I must stop now. Dad has just shouted up the stairs to say there is some sort of dog out by the back fence and it will be into the bins soon and the bins are my job and he is busy, and the wind is getting up so it will probably rain, so I should go and chase it away now before I get wet and it rips the bags. I have opened my bedroom window to shout at it, but it hasn't done any good. I can hear it panting, and there is some sort of cow bellowing, so maybe it has been chasing the dog out of the mountains, or something. The dog sounds big. It must have got into one of the bins already, because even from up here at the window I can see that there are flies everywhere, and there is a terrible stink of brimstone and corruption.

There goes the doorbell. That will be Craig. I'll give him this and then I'll do the bins. It's been quite interesting to write, after all. That dog is really, really barking. I wonder what it wants? Soon find out.

SAM LLEWELLYN

This is the 'Days in the Life Diary' handed in by Craig Evans to Mrs Preece, with his own work, at five o'clock on April 13th. At five-past five on the same evening, the Davies house was destroyed by a freak whirlwind. The entire Davies family vanished, and no trace of them has been seen since.

THE GHOST
WALK

Matt Haig

THE GHOST WALK

'Did you know,' said Oscar's dad, looking at the second-hand guidebook, 'there are meant to be more ghosts in York, for its size, than any other city in the world?'

Oscar wasn't impressed. He was still fiddling with the remote control in the hotel room, trying to get the rubbish TV to work.

'Oh, don't tell me that,' laughed Oscar's mum, her head upside down between her legs in a yoga pose. 'I won't be able to sleep tonight.'

'I can't get any channels,' said Oscar, ignoring what his parents were saying.

His dad sighed. 'Oh, well, don't worry. We're going out in a minute. We can do something more interesting than watch TV.'

'Yeah, right,' said Oscar. 'Interesting? In York?'

He knew he was sounding grumpy, but the trouble was he was having the worst holiday ever. If you could even call it a holiday. Holidays were normally about beaches and swimming pools and theme parks and bike rides and exotic food and hot weather. Not about going one hundred miles up the motorway to a town that was just as boring as the one they'd come from, only with worse weather and rubbish restaurants and zero friends.

And OK, so his dad couldn't help it that he'd lost his job and now had to work from home, creating websites for people who paid even less money than the people who paid for his mum's yoga classes. But surely even poor people could have a better holiday than *this*? And if it was all about money why did his mum insist that they spend all day going around *gift shops*? (The words 'gift shop' had become far scarier than the word 'ghost' for Oscar, because they meant Death by Boredom, and that was a particularly slow and nasty way to die.)

'Well, *this* sounds interesting', his dad went on, still sitting at the end of the hotel bed, reading the guidebook. '*The Ghost Walk. A haunted tour of York, which takes place every evening.*'

'Ooh, I don't know about that,' said Oscar's mum, who was now struggling with her yogic breathing.

'Come on, it'll be fun. It says everyone meets up at eight o'clock by the river, just outside the King's Head pub.' Then he read an extract from the guidebook. *'Expect to be frightened out of your skin as legendary ghost-tour guide Dorian Deadwater takes you to horribly haunted graveyards, spooky inns, medical manor houses and other sites roamed by York's most famous ghosts.'*

'Dorian Deadwater,' scoffed Oscar. 'That is *so* a made-up name.'

'Probably,' said his dad, laughing, 'but it will be a bit of fun. And you never know, we might actually see a real ghost.'

'Yeah, very likely, except for the fact that ghosts don't actually exist,' said Oscar, switching off the flickering TV in frustration. But then he looked at his dad's face, and he realised he was only trying to cheer him up and take his mind off the fact that, when this holiday was over, Oscar had to start a new school. A new school which was known to have some very big and scary kids, kids who hated people who went to posh schools like Horton Boys' School, which was where Oscar had been up until the end of last term, when his parents told him they no longer had enough money to send him there.

So Oscar tried to be a bit less grumpy. 'No, it sounds fun, Dad.' And now he thought about it, as he read the entry on the yellowing page of the guidebook, it *did* sound fun. Or, at least, more fun than spending a night in front of a broken TV.

Oscar's mum stopped brushing her hair and went over to look at the guidebook. 'Hold on, though,' she said, 'this is a very old book. It was last updated ten years ago. That tour's probably not even going any more. Perhaps we should check at the tourist office.'

'It says here the Ghost Walk has been going for thirty years, so I'm sure they've managed another ten,' said Oscar's dad, pointing at the page. 'Anyway, there's no harm in going to have a look, is there?'

'No, I suppose not.'

'If there's no one there we'll just go for a wander and grab a bite to eat.'

Oscar looked at his mum and saw she was really hoping the guidebook was out of date on this matter. 'Don't worry, Mum, we'll look after you.'

Their hotel was quite a long way from the River Ouse. They walked past the gigantic York Minster, which was lit at night in a way that made the whole building itself look like a ghost. They went down a scruffy-looking higgledy-piggledy street appropriately called The Shambles, which they'd been down earlier to visit more gift shops and to eat the most disgusting pizza Oscar had ever tasted. They passed another street called Whip-Ma-Whop-Ma-Gate.

This really is a weird city, thought Oscar, as his dad kept looking in the guidebook.

'*Whip-Ma-Whop-Ma-Gate is the smallest street in York, and the name means "Neither One Thing Nor the Other", and dates back to Viking times . . .*'

Before they got to the river, it started to rain heavily. But Oscar's mum had heard the weather forecast and bought two umbrellas earlier that day at a shop next to the Minster.

'See, gift shops come in handy sometimes.'

Oscar could tell she loved saying that.

And then they were there.

A big sign, creaking in the wind and battered by rain, had a picture of a calm, wise king, his painted face oblivious to the weather. Below his image were the words 'The King's Head'.

But there was no one else around.

'See, I was right,' said Oscar's mum. 'It's finished. Oh, well, let's go and grab a bite to eat.'

'Hold on,' said Oscar's dad. 'Look at that.'

He was pointing over to the old stone wall next to the pub. There was a painted sign on it, which was hard to read as it was weather-worn and the paint was peeling off. It said:

THE GHOST WALK

8.pm., nightly. Meeting here.

Adults £5, Under 16s £3

Join Dorian Deadwater as he takes you
on a tour of the city's restless dead.

Be afraid . . .

'Well the price isn't too scary,' said Oscar's dad, who was always worrying about money these days. 'Either they haven't put it up for ten years, or "Mr Deadwater" isn't worth paying much more,' he laughed.

'Please, call me Dorian.'

The voice came from nowhere, or seemed to. Oscar turned round with his parents to see a man standing there, with rain falling hard into the River Ouse behind him.

'Oops, sorry,' said Oscar's dad, looking rather embarrassed. 'I didn't see you there.'

'My goodness,' said Oscar's mum, with a gasp. 'You gave me the fright of my life.'

Oscar looked at the man and almost laughed.

Dorian Deadwater was dressed in a long Victorian tail coat. He had a grey goatee beard which was cut into a little point below his chin. If it wasn't for his very normal-looking modern glasses and his small silver earring it would be easy to believe he had stepped out of the nineteenth century. But there was something a bit too theatrical about him to be truly scary. Indeed, Oscar thought he looked like someone out of a pantomime.

The man turned back for a moment, watching the rain land on the river.

'There's a ghost of a little girl called Polly Mae who sometimes appears on that river,' he said, sounding tired before he'd even begun. '1652 had been a very cold winter. The Ouse had turned to ice . . . She died trying to cross. And now she sometimes calls out, asking for help. To hear her you would think she was really there, more alive than you or I. People have often believed it to be true, jumping in the Ouse to try and save her out of a simple human kindness.'

'How sad,' said Oscar's mum, but Dorian Deadwater didn't comment.

'That's not an official part of the tour,' said Dorian. 'I just thought I'd let you know. Anyway, it looks like you're the only ones, so follow me,' he said in a deep and quiet voice which struggled against the rain to be heard. 'Time to show you some ghosts.'

They began to walk across the slippery cobbles, following the tour guide as he took slow and steady steps towards their first destination. Oscar's mum held her son's arm tightly.

'I'm scared,' she said, half-joking, but only half.

Oscar wasn't scared. Not yet, anyway. But his heart was racing a little with excitement. Maybe York wasn't going to turn out to be such a bad place, after all.

They turned the corner and saw a hill with a large, round ruined stone tower, floodlit against the night.

'Ah, that's Clifford's Tower,' said Oscar's dad, consulting the guidebook for the 786th time that day. 'The only part of York Castle that's still standing, apparently...'

Dorian Deadwater stopped suddenly in front of them, as if at a gunshot, and turned. His eyes widened and stared straight at Oscar as he began to speak, with the tower hovering high and white above him like a giant crown. Suddenly he seemed very awake, far more alert than he'd been by the water's edge.

'On the sixteenth of March in the year 1190, over a hundred people died in this tower behind me,' he said, with water dripping off his nose and eyebrows and ears. As he carried on talking, Oscar felt chilled by his words. 'Men, women, children, who had all been hiding from an angry mob. This mob had burned down their houses to kill them just because they were Jews. Back in those days the castle was made of wood, not stone, and rather than be killed at the hands of the mob and sword-wielding knights who were coming for them, the poor Jews decided to set the castle, and so themselves, on fire. They all perished in the flames.'

'My goodness,' gasped Oscar's mum.

Dorian Deadwater waited a moment. He was soaked. His eyes were still staring at Oscar. The kind of sad, lost eyes that belong at funerals.

'Every so often at around about this time in the evening, people can still hear the screams of those poor trapped souls, burning alive...'

Oscar listened. He couldn't hear anything but the softening rain and distant traffic. Neither could his parents.

The rain got heavier. Oscar's mum offered Dorian the York Minster umbrella she was holding. He smiled, a soft sadness shining in his eyes, and took the umbrella. 'You are kind. But don't be too kind. It can kill you in this city. Kindness.'

They carried on walking around the old city, feeling a bit worried and confused by what Dorian was talking about. Then they came to a place called St William's College. They walked along its pathways, as Dorian talked about how many locals never went there because of a wailing ghost. The wailing ghost was a murderer.

'He and his brother killed and robbed a priest over five hundred years ago,' said Dorian, who was now shivering with cold from his wet clothes. 'And the younger brother felt guilty for their crime and wanted to confess. So the older brother went to the authorities and said his younger brother had committed the crime. The younger brother was hanged.'

'So, it's the younger brother who's the ghost?' asked Oscar.

'No. The older brother.' Dorian sighed with the cool sadness of a winter's breeze. 'Guilt creates more ghosts than anger ever can. So every night he walks these pathways, moaning...'

Oscar watched as Dorian pretended to see someone again, his eyes moving slowly as if to follow the ghost's walk. 'Can you see him? There. There in the dark.'

'I can't,' said Oscar's dad.

'Neither can I,' said his mum.

'Nor me,' said Oscar.

MATT HAIG

On the way to the next place, which Oscar hoped –
out of boredom rather than fear – would be the last, he
decided to ask the guide another question.

'Is Dorian Deadwater your real name?'

The man smiled for the first time all evening. 'No.'

'What is it then?'

His mum tutted. 'Oscar, don't be cheeky.'

'I'm just interested,' Oscar said, knowing that if
Dorian's name was fake then everything else was likely
to be fake too.

'My real name's Stephen. Stephen Holt.'

The laugh that Oscar had banned himself from
having now broke free into the night air.

'I know,' said Dorian – or Stephen, rather. 'Not very
scary. That's why I changed it.'

'So how did you get interested in ghosts?'

'I don't know,' he said solemnly. 'It was just a job I
suppose. I didn't believe at first. Not until...'

'You saw one yourself?' asked Oscar, sensing this
was part of the act.

'Yeah, something like that.' Then he suddenly seemed
alert. 'You see, life and death are really just two islands
very far apart. And there's a whole sea of nothingness in
between. And it's a vast sea, full of souls who aren't dead
or alive. They're neither one thing nor another.'

This time it was Oscar's dad who laughed. 'Or
Whip-Ma-Whop-Ma-Gate, as the Vikings would say.'
But his laugh soon died under the guide's serious stare.

'Yes,' said Stephen, still looking soaked even though he had now been sheltering with the umbrella for over half an hour.

The tour kept going, and at each stop a very spooky ghost was described but never seen.

At All Saints' Church, Oscar strained his eyes until they hurt looking for a girl his own age who had died but never had a proper burial.

'She wanders around,' said Stephen sadly, 'looking for her own grave, but she can never find it because it isn't there. She was a friend of Polly Mae – the girl on the river. They died within a week of each other.'

And even Oscar was a little creeped out when Stephen stared over to the far end of the graveyard and the yew trees that blew in the wind.

Oscar's mum saw Stephen shivering. 'You're still wet. I feel guilty, you having to do this tour when there are only three of us.'

'Don't worry,' Stephen said, smiling softly. 'I enjoy it. It's like being with friends.'

And when he said this, neither Oscar nor his parents knew if Stephen was speaking about his friends being *them* or the *ghosts* he was pretending to see. Either way it made Oscar shiver from more than just the cold.

They went to more places. To a medieval manor house where one of Henry VIII's wives is meant to float about. To a street called Goodramgate where a man called Thomas Percy apparently walks around with his head under his arm. His head had been chopped off at the orders of Elizabeth I because he'd tried to start a rebellion.

'I can't see him,' said Oscar, as the wind picked up, the cold, harsh air scrubbing against his face.

'I can,' said Stephen, sadly. 'His head always whispers...'

Oscar shook his own head. For a moment he had been starting to believe, but this was getting silly. Yet then, just at that moment of doubt, he heard something.

'*There is a life after death.*'

It was very quiet but Oscar felt cool breath next to his ear. Breath which felt different and closer than the wind. And then Stephen finished the sentence he was halfway through, '"...there is a life after death". That's what he says.' And Stephen was staring straight into Oscar's eyes, with a kind of knowing stare.

'Dad, Mum, did you hear that?'

'Hear what?' they asked together.

Oscar looked around, saw no sign of a man carrying a head under his arm, and realised his old English teacher, Mrs Gooding, had been right. He really did have an over-active imagination.

'You have been kind, keeping me company,' said Stephen, from somewhere. 'It gets very lonely sometimes.'

Then they heard wet footsteps, fading. They turned to see Stephen Holt walking away, his long sweeping coat disappearing out of view as he turned a corner.

'Wait! Where are you going?' Oscar's dad asked, starting to run after him. 'We haven't settled yet. We haven't paid you.'

Oscar and his mum jogged towards Dad, wondering why he was just standing at the corner, looking confused.

'Dad?'

'It's impossible.'

Oscar was there now, so he could see it too. Or rather, *not* see it. It was just a long narrow street with cobbles shining from the rain. Stephen was nowhere to be seen.

'Stephen?' called Oscar's dad. 'We owe you money.'

'And you've got my new umbrella,' whispered Oscar's mum.

But there came no reply. Just the rise and fall of a distant ambulance siren.

'Guess it's time to go back,' said Oscar's mum.

The next morning, over a hotel breakfast of Crunchy Nut Cornflakes (out of those little boxes that only seem to exist in hotels), Oscar's dad said, 'I feel really bad about not settling with Stephen yesterday. Perhaps he heard my joke about him not being worth paying.'

'But the walk was pretty rubbish,' said Oscar, 'we didn't see any ghosts and then he ran off.'

Of course, Oscar heard a ghost, but he had now convinced himself he'd just *thought* he'd heard a ghost. Which was a big difference. And, anyway, he knew how his mum and dad didn't have very much money these days, and he didn't want them to have to waste it on a silly walk in the dark.

'That's not the point,' his dad went on, talking with his mouth full as always. 'The point is it cost thirteen pounds last night, so we should have paid thirteen pounds. Money might not exactly grow on trees any more, but we've still got our principles, Oscar. That's the main thing.'

Oscar didn't argue.

'We should go to the tourist office,' his dad continued, chewing on a piece of toast and Marmite. 'I bet they organise it.'

His mum nodded, 'And I might be able to get my new umbrella back. It was a nice one. And not cheap. That cost almost as much as the ghost tour. In fact, I think it was the same price. How strange.'

The tourist office was bright and modern, full of lots of shiny leaflets about York Minster and the Jorvik Viking Centre and fun-looking theatre shows.

There were two members of staff behind the desk. An old, grumpy-looking man eating an apple and tapping away on his computer. And a younger, happier-looking woman who was chatting to two equally friendly looking Japanese women.

Oscar and his family waited. And at least they knew they'd come to the right place. Because there on the wall behind the desk was a large photograph of a man with a pointy little beard and glasses, with sad eyes. Underneath the photo it said: *York's Legendary Ghost Walker, Dorian Deadwater*.

Five minutes later it was their turn to see the woman behind the desk.

'Oh hello there,' said Oscar's dad, 'we're here because we need to pay for something. It's a bit embarrassing, really, but we went on the ghost walk last night and we never paid the man his money for the tour.'

'And he went off with my new umbrella,' added Oscar's mum.

The woman was looking cross or confused. 'What tour?'

'Sorry?' said Oscar's dad. 'The ghost tour. I mean, walk. Whatever it's called.'

Then, to make himself even clearer, he pointed at the framed poster on the wall. 'With him. "Dorian Deadwater." Or Stephen, rather.'

This time the woman looked perfectly blank. 'There isn't a ghost walk as far as I know. I'm sorry.'

'But that's ridiculous, of course there is. We were on it last night. With Dorian ... I mean, Stephen ... Stephen Holt. That was his real name. He was soaked, poor man.'

And at the sound of the name 'Holt', there was a

sudden gasp from the other person behind the desk. The man, who had finished eating his apple.

Even though they were in the middle of a warm, bright, colourful tourist office, Oscar felt himself go colder than he'd felt at any point the night before.

'I'm sorry,' said the man, standing up and looking suddenly very pale, 'I think you've made a mistake.'

'But we couldn't have,' said Oscar's mum, laughing at the ridiculousness of the situation. 'Look, you advertise the ghost walk right here on your wall.'

'That's not an advert,' the man said. 'It's a mark of remembrance.'

Oscar's dad looked confused. 'What are you talking about?'

'We keep it here to remember Stephen. He died ten years ago next January. It had been a ... The river had frozen over... And he'd walked out onto it, for some strange reason. No-one knows why... It wasn't like Stephen. He was a very sensible person. A good person. And he loved doing the ghost walk.' The man stared at the picture on the wall. 'But once he died, we stopped it. No one could do it like him.'

Things from last night flooded Oscar's brain.

The out-of-date guidebook.

The way Dorian was dripping wet, even with the umbrella, and then when the rain stopped he was unable to dry off.

Neither one thing nor another...

The story of Polly Mae. The girl who appeared on the river, asking to be saved. *It can kill you in this city. Kindness.*

'Yes,' the man was saying, shaking his head with an infinite sadness. 'He would have helped anyone. He's buried in the graveyard at All Saints.'

'Right,' said Oscar's dad, his voice wavering. 'Thank you.'

Outside the tourist office, Oscar and his parents stared at each other, speechless.

'We should go and look,' said Oscar, half-surprised by the courage of the words that had come from his mouth. 'That was the graveyard we were in yesterday.'

'I don't know,' said Oscar's mum. 'I think I'm in shock.'

'Yes,' said Oscar's dad. 'I know the feeling. But if we don't find out the truth there's going to be a big doubt buzzing around our heads. The kind of doubt that keeps you awake at three in the morning. Let's get to the bottom of this.'

They found their way back to the graveyard and walked through it on the thin, withered Tarmac path, checking headstones as they went.

Then: 'Oh my God,' cried Oscar's mum suddenly. 'It can't be.'

'What can't be?' asked Oscar's dad.

'The umbrella.' Oscar's mum was looking deathly pale as she raised her hand towards a gravestone. And she was right. There, leaning against the grave, was the York Minster umbrella she had lent Stephen Holt.

'How did that get there?' she asked, scared of an answer.

Oscar read the inscription on the gravestone as fear crept like a shadow over him.

IN LOVING MEMORY

STEPHEN HOLT
1960–2002

Drowned on 4th January
in the River Ouse.

YOU WILL LIVE FOR EVER
IN OUR HEARTS

'Right,' said Oscar's dad, his voice sounding weaker than normal. 'Let's, erm, take the umbrella and go home.'

And as they walked out of the graveyard, mute with shock, Oscar realised that he wouldn't be the slightest bit scared of his new school.

'Well,' said his mum, eventually finding the comfort of words. 'I think we'll save up and go on a beach holiday next year.'

They all agreed it sounded like a very good idea.

THE GHOST
WOOD

Philip Reeve

THE GHOST
WOOD

It was the last day of Will's holiday, and although the sun was shining and the moor was his favourite place in the world, everything was made sad by the weight of knowing that tomorrow there would be the long drive home, the shops and houses squeezing in closer and closer on each side of the busy roads, the sky getting tangled and trapped behind nets of wires and overhead cables. On the last day of the holiday, he thought, you had to look harder at everything; listen carefully to all the sounds, and breathe in all the smells; try to fix the wild places in your memory so that they would last you through a whole year back in the town.

Maybe that was what made the wood feel so strange. Maybe he had looked too hard, or listened too intently. It was only a little, stunted tangle of low oaks which straggled for a mile or so along the hillside above a clattering river, but as soon as he stepped into its shadows, running ahead of Mum and Dad down the footpath from the rocks on the hilltop, he had thought, *I love this place*, because it looked like a place for elves and orcs and wonderful adventures. Now, exploring alone among the trees while Mum did a drawing and Dad sat studying the Ordnance Survey map, he was starting to wonder if 'love' was the right word for what he was feeling. He couldn't imagine ever saying, 'I love Poldavy Wood,' in the way he sometimes said, 'I love chocolate biscuits' or, 'I love Warhammer'; the wood was too old and strange and somehow serious for that.

Wreaths of mist were rising into the sunbeams from the wet moss which covered all the tree trunks and the rocks between them, and the shadows of the twisty branches reached down through the mist, and the dry leaves whispered, and everything shone with the wetness of the shower that had just passed. Beards of grey lichen trailed from the branches, brushing Will's face and catching at his hair as he ducked under them, climbing uphill towards the top of the wood. The cry of the river came clearly through the trees behind him. He'd got that phrase out of dad's guidebook: *the cry of the river*. And when you heard it like this, the sound muffled by trees and tugged about by the breeze, it *did* sound like voices calling. He thought how, if he was in a story, like *The Hobbit* or something, the river might have started speaking to him, telling him things. He even stopped and listened, to see if he could make out words, but if the water was talking to him it spoke in its own language, one that Will did not understand.

'Will,' called another voice, much closer.

Will started. Dad had come quietly through the wood while Will was daydreaming, and now he laughed and said, 'Sorry, Will, I didn't mean to make you jump. Mum's about ready. We'd better push on. Tea at the pub tonight?'

'Yeah,' said Will, trying to look keen. He *was* keen; he liked eating at the pub. It was something they always did on the Friday of these autumn half-term holidays, and he liked the food and the feeling of being allowed into that secret grown-up place, the smell of the wood fires and the burr in the voices of the old farmers who sat at the bar. But thinking about it now reminded him that this was the last day of the holiday and that he wouldn't see real hills for another whole year.

Dad had been reading the guidebook. He said, 'Seems this was once part of the forests that covered the whole moor back in the old days. The whole of England, probably.'

'When was that? In Roman times?'

'Oh, long before the Romans. There are only a couple of scraps of the old wildwood left now, and this is the largest. It's meant to be haunted, of course. They say the devil kennels his hounds under the boulders.'

Will looked about. Beneath their thick, shaggy coats of moss the boulders themselves looked like sleeping beasts, and the steam that rose from them where the warm sun touched was their hot breath. The trees crouched over them, watching, waiting. It wasn't hard to see why people had believed this place was haunted, Will thought, and he shivered.

'Come on,' said Dad, starting downhill, arms stretched wide to help him balance as he stepped from rock to rock.

'Coming,' said Will, with a last, long look into the green shadows under the trees and all the secret corners of the wood that he might never get to explore.

Nearby a tree had fallen; brought down perhaps by the sheer weight of moss and lichen that had gathered on its branches. Its ragged roots stuck up into the air, with ferns still growing out of them, and little mushrooms shining wetly as the sun touched them. Down in the dark, peaty hollow where the tree had stood, something else gleamed too, and Will crouched down and tugged it from the soft earth. It was a smooth, dark stone; a river stone; small, but heavy in his hand. At one end there was a hole, and Will thought at once that if you threaded a string through it you could wear it around your neck, although the hole was smooth-edged and natural-looking, not like something anyone had bored.

How had it come there, he wondered, so far up the hill from the river? Surely someone must have put it there, back before the tree grew, however long ago that was. Or perhaps an animal. His friend Jon's dog carried stones about in her mouth when she went to the beach sometimes.

'Will!' called Dad, way down through the wood.

'Will!' called Mum.

He slipped the stone into his pocket for a keepsake and hurried after them.

That night in his room under the low, slanting roof of the holiday cottage Will's dreams were filled with creaks and rustlings, with wordless whispers and the soft, small trickling of water. He dreamed of a smell he could not name; a wet earth smell, and a mushroom smell, and some other smell mixed in with it that was familiar but strange at the same time. Something moved on the landing outside his door. He woke, and he could feel it there; something big and motionless and quiet. He lay very still, listening, trying to filter out all the noises that he knew were just the noises of his own body, his heartbeat, and the whoosh of his blood through his veins. He listened, and he heard something scratch at the door. The door handle made a clunking sound, but that was just the weight of the thing outside pressing against the door and making it move slightly; the thing outside didn't know how to turn the handle;

all it could do was reach out its thick, heavy claws and run them down the wood of the door: *scratch, scratch, scratch*.

'Mum!' shouted Will, throwing off the duvet and scrambling upright on the bed...

...and there was sunlight coming in around the edges of the curtain, and Mum opening the door and smiling at him, saying, 'Will, whatever's wrong? Was it a nightmare? You've been asleep for ages. That hike up to the wood yesterday must have worn you out. Come and have breakfast. Dad's packing the car.'

Only a dream. When she had gone back downstairs Will went on to the landing and looked at the outside of his bedroom door, half expecting to see it covered in claw marks, but the thick, shiny paint was undamaged, and a smell of toast was wafting up the stairs.

And then, as if by magic, they were home. Well, not really by magic; it wasn't a question of snapping their fingers and saying some Harry Potter spell; just four hours in the car while Mum and Dad complained about the traffic and Will leafed through magazines and stared at the backs of their heads. But it felt like magic, to be home again; houses on the skyline instead of hedges, the town still there just as they had left it, the steady roar of the traffic on the main road. There were no trees here unless you counted the little clumps of spindly looking birches that had been planted outside the entrance to the supermarket, and Will thought those were worse than no trees at all.

The house was just as they had left it too, though it seemed bigger than usual after the tiny holiday cottage. As Will stepped over the threshold he caught for a moment the odd, comforting smell of home; the Mum-and-Dad-and-Will smell which he only ever noticed when he'd been away. In another minute or so he would stop noticing it, and then he would know the holiday was over.

'A nice quiet day tomorrow,' said Mum, bringing some bags in, 'and back to school on Monday.'

Will went up to his room with his rucksack. There were all his things; his models and books; his Lego space hotel. He'd not exactly forgotten them while he was away, but he had not thought about them, and now it was good to be reminded of them, and to pick them up and look at them again as if they were new. He emptied out his rucksack. He took the special models which had had to go on holiday with him out of the egg box they'd travelled in and set them carefully back on the shelf beside the others. He took his dirty socks and pants and shirts to the laundry basket in the bathroom. At the bottom of one of the pockets of the rucksack he found the stone. He'd put it there the previous night, when he was changing out of his wet walking trousers ready to go to the pub. It did not look half so interesting now that it was dry, but it was still a treasure; a little

PHILIP REEVE

piece of Poldavy Wood come home with him. If you pretended that the hole near one end was an eye then you could imagine the stone was an animal. It had a swift, leaping look; a wolf or a dog running fast with its tail stretched out straight behind. He set it on the bookcase beside his bed, next to his half an ammonite and his maybe-a-dinosaur's tooth, and went downstairs to see what was for tea.

That night, again, he dreamed noises.

His bedroom at home was different from the one in the holiday cottage. It was full of noises most nights, anyway. They were town noises: the sound of the cars on the busy main road three streets away, and other cars, closer, driving at all hours up the quiet side streets; car doors slamming; people's voices; far-off sirens; bursts of laughter; the sullen throb of music turned up way too loud in someone else's house. But that night, in that dream-that-was-not-quite-a-dream, Will could hear none of those things. Instead his room was filled with the deep, undersea sounds of a wood at night; the slow creak and rub of branches, the dry rustle of leaves. The room was very dark. He waited for a car to pass, because the glow of the headlamps as they swept around the angles of walls and ceiling was comforting, but no cars came, and slowly, as he lay there, he started to realise that the light coming in through his curtains was not the yellow glow of the streetlamp on the corner

274

but snail-silver moonlight, and where a stripe of it lay slantwise down the wall beside the window it was crisscrossed with the shadows of twigs and branches.

And then he thought that he could not be awake but must have only dreamed of waking, because there was no moon that night, and there were no trees anywhere near his house.

Dreaming or not, he slid out from under his duvet and went to the window. He twitched aside the curtain and peeped through. The twigs of a tree were brushing against his windowpane like little fingers, making faint, glassy squeaking sounds; winter twigs, holding up a few old papery leaves like tattered trophies. He could tell from the shape of the leaves that it was an oak tree. It was not one of the little, wind-writhen, goblinish oaks of Poldavy Wood, but a tall, strong, sturdy, forest tree, and through the gaps between its branches he saw more like it. They crowded close all round his house, creaking and whispering, shifting and rustling. A wood far bigger than Poldavy stretched away and away from him under the moon – a forest that had filled his road and engulfed all the neighbours' houses. The steep streets beyond the main road were wooded hills now, hummocks rising from a dark and scratchy sea of autumn branches; a sea of trees. Far away the town centre, office blocks poked up through the oak tops, their plate-glass windows burnished by the moon, looking like the sort of towers where princesses got imprisoned in fairy tales.

A movement made him glance down towards the ground. It was mostly hidden by a fretwork of shadows, but here and there he could see a patch of moonlit pavement, and across one of these patches something big and black slid suddenly; too fast to see a shape or to know what it was, just an impression of size and loping movement and then, for a heartbeat, the moonlight catching pale in two eyes as it looked up at Will's window. As it looked up at Will.

He jumped back, and the curtain fell with a swish. He sat on his bed and listened to the twigs scraping their little fingers over the windows and the wind hissing through the tree tops, and under it all he thought he heard the sounds of something padding round the house. *It's all right*, he told himself, *it can't get in; it can't possibly get in*. But then, there couldn't possibly be a forest outside, either, and there was; he could see the dim silhouettes of the swaying branches through his curtain. And now into his room crept that smell that he had smelled the night before; that wet earth and mushrooms smell, and the other smell mixed in with it, and he knew that the black thing had come into his house. He heard its snuffling breath outside his door. He sensed the door give slightly as a big weight pushed softly against it, and then, as he had known he would, he heard the long, slow, almost thoughtful scrape of claws.

He opened his mouth. He drew in a deep breath, and was about to let it out again as a shout when suddenly from somewhere outside the house there came the familiar warbling of a car alarm, and then, as if God had thrown a switch to turn the everyday world back on, the other sounds came flooding in; traffic on the main road, the rattle of a train on the viaduct. Yellow streetlamp light showed through the fabric of the curtain. He let out the breath as a long, shaky sigh and cautiously, cautiously, opened the door.

The smell of wet earth and rotted wood and some big animal hung in the air of the landing, but it was fading quickly, and soon it was only a memory.

The next morning, after breakfast, Will took the Poldavy Wood stone and went outside with it. He peered at the road and the pavements, looking for cracks which roots might have made; fallen leaves, dead twigs, dropped acorns. There was nothing.

He'd planned to leave the stone in a gutter, or drop it down the drain, but it seemed wrong somehow, so in the end he crossed the road to where the houses were older and set back behind gardens, and stuffed it in among the roots of someone's hedge. It ought to be among earth and growing things, that stone, he thought. It seemed to look up at him reproachfully with its empty eye, so he hid it under dead leaves and other stones and walked quickly away.

Later, on Dad's laptop, he scrolled through the ghost sites; back and forth, back and forth, the words rising up the screen like smoke, sliding down like rain on a window; *ghosttracker.com*, *spookseeker.com*, *famous hauntings.co.uk*. Hundreds of 'True Ghost Stories' which even Will could tell weren't really true. Stories of haunted inns and phantom airmen, friendly ghosts and deadly ones.

'What are you looking at, Will?' his Mum asked.

'Ghosts, Mum. It's for school.'

'More homework? You never said.'

'I forgot.'

She came and looked critically over his shoulder at *www.apparition.com*. 'Headless horsemen and ghostly nuns? I hope you don't believe any of this stuff, Will.'

'Course not,' said Will. And he didn't. There was nothing on any of these sites about the ghosts of trees; nothing about someone being haunted by the ghost of a whole forest. For a moment he thought he would tell her about what he had seen and heard in the night, but it would have sounded silly there in the daylight, with Radio Two blaring in the kitchen.

'Well, don't give yourself nightmares,' said Mum, and left him to it. He typed *Poldavy Wood* into the search engine of *greatbritishghosts.com*. Up came a picture of those familiar twisty trees under a stormy sky. The text retold the same legend Will already knew from Dad's guidebook, about the Devil kennelling his pack of haunted hounds beneath the boulders in the wood. Underneath that it said, *Black Dogs have been seen on the old funeral path which passes through the western corner of the wood.* 'Black Dogs' was a link, and by clicking on it Will found his way to another part of the site, where a whole list of stories about ghostly black dogs had been gathered.

He closed the site and shut down the computer. He felt cold, and had the uneasy sense that someone was watching him, although Mum was clattering about in the kitchen and Dad was outside washing moorland mud off the car. And when he checked behind him there was nothing there. He thought of the dog-shaped stone, and of the black creature he had seen cross that patch of moonlight, slipping between the phantom trees. Black dogs; the Devil's hunting hounds; harbingers of death. He shivered; told himself not to be so silly. It was a dream, that was all, and if it wasn't, well, he'd got rid of that stone, hadn't he? Poldavy Wood could not haunt him any more.

But that night when he woke he knew at once that the trees were back. The silver moonlight lay upon his wall; the twig-tips muttered at the glass. The damp-earth smell was in the room again, and as he lay there he slowly became aware that there was a great, warm weight on his bed; something was pressing down on his feet the way a well-filled stocking did on Christmas morning, only this was not Christmas morning, and Will knew that this something was alive. He could hear its breath; the soft, snuffling, steady breath of something awake and waiting.

Moving nothing but his eyes, he saw that the door stood ajar. Between his bed and the door a stripe of moonlight lay across the carpet, and in the moonlight, smooth and familiar and glistening wet, lay the dog-shaped stone he had taken from Poldavy Wood.

He lifted his head just a millimetre off the pillow, waiting to see what the thing on his bed would do. It did nothing. He peeked over the edge of the duvet and saw a darkness there. The smell was very powerful, and he knew now that it was an animal smell; Jon's dog smelled like that sometimes, when she had been for a long walk and rolled herself about in wet earth and badger poo and stuff. He stared at the thing, and the thing raised its head and stared back at him, and moonlight reflected palely from its eyes and two black ears pricked up, pointy as cartoon tents against the grainy greyness of the dark behind it.

It's a dog, he thought. And he knew that it was not some stray that had crept in out of the streets; it wasn't an ordinary sort of dog at all, any more than Poldavy Wood was an ordinary sort of wood. It was as old and strange as those ancient trees; a dog from a time when dogs had only just stopped being wolves.

He did not know how long he lay there, stone still, looking at it, while it looked back at him. His neck started to ache. His heartbeat pounded so loudly in his ears that he was sure the dog must hear it too. He wanted to shout for Mum and Dad, but he was afraid that if he made a sound the thing would spring at him. An animal so big, so heavy, think of the power it would have in its jaws! Think of its teeth!

But all it did was watch him. Then something thick and weighty slapped his feet through the duvet, and slapped them again, and again, and he heard the sound it made, a soft shushing beat against the duvet cover, and he realised that the black dog was wagging its tail.

A dog wouldn't do that if it was about to attack. He remembered dogs in books and films. Its tail would go down. And its ears wouldn't keep sticking up like that, either; they'd lie back flat, and it would growl.

Slowly, slowly, he drew one hand out from under the duvet and reached towards the waiting thing. After a moment he felt a cool, wet nose go snuffling over his fingers; and after another, like the swipe of a warm flannel, a long, wet tongue started to lick his hand.

'Good boy,' he said, in the tiniest of whispers, not so much scared of the dog now as scared that his parents would hear him and come and take the dog away. Mum and Dad had always said they couldn't have a dog; that it wouldn't be fair to keep a dog in the town, in a house with no garden, where everyone was out at work or school all day. 'Good dog,' he whispered, and it moved its head in the darkness and his hand went smoothing over the big, knobbly dome of its head, over the soft fur.

Carefully he slid his feet out from under the warm bulk of it and swung them off the bed and sat up. The dog climbed down with a big, soft sound and padded to where the stone lay in the bar of moonlight. It picked up the stone in its mouth and turned back and pushed it, all wet with dog slobber, into Will's hand. Then it turned again, shoved the door open with its head and went out onto the landing. There it stood waiting for him, its tail wagging so hard that Will felt sure the *swoosh swoosh swoosh* of it would wake his parents.

He slid his bare feet into trainers, tugged on a hoodie over his pyjama top. 'It's all right,' he whispered, 'I'm coming.'

On the way downstairs the uneasy thought came to him that maybe the dog was only pretending to be friendly; maybe it was just luring him outside to do him harm. But the warm tongue that rasped at his hand while he unlocked the front door did not feel like the tongue of a creature with secrets to hide, or an appetite for eleven-year-old boys. He opened the door and they stood there for a moment together on the step while the damp smells of the wood came into the house. Then Will drew back his hand and threw the stone, and the dog brushed past his legs like a soft wind, bounding out after it into the street; into the forest.

Will followed it. All around him the ghostly trees towered, and above his head they spread their branches, and everywhere there was the same watchful, waiting feeling that he had sensed that day in Poldavy Wood. Dead leaves lay heaped knee-deep between the knobbly roots, crackling and crunching like drifts of cornflakes as the dog bounded through them; but they were only the ghosts of leaves; as he went kicking after the dog Will looked down and saw the pavement showing faintly through them. The huge roots had not cracked the Tarmac or pushed the paving slabs aside.

The dog found its stone and brought it back to Will, and Will threw it again and they went on, further down the street, deeper into the forest. Now he could see that some of the moss-furry boulders which lay between the trees were not boulders at all but his neighbours' cars. Streetlamps shone dimly, twined with ivy and crowned with long, grey, trailing wigs of lichen. There was lichen too on the house fronts, which rose like dark rock faces behind the branches; lichen hanging from the gutterings; moss thick as green carpet on their walls and roofs, small trees sprouting from caves and window ledges. Will turned a corner and then another, and the huge dog sometimes trotted beside him and sometimes ran on ahead, and he thought, *How could anyone ever have been scared of him? He only wants to play.* The dog wasn't even black, not when you really looked at it; just a deep, deep grey, like dark smoke, and transparent like smoke sometimes too.

A sound came through the trees ahead; a steady rushing, a soft roaring that was almost like a voice.

The ghost-dog stopped and pricked up its ears. At first Will thought it was the river that they could hear, but any rivers that ran through the town had long ago been buried in tunnels and sewers. It was the main road, still busy with traffic, and as he drew nearer to it he could see it faintly, a smear of moving light between the trees. If he looked hard he could make out the faint, vague shapes of the passing vehicles. He paused a moment, watching, while the dog snuffled about finding fascinating scents among the leaf litter. Then, taking a deep breath, he stepped out into the stream of light.

He half expected horns to blare and brakes to squeal, but the cars kept moving, the tired, frowning faces of their drivers visible behind the windscreens like the faces of ghosts. He held out his arm and watched a bus pass through it as if his hand, or the bus, were made of light. The dog looked up at him, curious, tail swinging from side to side, waiting to see what they would do next. And Will laughed, thinking of all those poor, silly drivers hurtling along the road under the blinking glare of the streetlamps with no idea that he and the dog and the forest were here. This wasn't a dream or, if it was, it was not his dream. Maybe beneath the road, down under all the concrete and clutter that people had spread over it, the land itself was dreaming of the days when it was still all forest; when a squirrel could run from branch to branch all the way from here to the furthest tip of Cornwall and never have to touch the ground.

The dog barked; it was tired of waiting for him. Will found a stick and flung it, and together they went haring, leaping, bounding, tumbling through the ghostly trees until Will was tired out from running and laughing, and so far from his house that only the dog, with its clever nose, could find their way home.

'There's a peculiar smell in Will's room,' said Mum at breakfast.

'That's Will,' said Dad. 'Will's trainers, anyway.'

'Sort of a musty, earthy smell...It's quite nice, really. So it can't be Will's trainers.'

'Damp, probably,' said Dad, who was getting ready to go to work and wasn't really listening. 'Have to get it looked at.'

'I like it,' said Will.

'Come on, you,' said Mum. 'School.'

He ran upstairs to find his book bag. Mum had opened the window to air the room. The dog-stone lay on his bedside table. Outside, the houses were all themselves again; there was no trace of the trees. There was no trace of tiredness in Will's body, either; he felt as refreshed as if he'd slept a good night's sleep instead of running through a ghost-wood with a ghost-dog. Maybe, when he was in the wood, he became a sort of ghost too...

Mum called him again. He could not see the dog, but he sensed it was close, so he said, 'I'll see you later, dog,' before he swung his bag onto his shoulder and hurried downstairs and out into the street; the ordinary, boring, treeless street. He didn't mind it now. He had a feeling that that night, and the next night, and on all the nights from now on, his black dog would come and wake him.

The dog watched Will go. It heard the front door slam behind him. It lay among the roots of the trees which had grown ten thousand years ago on the ground where Will's house stood; the trees which grew there still, if you knew how to see them. The dog was happy. Once, long ago, there had been a boy in the wood who had played with it, a boy at whose side it had slept by some leaping campfire in lost autumns. The boy had loved it; and it had loved the boy. The two of them had been among the very first to sense that special bond that exists between boys and dogs. It was the boy who had found that dark river stone and had worn it around his neck because its shape made him think of the shape of the dog. Perhaps some of his love for the dog had got into the stone, seeped into it somehow along with his sweat and the scent of his skin. Perhaps that was why the dog had remained, long after the boy had gone beneath the ground. Alone it had waited, sleeping mostly, while centuries fell past it like dead leaves.

Sometimes, hearing people coming near the wood, it had roused itself and gone to greet them and been confused and saddened when they did not want to play. Most of them had not even seen the dog; the ones who did had run and not come back.

Now, at last, there was a new boy. He had found the stone. He understood. The dog would stay with him until he was too grown-up to run and play and laugh, and then perhaps he would pass the stone onto another boy, and another...

The dog closed its eyes and tucked its nose under its tail, and dozed, waiting for its boy to come home; waiting for the friendly dark, when they would run again together through the long dream of the woods.

THE LITTLE SHIP'S BOY

Berlie Doherty

THE LITTLE
SHIP'S BOY

Jez was spending the school holidays at his Uncle Jack's cottage in Cornwall. He and Auntie May lived right by the sea, not far from Cape Cornwall, which is the most westerly point of England. The cottage was near the edge of the cliff, and looked right out to sea. He could always see it. Sometimes the waves were so high that they towered right up to the top of the cliff, and sometimes they were so calm that the sea stretched out to the horizon like a sheet of gleaming silk. Jez could always hear the sea, day and night, when he was in the cottage. Even though the granite walls were four feet thick, he could hear it. And every morning he woke to the sound of gulls, heckling each other or pouring out their sobbing cries.

One night when Jez was in bed a hectic storm blew up. The wind was so violent that it made the windows rattle like loose bones, and the rain scratched and hissed against the panes as if a wild animal was out there, desperate to fight its way in. Jez pulled the covers up over his head, but still he could hear it. The wind tore and wrenched against the cottage as though it would pull it up by its roots and toss it over the cliff into the waves of the Atlantic Ocean. There would be nowhere for it to touch land again until it reached America. And through all the roaring, the spattering and howling, he could hear a voice, low and moaning, a voice of utter despair; and it seemed to be the voice of a child.

He clambered out of bed and ran to the window, sure that the child would be standing just outside the cottage, wet to his very bones, and with his hair streaming like seaweed around him, desperate to be let in to be warm and dry and safe. But there was nothing to see out there, only blackness; black sky, black rocks, black sea. Yet, as he watched, he felt sure he could see a light, hiding and winking as if the moon had fallen into the sea and was being flung this way and that by the waves. It seemed to be behind the craggy rocks that were known as the Brisons. It must be a fishing boat, he thought. The fishermen must be having a very bad time of it in this storm.

Jez tried to open his window, but the squall of rain flung itself in at him as though the sea itself was breaking through, and he had to struggle to shut it again without it slamming and breaking. He climbed back into his bed, and still he heard the voice, moaning, moaning. He daren't close his eyes, he daren't move in his bed, but lay there rigid, listening with every bit of himself to the voices of the wind, the rain, the sea; and a lost child.

But he must have gone to sleep eventually. When he woke up the sea was still and blue, the day was calm and newly washed. Auntie May had gone into Penzance on the early bus to spend a couple of days with her sister, so only Uncle Jack was in the cottage, tuning his violin. He was a fisherman, but sometimes he helped Old Sammy on the farm next door. When he wasn't out on the boat or in Sammy's fields, he played fiddle in a local band. He always seemed to have a tune in his head. He was forever whistling, or tapping his feet, or jigging his fingers across the table top.

'Will you just stop it now?' his wife sometimes said. 'You're worse than a cat with fleas!' And sometimes she smiled and did a few prancing steps herself, like a little girl, and said, 'Play me that new tune of yours, Jack. It'll make me merry.'

'Well, and how did you sleep?' Uncle Jack asked, when Jez went down for breakfast. 'Not a wink, I'll bet!'

'I think I did, in the end. But the storm kept me awake most of the night,' said Jez. 'And I felt sure someone was outside my window, crying to come in.

But I couldn't see anyone.'

'You heard the fog warning from the lighthouse at Wolf Rock, most like. I call her Moaning Minnie. She gives a howl every thirty seconds, but you don't always hear her, of course. Sometimes she carries on for days on end, till you could pull your ears off. Look, there she is, out there.' He led Jez to the window and pointed to the far horizon. Jez could just make out a smudge. It could have been a boat, or a rock, or a whale, for all he could tell.

'Wouldn't believe there's a helicopter pad on top of it, would you? There's wicked rocks round this coast, and on nights like last night, when the visibility is so bad, you hear the Wolf Rock lighthouse moaning out a warning to keep the ships away. If they come in too near, they'd be smashed to bits like the shell of an egg.'

'Have there been any shipwrecks round here?' Jez asked.

Jack laughed. He stretched up his arms so they nearly touched the low ceiling. 'Plenty. Hundreds, they reckon, round these coasts. Most have never been found again. Some of the sailors were rescued and, settled down to live here. And one of the boats haunts the seas, and has done for a hundred years or more.'

'Like a ghost ship?'

'I suppose it is. A ghost ship.'

'Have you ever seen it?' Jez asked nervously.

'Oh yes. Makes my bones go cold to think about it.

I've seen the name of it painted on the side. *Merandee*. It's only ever seen in times of fierce storms, and it seems to be searching for something. Glides out of the mist, glides away again. Oh, and some say they hear the voices of the ghost sailors singing. Why, you've gone so white, you look like a ghost yourself, boy. I can see right through you!'

He turned to the cooker and scraped some porridge out of a pan into Jez's bowl. 'Here, your aunt made you this before she went out. Looks like something Oliver Twist had to eat, but she tells me you like the stuff, coming from up north. I'm a herring man myself. But you get it down you, if you can, and perhaps you'll turn back into a living boy again.'

Jez sat at the table and ate slowly, doodling his spoon through the thick porridge. He couldn't get the thought of the shipwrecks out of his head.

'Could we go to see one, Uncle Jack?' he asked.

'Huh?' Jack was working out a new tune on his fiddle. Sometimes, when he was playing, his face was so tight with concentration he only half heard what anyone was saying to him. Jez took his grunt for a yes.

'Can we go now?'

Jack put his fiddle carefully into its cradle and loosened his bow. 'Go where?'

'To see one of the wrecks.'

'Well, there's a rusty iron hull of a Russian ship that was swept up a few years ago. What's left of it is high on the rocks near Land's End. We could chug down along Mayon cliff to see that, but *Mayfly's* motor's packed up and we'll have to wait till I can get a new battery. Too far to walk from here today. But we could take the van to Sennen and walk along the coast path from there to see it.'

Jez shook his head, disappointed. 'I mean an old wreck, a ship of long ago.'

Jack laughed at that. 'Oh, that's different. You'd have to turn into a fish or a seal to see one of those. There's nothing left of any of them, except deep under the sea and rotting on the bed. Tell you what; I'll take you out in the *Mayfly*, before high tide comes in. We can row out to the Brisons this morning; it's slack tide and running calm just now. I'll show you where many and many a ship has foundered on the rocks there. But we'll have to move fast, be turning back about one. Take a look out to the horizon. It's not a straight line, is it? Not today.'

Jez did what Jack did, rolling up his hands into a tube and peering through them as if they were a tele-scope. 'It looks as if there's land out there. Is it the Scillies?'

'No, too far over. Look again.'

'It's rocks. They look as if they're moving. Big rocks, moving.'

'Not rocks, Jez; but moving that's for sure. That's because the breakers out there are so high. Five miles out and yet we can see them. High as houses! It's a spring tide this week – because there's a full moon in a couple of nights, when she cares to show herself. That means the tides are very high. We've got three or four hours, and then I wouldn't trust my *Mayfly* anywhere near those Brisons, motor or no motor, and certainly not when I'm rowing. What kind of muscles you got?'

He squeezed the top of Jez's arm. 'Call them muscles? Look more like cockles to me. You eat too much of that soggy porridge, that's your trouble.'

Soon after breakfast Jez and Jack hurried down to the little cove where *Mayfly* was moored high on the slipway. A three-legged mongrel pattered after them. He belonged to a fisherman who was drowned months ago, Jack told Jez, and he still spent all day down in Priest's Cove waiting for his master to come home with the tide. Jack put some scraps out for him, then went up to one of the little sheds that were perched on the rocks above the cove. He rummaged through his lobster pots and creels, and drew out a pair of oars, which he handed to Jez. Then he slung a couple of life jackets over his arm.

Together they untied the rope that attached the *Mayfly* to a ring set in the slipway, and carried the boat down to the water. A mile out to sea, they could see the Brisons, which looked just like a man with a big nose and a huge belly lying on his back.

'Not going to be seasick, are you?' Jack asked.

'After that porridge stuff? Sea's a bit jumpy, even now. Always is just here in the cove.'

Jez shook his head, gazing at the wet chunks of rock around them, each with its ruff of lacy white foam. 'I'm never sick even on the biggest rides in the fairground.' Besides, he promised himself, he was too excited to be seasick.

Uncle Jack drove his oars into the water and headed off towards the Brisons. They towered above them, massive now, and dangerously jagged. Gulls screamed round the boat as if trying to frighten the humans away from their sanctuary. Seals slithered down from the rocks and sank like black shadows. Below them in the water Jez could see the points of more rocks, like the jagged black teeth of some sea monster.

'A bigger boat than mine would go down on those,' Jack had to shout over the noise of the sea birds. 'Nothing of any great size would want to come as near as this. But some boats have, blown in by high seas, or cheated by lights on shore, and they've come to grief here, and many a man drowned too. You can see, nothing lives here except gulls and seals.'

He swung the *Mayfly* away from the rocks. 'That's it now. Tide's coming in fast, and it's dangerous even for us to be here. I'll row back in on the tide, but I need to get away from these rocks as fast as I can or we'll just smash onto them.' He lifted his oars and swung the boat round. Jez leaned over the side, imagining he could see the masts and riggings of wrecked ships lying on the ocean bed far below him. And it was there, in the cream and swell of waves breaking against the rocks, that he saw the boy's face in the water.

'Stop!' he shouted to Jack. 'Stop! There's a boy in the water.'

It seemed that his uncle couldn't hear him. Jack set his face hard against the feathering spray and didn't turn his head, even when Jez crawled along to reach his uncle, pulling him by the arm to try to stop him.

'A boy in the water!' Jez shouted. 'You must stop. You must!'

Jack half turned his head, and turned away again. And it was then that Jez knew that his uncle *had* heard him, but that he had no intention of stopping.

'Please!' Jez screamed into the wind, but his uncle carried on rhythmically and grimly rowing so the boat bounced away from the rocks. He didn't pause until they had come back to the Priest's Cove slipway, where he eased the *Mayfly* gently home. Only when they were safely on land, and the boat hauled back to its mooring rope, did Jack look at Jez again.

'I didn't want you to see that,' he said. 'I didn't expect it today, not when it's as mild as this.'

'Why wouldn't you stop for him? We've got to get help!' Jez shouted, but even as he said it he knew it was too late. Surely nobody could still be alive in that water.

'You should have stopped,' he sobbed.

Jack strode off to his shed and threw the oars and life jackets inside, not bothering to lock the door. Then he turned back.

'Jez, you haven't seen a boy. Do you hear me? It's some spooked thing that happens now and again, but usually it's when there's a storm. That's what I've been told. I've never seen it myself. I didn't today. But you're not the first to see it.'

'I don't understand.'

'They say it's a drowned child. That's the tale some fishermen tell. Nobody knows who he was, or how he's there, or why. But it's not a real child, Jez. He's from long ago. It's a ghost.'

Jez was too upset to do anything much that day. Uncle Jack had been right about the weather. The early afternoon tide had brought the high waves in with it, though it wasn't stormy like it had been the night before. He wandered round his uncle's field at the back of the golf course, hunting in the grass for lost balls. His uncle told him he could keep them, so he spent a bit of time rolling them in the lane, like marbles, and then put them all in a bag. He ran to the clubhouse and gave them to a woman who was just setting off with her clubs for a round of golf. She was so pleased that she gave him a five-pound note for them. It should have cheered him up, but it didn't. What good is money, he thought, when there's a drowned boy out there? Drowned for ever. Why? And was he something to do with the ghost ship, *Merandee,* that Uncle Jack had mentioned? Nobody knew, apparently. Nobody wanted to know.

That night he went to bed quite late, thinking it might help him to sleep better. Whatever he heard, Jez decided, he wasn't going to look out of the window. He slept well at first, but in the early hours he was woken again by the sound of the night tide, and this time the storm had come back; the wind and the rain, and that haunting, crying voice. He couldn't help it – in spite of himself, he ran to the window and looked out.

The moon was completely covered by clouds. So there was nothing, nothing in all that howling blackness, except a strange glimmer of light coming and going behind the Brisons. Could it be a fishing boat again? But why was it moving like that, backwards and forward behind the rocks? And why was its light so dim and peculiar? He pulled the curtains firmly closed. Now, very faintly, he could hear voices singing, so far away that he could only just make out the words.

And the little ship's boy called Davey'o
He slid to the side and away did go
All into the grey sea down below
A-fallling into the ocean.

Jez switched on his bedroom light and went to get his iPod, thinking he would listen to some music to drown out everything that was going on outside. He rummaged in his drawer, and glanced up at the mirror on the top of the chest. And there he saw a white face; not his face at all; blank eyes, hair streaming with water.

He yelled and barged through his door onto the landing. Uncle Jack came stumbling out of his room opposite.

'What's the matter, Jez?'

'There's a face in my mirror!'

'Well, there would be!' Uncle Jack smiled, but Jez grabbed his arm and pushed him into the bedroom. His uncle looked in the glass, and turned back, still smiling. 'Well I know it's pretty ugly, and enough to give anyone a fright, but there's only my face there. Have a look, and you'll see yourself, like always.'

Nervous, Jez risked a glance and saw his own white face, his eyes wide with fright and his hair sticking up with the untidiness of sleep.

'All right?' Uncle Jack asked gently. 'Nothing more scary than your own mug, is there?'

Jez nodded. He was still dithering with fright. Uncle Jack took him to the kitchen and made him some cocoa and buttered toast, thick with marmalade.

'You had a fright this morning and it's given you nightmares, that's all,' he told Jez. 'How about if we swap rooms for tonight, as May's not here? It's a bit quieter at the back, though you might still hear Moaning Minnie. But there's no mirror, because my own face isn't worth looking at and May's not too keen on hers these days; and no sea to stare at, only fields. Off you go, and I'm sorry about my fishy socks hanging off the bedrail.'

Jez slept, but as soon as he woke up he remembered everything. He couldn't get the thought of the ghost of the drowned boy out of his mind. Had he imagined it, or was it real? Had he imagined the wet, white face in the mirror? Must he sleep in that room again, and wait for it to come back?

His uncle had a go at making him some porridge, but it wasn't very good, and he didn't feel like eating, anyway.

'I'm going into Newlyn to collect a new battery for the engine.' Uncle Jack scraped the burned porridge remains out of the pan. 'I'll go on to Penzance from there to bring May back home. I'll be gone a few hours. Coming for the ride?'

'Can I stay here?' Jez asked lightly. 'I could help Sammy on the farm, or look for more golf balls.'

'We'll eat out on your takings then. You'll be wealthy by the end of the week.'

It was a calm day, just as it had been the day before. Jez knew exactly what he wanted to do. He wanted to find the ghost boy again. He wanted to help him. He stood by the window with his hands cupped like a telescope, and looked out to the horizon. It was a bit bumpy, he thought, but not too bad. He calculated that the tide would be an hour later than it had been yesterday, so it would be at its height at about three. He was going to row out to the Brisons. It would take him at least twice as long to row out as it had taken Uncle Jack, who was right about his muscles. He might not manage to get that far, but he could always turn back again. He would take it slowly, and if he did make it as far as the Brisons, he would come back in on the tide, like Uncle Jack had done, and so the return trip would be much faster. He felt his stomach clenching with fear. He had to do it.

He waited impatiently till he heard the sound of the van pulling away, and then ran straight down to the cove. The three-legged dog was there, gazing out to sea. Jez gave him the scraps that he'd brought from the kitchen, and then ran to Uncle Jack's shed for the oars and the life jacket. He untied the mooring rope and pushed and pulled the *Mayfly* till he got her into the sea. That was such hard work that he felt sure he'd used up all his strength, but once he was out of the choppy little cove he found the sea calmer than it had been yesterday. Rowing was surprisingly easy, once he'd got into the rhythm of it. He kept glancing over his shoulder to make sure he was still heading for the Brisons. He didn't want to give himself any more work to do than he had to, by going off course. When his arms started to ache he shipped the oars and rested a bit. The sea was a peculiar olive-green, sparkling around him in the sunlight.

At last he was near enough for the final effort. There was no turning back. He knew he could make it now. He rowed with all his strength towards the rocks. As he drew near, gulls with huge grey wings flapped round him, their yellow beaks opened wide. Jez paused and shipped his oars again, letting the *Mayfly* drift slowly round in the slack water. He looked fearfully over the side of the boat. Nothing to see under the slop of the waves. He closed his eyes, waiting, waiting, listening to the cry of the gulls and the low, singing moan that the seals made. There was nothing else. He should go. Just as he was leaning forward to pick up his oars, he felt a deep coldness stealing over him, chilling him right to the bone. He knew someone was there. He looked round, and there was the boy perched on a rock. But he wasn't a boy, not a real boy at all. He was like a statue of glass, completely transparent, and yet with water running down him. He was made of green water. Jez could see right through him, could see the pale cream of waves behind him as if he wasn't there at all. But he was there.

Jez shouted out involuntarily. He wanted to lift his oars and row away from the Brisons as fast as he could. He clenched his fists against the sides of the *Mayfly*, and took a deep, steadying breath.

'Who are you?' he asked.

'I'm the little ship's boy. I'm Davey.' The voice was thin and hollow, hardly there at all. It could have been the cry of a gull, or the *sheesh* of waves against the rocks. It could have been in Jez's own head. The boy wasn't looking at him, but away towards the towering rocks of the Brisons – as if he was looking through them, as if he could see what was on the other side.

'Why are you here? What are you waiting for?'

'*Merandee. Merandee.*'

'Is that why the ghost ship comes? Is it looking for you?'

'Help me! Save me!'

The sound came like a wail, like the sobbing cry Jez had heard in the night. Then with a slipping movement the boy lost his shape. He poured into the sea, like a cascading waterfall, and disappeared. Jez stared at the rock where the boy had been sitting. Perhaps he had never been there at all. Perhaps what he had seen was one of those green waves, breaking against the rock and streaming over it.

Jez dipped his oars gently into the water and turned the *Mayfly* slowly round. There was no sign, anywhere, of the ship's boy Davey, no face in the water, nothing. He could feel his throat tight with fear, his tongue dry and sticking to the roof of his mouth. Now he could see the urgent waves licking and rocking his boat. The tide was coming in. He had to go, before it rose too quickly for him to steer away from the rocks.

Once he was past the rocks the rowing was quite easy. The tide was streaming fast, and all he had to do was dip his oars in and out and ride it like a windsurfer until he drew near to the slipway of the Priest's Cove. He had to keep glancing over his shoulder, to gauge where the rocks were, and then to steer his oars with a massive burst of strength which just brought him to the edge of the slipway. He grabbed the *Mayfly's* rope and swung himself over the side, knee deep in chilly water, and somehow caught the prow of the boat before it slammed against a rock. He heaved her onto the slipway and dragged her up to mooring. He was utterly exhausted. On his hands and knees he tied the boat to the ring. Then he collapsed on his back.

He was awakened by a slurping sound around his ears, and opened his eyes to see the three-legged mongrel nudging him with its wet muzzle. The dog tried to lick him all round his face, and Jez sat up, laughing and pushing him away.

'All right, all right, I'm alive!'

He heard the sound of a van door slamming. He stood up quickly and yanked the oars out of the bottom of the boat, ran up to Uncle Jack's shed with them and threw them in, along with the life jacket. The dog was leaping round him, eager for a game, and Jez saw that it had picked up a plastic bobbin that had fallen off a frayed buoy rope. It dropped the bobbin at Jez's feet and turned its panting face up to him.

'OK. OK.' Jez flung the bobbin across the boulders in the cove, and the dog leaped after it, barking with joy. Jez ran down the slipway just as Uncle Jack came staggering down, cradling a new battery.

'See you've made a friend,' he said. 'You can give me a hand with this, Jez, and then I've promised Sammy some help. Did you go over there?'

'No,' Jez had completely forgotten about his promise. 'I've just been round here all the time.' It was nearly true.

Uncle Jack wasn't really listening. '*Mayfly's* a bit wet inside. Must have rained a lot in the night.' He looked round, puzzled, at the other boats on the slipway. The dog came bounding back to Jez and laid the slimy bobbin at his feet, gazing up at him, shiny-eyed. Uncle Jack laughed.

'Run up to the house and tell May to leave some meat aside. We might be feeding this dog properly soon.'

Jez enjoyed helping Uncle Jack and Sammy that afternoon. There were lots of farm jobs to be done that didn't involve digging, which he was pleased about as his arms were aching from the morning's rowing. The dog lollopped beside him for most of the time, but then ran off to the slipway to keep its watch there. After his evening meal Jez ran over with some scraps and the dog wolfed them down eagerly and then sat on its haunches, gazing out to sea again. Jez stood beside it, watching the white fling of spray against the Brisons. Was the boy there again? he wondered. Was the ghost ship there, invisible, searching the seas? He tried to calculate when the next high tide would be. He thought it would be about half-past three in the morning.

He was to sleep back in his own room again that night. He closed the curtains firmly, and hung a pillowcase across the mirror. He put his earphones in and listened to his favourite band. He kept his light on, and stared up at the ceiling, hour after hour. He couldn't sleep. At last he made his way downstairs and switched the kettle on. He made himself a cup of cocoa and ate one of the scones that May had brought back from Penzance. He didn't feel tired. Not one bit. He kept his earphones in, so he couldn't hear the wind or the rain or any sobbing voice. He was going to be all right. He had kept the ghost away. He ran some water into the washing-up bowl to rinse out the mug. And when he looked down, there was the boy's face in the water, staring up at him.

Auntie May put him back to bed and stayed with him till he was asleep. After breakfast she took him to St Ives for the day, while Uncle Jack went out fishing.

'Aunty May,' he said. 'Do you know about the ghost ship *Merandee*?'

'Of course I do,' she sighed. 'Everyone does. But you mustn't get worried about it, Jez.'

'But Uncle Jack said he's seen it!'

'You don't want to believe everything your Uncle Jack says!' she laughed. 'I certainly don't!'

Jez was silent for a bit, watching the glints of sea coming and going as the car wound its way round the headland.

'But just supposing it was true,' he said. 'What do you think it might be there for?'

His aunt smiled. 'Well, supposing someone had fallen overboard? Supposing the boat was searching for one of the crew? That's what I think.'

'That's what I think too,' said Jez.

'Now, we won't talk about it again,' Aunty May said firmly. 'We're going to forget all about it, aren't we?'

Jez nodded. But a plan was already forming in his head. He was going to help the ghost boy.

They ate together that night, lovely fish stew, and then Uncle Jack took him along to a practice with his ceilidh band. Jez knew how to play a recorder, and so when his uncle gave him a penny whistle he found he could play it easily. He could pick up all the tunes in no time, and he enjoyed joining in. There was another boy of his age in the band, playing a concertina. After a bit they swapped instruments and giggled a lot over their mistakes. On the way home the full moon was blazing like a lantern over the sea. It was a night of brilliant stars. Jez couldn't stop talking and humming and tinkering with the whistle on the tune that Uncle Jack had written and wanted some words for. During their late supper of lardy cake and cocoa Aunty May and Uncle Jack smiled over Jez's head. They had made him better, their eyes said. He's made a friend in the band, he's full of himself. He's all right now.

But they couldn't read Jez's mind. He was planning something that was so frightening that he couldn't even put his thoughts to it. All he knew for certain was that he wasn't going to wait for the drowned boy to haunt him again. He was going to get him back to the *Merandee*. He didn't know how he was going to manage it, but one thing was for sure, he would have to row out to the rocks that night by the light of the full moon.

Soon after two o'clock in the morning Jez crept downstairs and ran to the cove. The dog was there and loped up to him, and Jez threw him the handful of biscuits he'd brought in his pocket. When Jez pulled the *Mayfly* into the water the dog jumped inside it. Jez was quite pleased. At least he had company. This time he found the rowing much easier than before, and with the full moon he could see clearly where he was heading. He reached the Brisons without having too many pauses, and edged the boat towards the rock where the drowned boy had been. Now the silence was eerie. The dog cowered in the bottom of the boat, his ears pricked, moaning softly. Jez felt a chill creeping over him. A strange kind of phosphorescent light was drifting towards the Brisons. He shipped his oars as silently as he could, and waited.

After a while he could hear a groaning and creaking, and then he could see a glow of lights high above the sea. The dim shape of a ship came riding the waves, its lanterns swinging. And out of the night he heard faint voices, singing:

And the little ship's boy called Davey-o
He slid to the side and away did go
All into the grey sea down below
We were sailing over the ocean.

Jez could make out the dark rigging, and the straining, pale sails. It swung about, and about again, and now in the moonlight Jez could read the name on the side. *Merandee.* Jez knew that the ship couldn't come any nearer because of the rocks of the Brisons. And the boy might only be yards away, only the other side of the rocks.

'Davey! Davey, where are you?' Jez whispered. He saw the water around the boat ripple and shiver. Something white floated in the ripples; a face with staring eyes and moving lips.

'He's here, he's here!' Jez shouted, cupping his hands round his mouth, but he knew it was useless. Could the sailors on the ghost ship see him? Could they hear him? And even if they could, there was no way they would bring that huge ship so near to the rocks.

'Don't go. Don't leave him again!' he yelled.

He reached his hand down into the water, but all he could feel was the cold, wet sea. And then he saw the boy's white face lifting itself up out of the water, and the shape of a body heaving itself inside a wave that swayed and swung against the rocks, then gathered itself and towered over the side of the *Mayfly*. Sea water showered into the boat.

The dog sat up, howling now, shaking, and pressing his back against Jez's legs. Jez was so frightened he hardly dared to grope his hands into the water that was swilling round his feet. But he did. He found the oars and began to row, glancing over his shoulder to avoid the rocks, and kept on rowing until he was right beside the ghost ship. The glow was so bright now that he had to keep his eyes closed. The dog set up a fierce barking, and there were voices, men's voices, calling and shouting, and without realising what he was doing, Jez was shouting too, 'He's here, he's here! Throw a ladder!'

Next minute a rope ladder came thumping down the side of the *Merandee*. Jez nudged the *Mayfly* right up to it. The little boat rocked dangerously, and Jez had to cling onto the sides. The water in the bottom of the boat swayed and gathered itself into the shape of a child, then plunged over the side, and then everything was still. Jez could just make out the slight figure of a boy hauling himself up the ladder, and hands reaching down, pulling him to safety. And then, white in the moonlight, a small hand waving, a thin voice calling; 'I thank thee, boy. I thank thee.'

At that moment Jez felt a dreadful sense of loss, as if part of himself had gone. He pulled away with the oars and looked up at the *Merandee*. Its lights were fading so fast that it was almost invisible now. He strained his eyes to see it, he strained his ears to hear it, but the big sailing ship had gone completely, as if it had never been.

Now a steady rhythmic slapping of waves warned Jez that the tide was beginning to turn. Gulls lifted themselves off the Brisons, sobbing and screaming. Clouds raced across the moon, hiding its light. He knew he had get away from the Brisons as quickly as he could, but without the light of the moon he had no idea which way he should be rowing. Panicking, he splashed with his oars, struck a rock with one, had to push himself away. His heart was lurching now; his hands were shaking too much to grip the oars tightly. He bent his head down and closed his eyes.

The dog scrambled towards him and licked his face, muttering and whining softly. Jez looked up. Now he could see the light of a boat on the water. It was surely *Merandee*, guiding him away from the rocks. It had to be. He picked up his oars again and edged the boat round. He had his back to the light, but he kept looking over his shoulder to make sure he was heading towards it. The waves slapped him this way and that, and showered into the boat from time to time. He looked over his shoulder again, and realised that the light was coming towards him, not away from him. It seemed to be moving very fast. Now he could hear the sound of a motor, and knew that it wasn't the *Merandee* at all.

Yet it was heading straight for the Brisons. It came steadily nearer and nearer, and the dog stood up in the boat and barked furiously. Lights from the boat came sweeping over them, blinding Jez. He stopped rowing, and heard the engine of the lifeboat cutting out. Then he heard Uncle Jack's voice.

'Jez! Jez! You all right, boy?'

Jez spent most of the next morning in bed, with the three-legged dog sprawled across his lap. At lunch time Aunty May called them both down for a meat stew.

'Good job your Uncle Jack had decided to do a bit of night fishing,' she told Jez. 'Or he'd never have known the *Mayfly* was missing till now. And, of course, he knew straight away who'd taken it, and where you'd be.'

'Is he very angry?'

'Not Jack. He's glad you're alive, and so am I. He's going to teach you how to use the engine, though, if you're going to do mad things like that again.'

'No. I won't be doing it again, will I, Merry?' said

Jez, stroking the dog. 'There's no need. Not any more.'

When his uncle came home later that evening, with a catch big enough to take to the market, he asked Jez what he'd been doing all day.

'Playing with Merry,' said Jez. 'And writing a song for that new tune of yours. It's about a ship called *Merandee*. It really existed, Uncle Jack. It really did.'

Oh, oh Merandee-o
Get her out to sea and away we'll go
With the little ship's boy called Davey-o
Sailing over the ocean

There was Captain Marr and all the crew
And the little ship's boy called Davey-o
And Turk the Cook and the bo'sun too
Sailing over the ocean
We kissed our girl, we kissed our wife
And we never looked back for a last goodbye
Our hearts were light, we were filled with life
Sailing over the ocean
Oh, oh Merandee-o etc.

So we set sail from Plymouth port
On the very first day of the month of May
And the breeze was fair and the sails were taut
Sailing over the ocean
But as we rounded Cape Cornwall
The seas rose up like a pack of wolves
We were this way and that in a night squall
Tossed all over the ocean
Oh, oh Merandee-o etc.

Then the little ship's boy called Davey-o
He slid to the side and away did go
All into the grey sea down below
A-falling into the ocean:
'Boy's in the water!' came the cry
And the ship hove-to in the streaming sea
And they leaned right down but they never could spy
The poor child in the ocean
Oh, oh Merandee-o etc.

Then the mist closed in and the ship was lost
She was lunged to the shore by the rolling tide
And before night came she was on the rocks
Not sailing over the ocean
Now sailors passing by that way
Can see a child's face in the waves they say
And they hear the brave song they sang that day
Sailing over the ocean
Oh, oh Merandee-o etc.

Now the wreck has sunk to the ocean bed
With Captain Marr and the cook 'tis said
And the bo'sun too and the whole ship's crew
All underneath the ocean
But when the mist is on the sea
You can still see the ship as it looks for me
For i was the little ship's boy Davey
Drowned in the cold grey ocean.
Oh, oh Merandee-o etc.

Merandee-o

Words: Berlie Doherty

Tune: Jerry Simon

Oh! Oh! Me - ran - dee - o, Get her out to sea and a - way we'll go, With the lit - tle ship's boy called Da - vey - o, Sai - ling o - ver the o - cean. Now the wreck has sunk to the o - cean bed, with Cap - tain Marr and the cook, 'tis said And the bo-'sun too, and the whole ship's crew All un - der - neath the o - cean. But when the mist is on the sea You can still see the ship as it looks for me, For I was the lit - tle ship's boy Da - vey, Sai - ling o - ver the o - cean. Oh! Oh! Me- ran - dee - o, get her out to sea and a - way we'll go, With a lit - tle ship's boy called Da - vey - o, Sai - ling o - ver the o - cean.

AUTHOR
BIOGRAPHIES

Joseph Delaney lives in Lancashire and is the author of the bestselling *Spook's Apprentice* books, so has spent a lot of time writing and thinking about ghosts. Does he believe in them? Most definitely. Has he seen one? Well, Joseph says he hasn't seen any, but he's definitely heard some and smelled some! What do they smell of? Joseph says it's not rotting flesh and the decay of the grave. We each have a personal smell – it's on our skin. After washing it is very faint. Don't shower for three days and it gets much stronger!

So that's what ghosts smell of – body odour!

Susan Cooper grew up in England but now lives in America on an island in a Massachusetts salt marsh. She is the author of the seminal *The Dark Is Rising* sequence and has won assorted awards including the Newbery Medal. As well as writing novels, Susan has also written screenplays and a Broadway play. She says, 'I believe in hauntings, from experience, but I've never come across a visible ghost. Yet.'

Mal Peet lives in Devon and his novels for young adults have won the Branford Boase Award, the Carnegie Medal and the Guardian Fiction Prize. Mal says, 'I don't know whether I believe in ghosts or not. I do believe they are very useful and interesting for writers, and I like the idea that they might be sinister and friendly at the same time. Once, long ago, I was in a house where I shouldn't have been and saw in a mirror the reflection of an old man sitting in a chair smiling at me. He wasn't there when I was brave enough to turn round. But that's another story...'

Jamila Gavin grew up in India. With an Indian father and an English mother, she inherited two rich cultures which run side by side throughout her life, and which always make her feel she belongs to both countries. She became a children's writer when her son and daughter were young and she won the Whitbread Prize for her wonderful novel *Coram Boy*. Jamila says: 'I don't believe in ghosts, yet over the years I've had interesting encounters that many people would describe as being ghostly. I've slept in a bedroom and seen the old man who used to sleep there, but who had died some time ago; I've heard someone playing my piano downstairs, and then seen three Victorian figures walk through a wall; I've swum in the sea over ancient ruins and heard people shouting. So, although I really don't believe in ghosts, strange things can happen which make me think.'

Eleanor Updale grew up in London, studied History at Oxford University and worked for the BBC before becoming a children's writer. She is the author of the award-winning *Montmorency* books and divides her time between her homes in Edinburgh and London. Eleanor says: 'I don't believe in ghosts now, but when I was young I had to walk past a bombed church and a ruined mansion on my way to school. There was something chillingly spooky about those places, even though they were in a busy London street. Maybe I'll put them in a story one day...'

Derek Landy is the author of the bestselling and award-winning *Skulduggery Pleasant* series. He has a black belt in Kenpo Karate, he trains in Krav Maga, and lives on the outskirts of Dublin with a variety of cats, a German Shepherd and two geriatric Staffordshire Bull Terriers, who keep peeing on his kitchen floor. Derek says, 'I don't actually believe in ghosts or the supernatural, but I really wish I did. That's probably why I write about the things I write about – it's my way of experiencing a side of life I've never allowed myself to live.'

Robin Jarvis lives in Greenwich and is the author of many fantasy novels for children, including the bestselling *Deptford Mice* series. He grew up in Liverpool, the youngest of four children, and he has a true ghost story to tell: 'When I was a toddler, my grandmother was staying with us. She was very ill and late one night my mother heard what sounded like a child pattering to her bedroom. Thinking it was me, she got up and checked. I was still fast asleep in my cot. Frightened that an intruder was in the house, she woke my father who checked every room with a truncheon in his hand. He found no one. Settling back into bed, they both heard the same child-like sounds walking back past their door. My father got up and checked again, but found nothing. A few days later my grandmother died. My mother always believed that the Angel of Death had come for her that night but they had disturbed it.

Sam Llewellyn was born on Tresco, Isles of Scilly where his ancestors lived for generations. He has worked as a journalist and also published lots of books for adults and children, including the much-loved *Little Darlings* series. He now lives in a house a thousand years old, far from neighbours and shadowed by the mountains of Wales. On still winter nights he hears doors close when there is nobody to close them. On such occasions he puts his fingers in his ears and hopes for spring.

Matt Haig writes adult and children's books. His first book for children, *Shadow Forest*, won the Smarties Prize and the Blue Peter Book Award. He lives in York with his wife and two children. When he was ten years old, Matt went to stay at his grandfather's creaky old wooden house on the Suffolk coast, and saw the ghost of an old lady in a white Victorian nightgown walk past his bedroom doorway, carrying a flickering nightlight. Or he thought he did. It might have been a dream, as he HAD been eating an awful lot of cheese.

Philip Reeve is an illustrator and author. He won the Smarties Prize for his novel *Mortal Engines*, and the Carnegie Medal for *Here Lies Arthur*. He lives with his wife and son on Dartmoor, a place rich in tales of ghosts and hauntings. He doesn't believe in ghosts, but is still quite scared of them.

Berlie Doherty was born in Liverpool and grew up in the Wirral, and has written over fifty books for children – and won the Carnegie Medal twice! Does she believe in ghosts? 'I was once confronted by a very frightening 'presence' in a room which I later discovered to be haunted – in all truth I hadn't been told beforehand that other visitors had been too frightened to sleep there – and I certainly won't stay in it again! And I am currently writing a play, "Thin Air", about a ghostly pre-World War One plane that keeps circling the Dark Peak of Derbyshire and appearing to crash – and there are many sightings of such planes. The area of Derbyshire where I live has many ghostly tales attached to it, and when the mists are low on the moors, it's easy to believe they're true.'

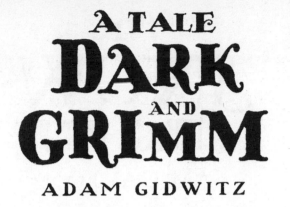

A TALE DARK AND GRIMM

ADAM GIDWITZ

Reader: beware!

Lurking within these covers are sorcerers with dark
spells, hunters with deadly aim and a baker with an oven
big enough to cook children in. But if you dare, pick up
this book and find out the true story of Hansel and
Gretel – the story behind (and beyond) the
breadcrumbs, the edible house and the outwitted witch.
Come on in. It may be frightening, it's certainly bloody,
and it's definitely not for the faint of heart, but unlike
those other fairy tales you know, this one is true.

'Gidwitz balances the grisly violence of the original
Grimms' fairy tales with a wonderful
sense of humour and narrative voice.
Check it out!'
Rick Riordan

'*A Tale Dark & Grimm* holds up to
multiple readings, like the classic I
think it will turn out to be.'
New York Times

9781849393706 £5.99

The SNOW MERCHANT

SAM GAYTON

Lettie Peppercorn lives in a house on stilts near the wind-swept coast of Albion, with no one to talk to but Periwinkle the pigeon. Her days are filled with floor-sweeping, bed-making and soup-stirring. Her nights are filled with dreams of her mother, who vanished long ago. Nothing incredible has ever happened to Lettie, until one winter's night.

The night the Snow Merchant comes.

He claims to be an alchemist – the greatest that ever lived – and in a mahogany suitcase, he carries his newest invention.

It is an invention that will change Lettie's life – and the world – forever.

It is an invention called snow.

The Snow Merchant is a fantasy filled with family secrets, magical transformations and wild adventure. Join Lettie on her journey to uncover the true meaning of snow, family and friendship.

Illustrated throughout by Tomislav Tomic

9781849393713 £12.99 Hardback

THE ISLAND OF THIEVES

JOSH LACEY

Buried treasure. Ruthless gangsters. An ancient clue . . .

Our Captayne took the pinnace ashore and I went with hym and six men also, who were sworne by God to be secret in al they saw. Here we buried five chests filled with gold.

Tom Trelawney was looking for excitement. Now he's found it. With his eccentric Uncle Harvey, he's travelling to South America on a quest for hidden gold. But Uncle Harvey has some dangerous enemies and they want the treasure too. Who will be the first to uncover the secrets of the mysterious island?

Praise for other books by this author:

'A delight'
The Times

'Smart and pacy'
Sunday Times

9781849392457 £5.99

When You Reach Me

REBECCA STEAD

Miranda's life is starting to unravel. Her best friend, Sal, gets punched by a kid on the street for what seems like no reason, and he shuts Miranda out of his life. Then the key Miranda's mum keeps hidden for emergencies is stolen, and a mysterious note arrives:

'I am coming to save your friend's life, and my own. I ask two favours. First, you must write me a letter.'

The notes keep coming, and whoever is leaving them knows things no one should know. Each message brings her closer to believing that only she can prevent a tragic death. Until the final note makes her think she's too late.

Winner of the John Newbery Medal 2010

Shortlisted for the Waterstone's Children's Book Prize

'Smart and mesmerising'
New York Times

9781849392129 £5.99

The GREAT DEATH

John Smelcer

When white strangers visit, they leave a deadly sickness of red spots and fever. Only thirteen–year–old Millie and her younger sister Maura survive. The two girls embark on an epic trek through the harsh Alaskan winter wilderness in search of fellow humans.

An extraordinary story of courage, endurance and survival.

'A must-read by an exciting new novelist: definitely one to watch.' Jake Hope, *Bookseller's Choice*

'An outstanding piece of writing and undoubtedly my favourite novel of the year.' Lindsey Stainer, *Bookseller's Choice*

9781842709191 £5.99

Treason

BERLIE DOHERTY

Who matters most? Your father or your king?

Will Montague is a page to Prince Edward, son of King Henry VIII. As the King's favourite, Will gains many enemies in Court. His enemies convince the King that Will's father has committed treason and he is thrown into Newgate Prison. Will flees Hampton Court and goes into hiding in the back streets of London. Lost and in mortal danger, he is rescued by a poor boy, Nick Drew. Together they must brave imprisonment and death as they embark on a great adventure to set Will's father free.

'Doherty paints a very vivid picture ... almost Shardlake for young readers.'
Independent on Sunday

'A beautifully paced and measured story. 5 stars.'
Books for Keeps

9781849391214 £5.99